Mark,

I have to leav~~_____~~me.
Please take ca~~_____~~

Ardie

Mark fought back panic. He could feel the wide-eyed stares of the little boy and girl on the couch. What did "a while" mean?

Desperation coiled in his stomach. He knew nothing about taking care of children.

"Where shall I put the baby for the night?" the sitter Ardie had left with the kids asked. She held a swaddled bundle in her arms.

Baby?

Mark stared at the chaos in the apartment, speechless. Toys and tiny clothes were—everywhere.

The little boy slipped off the couch and crept closer, looking up at Mark seemingly in awe.

Something in Mark's chest squeezed tight. He stared down into the child's hopeful gaze and made a decision. He ran a company with hundreds of employees—he could certainly deal with three small children.

After all, it was just for a little while....

ABOUT THE AUTHOR

Leona Karr loves to read and write, and her favorite books are romantic suspense. Every book she writes is an exciting discovery as she finds the right combination of romance and intrigue. She has authored over thirty novels, many of which, like *Mystery Dad*, are set in her home state, Colorado. When she's not reading and writing, she thoroughly enjoys spoiling her eight beautiful granddaughters.

Books by Leona Karr

HARLEQUIN INTRIGUE

Don't miss any of our special offers. Write to us at the following address for information on our newest releases.

Harlequin Reader Service
U.S.: 3010 Walden Ave., P.O. Box 1325, Buffalo, NY 14269
Canada: P.O. Box 609, Fort Erie, Ont. L2A 5X3

Mystery Dad
Leona Karr

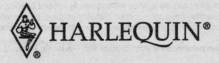

HARLEQUIN®

TORONTO • NEW YORK • LONDON
AMSTERDAM • PARIS • SYDNEY • HAMBURG
STOCKHOLM • ATHENS • TOKYO • MILAN • MADRID
PRAGUE • WARSAW • BUDAPEST • AUCKLAND

To Janet Grill, my dear friend,
In Heart and Spirit.

ISBN 0-373-22487-7

MYSTERY DAD

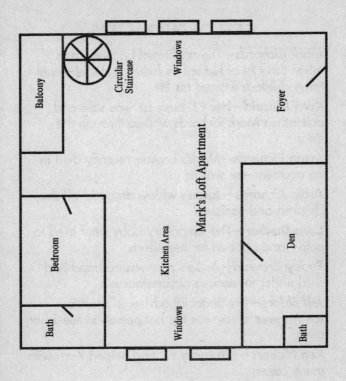

Mark's Loft Apartment

Balcony

Circular Staircase

Windows

Foyer

Bedroom

Bath

Kitchen Area

Windows

Den

Bath

CAST OF CHARACTERS

Mark Richards—The confirmed bachelor had never thought of himself as father material—until three children entered his life.

Kerri Kincaid—Her P.I. business was safe and dull—then Mark Richards walked through the door.

Jason Richards—Mark's brother recently died in an accident—or was it?

Ardie Richards—Jason's widow dropped off the children and vanished.

Cora Dunbar—The temporary baby-sitter tried to help—and got hurt for her efforts.

Buddy Browski—Ardie's previous husband had died under mysterious circumstances.

Jeff Elders—The financial adviser in Mark's Los Angeles office was the last person to see Jason alive.

Ken Nabors—The cocky P.I. had helped Kerri with many cases.

Dirk—His name frightened Timmy—was he the stranger lurking around Mark's apartment?

Timmy, Patti and Pammy—The three children just needed love and stability.

Chapter One

Mark Richards heard the baby's cry the minute he stepped out of the elevator. He paused for a moment, listening. The sound was intrusive, and frankly, annoying on this fifth floor of a fashionable loft apartment building in lower downtown Denver. Two bachelor pads spanned the whole top floor, his and one belonging to a middle-aged investment broker, Ted Winters. The quiet atmosphere of the newly renovated building was one of the joys of returning home from stressful business trips. He wondered who Ted's visitor with the baby might be and murmured a silent plea that their visit would be short. At thirty-five, he'd settled into a regimented routine of work and solitary pleasures, and he resented any intrusion into his well-ordered life.

Shifting his traveling case, he dug in his pockets for his keys, took a few steps down the hall and then stopped short. The baby's cries were getting louder. He couldn't believe his ears. The intrusive sound was coming from his own loft apartment.

"What in blazes—?" he swore. As he racked his brain, he couldn't think of a single person who should be in his apartment with a squalling kid. Most of his friends were single or divorced, and his only brother, who had died a couple of months earlier, had been married for only a short time, no kids. Besides, no one had any business being in his apartment while he was gone.

Mark strode to the carved mahogany door and angrily shoved his key into the lock. He didn't think about calling security or anyone else. The violation of his privacy was enough to send hot blood racing through his six-foot frame and stiffen every muscle. Flinging the door open, he strode across the foyer and into the wide-open space that was his living room.

A middle-aged, heavyset woman wearing tight jeans and large, plastic-framed glasses stood in the middle of the room. She was jiggling a five or six-month-old baby with one arm while readying a baby bottle with her free hand. "Thank heavens, you're home," she told Mark with an expression of utter relief.

He'd never seen her before.

Sitting down in his favorite lounge chair, she stuck a bottle in the baby's mouth. "There, there," she soothed and a blessed silence filled the room as the baby nursed the bottle.

Before Mark could release an explosive breath, a flicker of movement on his leather couch jerked his eyes in that direction. He saw two small children with toys and books piled between them, who looked as if a minute before they'd been laughing and playing. But now their wide eyes stared at him as if he were some creature complete with horns and dragon's tail. The little girl must have been about two years old, and the boy, five or six. They both had unruly curly blond hair, rounded blue eyes, and were dressed in wrinkled play clothes and dirty sneakers.

Mark felt as if his brain must have jumped a rail. For a weird moment, he thought he must be in the wrong loft apartment. But no, everything was familiar, cream-and-black leather furniture, ceiling-to-floor windows with a spectacular view of Denver's night skyline, and his favorite wall hangings and bookshelves. Everything was normal except for the woman and kids parked in his front room.

"Your office said your flight was due back at four o'clock," the woman said in an accusing tone. "It's nearly seven now. I didn't know what to do."

Disbelief made his voice strident. "Who are you? And what are you doing in my apartment?"

The woman brushed back a frizzy shock of bleached hair and frowned at him. Her frank eyes glinted with disapproval. "My name is Cora Dunbar. I was hired to stay with these children until you got back. Mrs. Richards said that you'd pay me for a whole day's wages, but since it's evening, you'll owe me for the extra hours, too."

"Mrs. Richards?"

"The children's mom. She said you were their uncle."

"I'm not anybody's uncle. My only brother didn't have any children."

She shrugged. "Ready-made families are nothing out of the ordinary. Nowadays, there's nothing simple like kids belonging to one set of parents. She said she hadn't been married to your brother very long but he really loved the children. He told her if she ever needed anything to come to you."

His brother had never mentioned that he was acquiring a ready-made family with his recent marriage. Out of the blue a few months back, Jason had called Mark to say he'd gotten married and was honeymooning in Reno. The marriage had been an utter surprise. Stunned and worried that his impulsive brother was headed for another dismal failure like his first two marriages, Mark tried to ask some questions about the new bride, but all Jason would say was, "She's wonderful! Wait 'til you meet her. Ardie's the best." The meeting had never taken place.

When his brother was killed a few months later in a freak car accident on a California freeway, Mark brought the body back to Colorado for burial, and he'd met his brother's wife then. She hadn't brought any children with her. His brother's widow was a small, light-haired woman who had kept her distance and made little effort to ingratiate herself with Mark. He'd never expected to see her again.

"There has to be a mistake," Mark repeated more fervently.

"You're Mr. Mark Richards, aren't you?" At his nod, Cora said shortly, "Then there's no mistake."

"I'm afraid there is," he said, with a determined jut of his chin as he ran a hand through the stylish cut of his light brown hair. "A big one. How did you get in here?"

"Mrs. Richards had a key."

Mark silently steamed. He'd given Jason a key so he could come and go when he was in Denver. No doubt, she'd held on to his brother's key after his death. Drawing in a deep breath, Mark endeavored to keep his voice even. "All right, explain. What are you doing in my apartment?"

"Tending the children 'til you got home. I came at nine o'clock this morning and Mrs. Richards told me to wait here 'til you got back and took them off my hands." Cora shifted the baby, reached into the pocket of her jeans, pulled out an envelope, and handed it to him. "She said to give you this."

The stationery was from his desk. Impatiently Mark

ripped the envelope open. The single sheet of paper had two lines of hasty writing on it. "Have to leave for a while. Don't try to find me. Ardie."

Mark read it through three times and still came up short of making any sense out of it. What in blazes? What did she mean by "leave for a while"? An hour? A night? A day or two? How dare the woman dump these strange kids on him for who knew how long? He couldn't believe the nerve of it. Mark's fist closed over the note.

He could feel the wide-eyed stare of the little boy and girl on the couch. Whatever they had been playing with lay between them, forgotten. The little girl had stuck her thumb in her mouth and pulled her chubby legs up under her Indian style. The boy's eyes were too large for his freckled nose and thin face, and the shape of his head was lost in his wild frenzy of hair.

"Well now, the little one's asleep," Cora said softly, as she put the baby over her shoulder and patted its bottom. "Where do you want me to put her down?"

"What?" Mark came out of his fog with a jolt.

"The baby. Where are you going to bed her down? And the other little ones? They're dead on their feet. I made them sandwiches for supper. Hope you didn't mind. Couldn't find much in your fridge. You'll have to order in some groceries. And some more milk. I'll tuck them in before I leave."

"Leave? You can't leave." Mark's jaw clenched in panic.

"Have to. Got my own family to look after. Just came on this job cause I was needing some extra money. Usually, I clean houses for the agency. When this baby-sitting job came up, they asked me if I'd like to take it. Doesn't pay as much as my regular assign-

ments but they didn't have me scheduled to go anywhere. Like I said, I wasn't supposed to work past five
o'clock. You owe me overtime.''

Mark fought back instant panic. He sure as hell
wasn't going to let this woman walk out and leave
him with a baby and two little kids. He'd brought off
million-dollar deals for his finance company when
there didn't seem to be a chance of snaring the investors, and the present situation was certainly one that
demanded his best persuasive powers.

He gave Cora Dunbar his best people-management
smile. ''Well now, I'm sure we can work something
out, Cora,'' he said smoothly. ''How about we add an
extra hundred dollars to your regular fee for helping
me out with the children tonight? Just tonight. If their
mother hasn't come back by morning then we'll work
something else out.''

Mark didn't have a clue what that would be. He
only knew he wasn't going to play patsy for some
brazen woman who thought she could dump her kids
on him. He pulled out his wallet and handed the baby-
sitter a handful of bills. ''Would this put us even?''

Cora fingered the bills and nodded, her expression
showing an inner battle going in her head. ''I don't
know if I should. My sister and her husband depend
upon me and all.''

''Surely, they wouldn't mind you bringing home
some extra money?'' Mark coaxed, desperation coiling
in his stomach. He knew absolutely nothing about taking care of kids and babies, and didn't want to. He'd
watched other men go the marriage-and-family route
without the least pang of envy. A confirmed bachelor
through and through, he enjoyed feminine companion-
ship when he wanted it, and often entertained a small

social circle of friends, but he liked his life the way it was, well-ordered and successful.

His mind raced ahead. "We could send a taxi to pick up an overnight bag for you. You and the children could take the bedroom and the pullout couch on the balcony. I'll bed down in the den." Not the best of sleeping arrangements, but the best he could offer. His deluxe bachelor pad was not made for family living. "Just tell me what you need, and I'll order it in," he promised.

Cora looked at the money one more time and then stuffed the bills in her jeans pocket. She nodded at Mark. "Seeing the way things are, I reckon I could stay. But if their mom comes back in the night, you ain't getting any money back."

"Agreed," said Mark, hiding a sigh of relief. Suddenly he realized that the little boy had slipped off the couch and was standing close to him. Mark was startled to see a broad grin on his little face. A shock of unruly blond hair fell over one eye as he held out something in his hand. Mark nearly choked when he saw what it was—his prized Rockies autographed baseball that he kept in a glass case in the den.

"Wanna play catch?" the boy asked shyly.

For a moment, Mark couldn't speak, then he said firmly, "That isn't the kind of baseball you play with."

"Why not?"

"Because it's a special ball. You can't play with it."

"Why not?"

"Because I said so," Mark answered shortly and took the ball away from him.

Cora pushed herself to her feet. Shifting the sleeping baby, she motioned to the other two children. "Come on, Timmy. Patti. Bedtime. Let's see who beds down where. I'll make that call to my sister after I settle them down," she told Mark.

He nodded and led the way to his bedroom. The spacious loft apartment had over 4,500 thousand square feet of living space, but it only had one enclosed bedroom with an adjoining bathroom. A kitchen and dining area was open to the large room, and a modest den with another small bathroom was partitioned off by panels of bookshelves. The walls were bare red brick with a series of ten-foot windows overlooking lower downtown Denver and the Rocky Mountain front range to the west. A wrought-iron circular staircase let to a small balcony that served as a sitting room or extra sleeping area. Jason had used the Hide-A-Bed couch when he was in town.

When Mark opened the door to his bedroom, he was hit with another surprise. Toys and clothes were strewn all over the floor and his king-size water bed was littered with half-opened suitcases and a diaper bag. Glasses and empty pop cans had already marked circles on his bedside tables. Several chiffonier drawers were slightly ajar and the door to his walk-in closet was fully open.

"Their mother told me to put the kids in here for their nap, so I did," Cora said defensively as a red flare mounted in Mark's neck. "I'll tidy it up a bit in the morning," she assured him.

Mark couldn't do anything but nod. If he'd uttered one word, his fury would have heated the room to five hundred degrees. One glance through the half-opened bathroom door was enough to assure him it had been taken over as completely as his bedroom.

"Timmy and Patti can sleep here," Cora said. "And I'll keep the baby with me on the balcony bed."

She gave him a tentative smile. "Mighty nice place you've got here, Mr. Richards. Awfully big for just one man, though."

Mark choked back a scathing retort. No use taking his fury out on the baby-sitter. It was Ardie Richards's neck he wanted to throttle with his strong fingers.

THE SEPTEMBER MORNING sunlight coming through the second-floor office window warmed Kerri Kincaid's face as she looked down at the busy Sixteenth Street mall. Shuttle buses deposited riders at the corners, pedestrians flowed through the crosswalks, and creative street entertainers collected gawking crowds. A beautiful Colorado autumn was in the making, and the brisk fall air seemed to put a bounce in everybody's step.

Kerri never tired of the scene, but she sighed, knowing she was stalling. Her intake basket was full of investigations in progress that were waiting for her attention. The growing success of her company, Finders, Inc., left her slightly discontented.

I must have autumn spring fever, she thought. She loved her work, but for some reason, her usual excitement and enthusiasm for the job had hit a low ebb. Searches for deadbeat dads, bill-collector dodgers, runaways, and adopted children looking for natural parents made up most of her clientele. Most cases simply required methodical checking of paper trails, and usually by the time she completed her checklist of government records, utility companies, employment records, work permits, former addresses and computerized records, she had zeroed in on the party in question.

Remembering the zest her Irish father had shown for his work, she felt guilty and a little cheated that she was finding the job quite humdrum. Patrick Kincaid had founded the business, managing it all by himself for years, spending most of his time as a private investigator, and wearing out his shoes checking out leads. But modern day access to all kinds of records had changed most of that. Thanks to her computer, when Kerri took over the business after her father's death five years earlier, she had a wealth of information at her fingertips. Now, Finders, Inc. was quickly growing almost beyond what she could handle with one receptionist-secretary. She'd been interviewing for an associate, but hadn't found anyone who really appealed to her. She used other investigative services when she could.

Sighing again, she brushed back the tendril of wavy black hair that had drifted down on her forehead, and turned away from the window. Summoning her laggard willpower, she sat down at her desk, and began to attack the stack of files.

A few minutes later, a buzz on the intercom interrupted her. "Mr. Mark Richards is here to see you," her young secretary said brightly. "Shall I send him in?"

Kerri frowned at Debbie's tone. Her secretary was a recent graduate of business college and had great computer skills, but the young woman had little success in hiding her likes and dislikes of people. Debbie's manner and speech gave her away every time, and Kerri could tell from the lift in her voice that the visitor had made a favorable impression on the young woman. Obviously Mr. Richards had sweet-talked Debbie out of the need to make an appointment, and Kerri would have resented the interruption if she'd been in more of a working mood. Lucky for Mr. Richards, she was ready to set aside a tedious report.

"Yes, I'll see him." Kerri leaned back in her office chair, waiting to see what kind of visitor had put that excited trill in her secretary's voice.

The new client opened and closed the door behind him with the assurance of someone accustomed to taking charge of a situation. "Ms. Kincaid?" he asked with a lift of an eyebrow.

She nodded. As he walked toward her, she noticed his solid six-foot build was balanced nicely with wide shoulders, a trim waist, and thighs that pulled at the creases of his pant legs. She had to admit his features were more than adequate for a magazine sportswear ad, masculine and damn sexy. He wore an expensive hand-tailored suit a shade darker than his light brown hair, a white shirt with button-down collar and silk paisley tie held by a narrow gold clip.

Money, thought Kerri. *And arrogance.*

As he handed her his business card, his dark brown eyes traveled over her as if he were doing an assessment of his own. Kerri entertained a moment of feminine regret that she hadn't worn the new cream linen suit she'd impulsively bought the weekend before. She resisted the urge to raise a hand and smooth the layered waves of her short dark hair. Then she took herself in hand, stood up, and held out her hand for a shake. "Mr. Richards."

"Thank you for seeing me without an appointment," he said smoothly.

"Please sit down." She nodded to a leather chair placed slightly to the side of her desk, and took her own seat. Swiveling her desk chair slightly toward him, she asked, "How may I help you?"

He leaned forward. His dark eyes met hers directly, and were arresting in their intensity. "I need to find someone. Right away."

She watched furrows deepen in his forehead. Worried and maybe even scared, she thought. His behavior was not unusual. This was familiar territory to her. Everyone who came to engage her services was caught in some kind of emotional turmoil. Almost always in the first interview, tension radiated from them like beaded sweat. This handsome man was no different. Had his wife run out on him? A son or daughter run away? Or had someone like a business associate disappeared?

Kerri put her hands on the desk in a relaxed clasp and smiled at him. "Whom is it you want to find, Mr. Richards?"

"My brother's widow." His full mouth tightened. "You were recommended by one of my acquaintances, Ed Salinger, as someone who works fast and is very successful in locating people."

"That's not always the case," she warned him. "Mr. Salinger's teenage son really wanted to be found. The boy told a half-dozen friends where he was going when he ran away. Sometimes it takes months—"

"Months," he snapped. "Even a week is too long."

"I see." Kerri reached for a missing person's profile form. Now, she was intrigued. He gave every indication that he was more than able to handle most situations himself, but he was obviously distraught. "What is the name of the missing person?"

"My brother called her Ardie."

"Is that her given name?"

"I don't know."

Kerri tried to keep her expression noncommittal. "And her name before she married your brother?"

"I don't know that, either. About four months before Jason died, he married this woman. My brother met her in Reno on a business trip, and he never brought her to Denver.''

"And you never heard her full name?'' she asked, her pen still poised above the form.

He stared at some point beyond her, his eyes narrowing in concentration. Then he shook his head. "No. Jason just called her Ardie. You see, my brother and I were business partners, Fidelity Financial Investors. Jason worked the West Coast, and I handled the Rocky Mountain region.'' We were very close when we were young, and after college, when our parents died, we went into partnership. On the whole it worked out well.'' Then his mouth tightened. "Then a couple of months ago, Jason was driving too fast on a California interstate, and missed a curve. The accident killed him.''

Kerri saw the pain in his eyes, and let a moment of silence go by before she continued the questioning. So far her intake form was nearly blank. "Do you know where they were married?''

"Reno, I think. That's where Jason called me from to tell me the good news.'' The gravel in his voice belied the happy announcement. "Jason had already gone through two divorces, and after several other disastrous romantic fiascos, he never brought his women home and I never asked about them. Until the day of the funeral, I'd never met this third wife. She kept her distance from me during the services, and left town after she found out that Jason left only debts and partnership life insurance.''

"And now you want to find her? Why?''

"Why?'' he echoed. "Because she dumped her three kids at my apartment and took off, that's why.''

Kerri put down her pen. Nothing about this interview was turning out to be routine, and she could feel her interest rising. She leaned back in her swivel chair. "Maybe you'd better start over."

He squared his shoulders. "I'm sorry. You'll have to forgive my confused state. I'm earnestly trying to make some sense out of all this, and not having much luck."

"Take your time," she said easily, and gave him a reassuring smile. "When did all this begin?"

"Last night." He took a deep breath. "I returned from a business trip around seven o'clock. After collecting my luggage and car, I drove to my loft apartment in lower downtown, and there they were! Three kids and a baby-sitter." He rubbed the back of his neck with an agitated hand. "She must have used the key I had given Jason. The baby was screaming its head off. The whole place was a disaster area. Clothes and toys strewn everywhere. I couldn't believe it." He looked grim. "I still can't."

"And what about the mother?"

"She left me a note. Said she had to go away for a while. No hint of where she's gone or when she'll be back. She just dumped the kids and took off. Some mother!"

"She must have thought you'd take care of them—"

"Well, she thought wrong," he interrupted. "I've never had time for a family of my own and even if they were my brother's children—and they're not—I'm in no position to assume responsibility for them. I want you to find this woman and put an end to this little con game of hers."

"You think it's a con game?"

"What else would you call sneaking her kids into my apartment and dumping her responsibilities on me?"

"An act of desperation?" she suggested quietly.

Mark didn't answer. His grief over his brother's death had found an outlet, and made him ready to believe the worst about the woman. For a long moment, he struggled with his strong bias, then he sighed and admitted to himself that, as difficult as it might be, maybe he owed it to Jason to try to keep an open mind about the woman he'd married.

Mark met Kerri Kincaid's Irish blue eyes, and asked, "You think she's in trouble?"

"It's a possibility."

"But what kind of trouble would make a mother do something like this?"

"Anything at this point is only a guess," Kerri admitted. "But Ardie could have wanted a safe haven for her children and decided to leave them with you."

"And then just take off? Giving me no warning? No clue as to what I would do with her kids? It doesn't make sense."

"Usually, nothing makes sense until you see the whole picture, but take it from me, there are lots of reasons why a person might want to disappear. Very often, it's because he or she is confronted with something they don't want to face."

"You think she's running away from somebody?" Mark looked skeptical. "More likely she decided to take advantage of my financial status, and decided to make her children my responsibility."

Kerri cautioned him. "Everything is just speculation at this point. When we find out why she took off, we'll have a better chance of finding your sister-in-law."

"But I don't know a blasted thing about her. Nothing. And I wouldn't know where to begin to start looking for her."

Kerri smiled. "I rather guess that's why you came

to me, Mr. Richards. There are ways of finding out all the things we need to know. But it takes time and patience. From what you've told me, your brother's widow was concerned about money. That might be a clue.''

''What do you mean?''

''People often try to disappear when there's no way to handle debts, or something more insidious, like blackmail,'' she told him evenly. ''Maybe the woman didn't have a choice. There's a possibility she had to run and wanted her children to be safe.''

The skin on Mark's neck suddenly tightened. The disappearance suddenly took on a different focus. He felt as if something ugly was about to change his whole life. ''You think she's in danger?''

''I have no way of knowing, but it's a possibility.''

''Why wouldn't she want us to try to find her if that was the case?''

''I don't know,'' Kerri said honestly. ''Sometimes people say they don't want to be found, but they really do. It's kind of like a cry for help.''

''If she's in some kind of serious trouble,'' Mark began thoughtfully, ''then we'd better find her as fast as we can.'' For the first time his concern went beyond his own involvement. ''We shouldn't waste any time.''

''I agree. I'll get things started here at the office and then I'd like to come and talk to the children. What's your address?''

He gave it to her. ''But I don't intend to keep the children there. I'll have to rent a place for them and hire someone to tend them for as long as it takes to find their mother.''

''I see. Who's with the children now?''

''The baby-sitter who was hired to watch them until

I got home. Fortunately I was able to persuade the woman to stay until other arrangements could be made." He surprised Kerri with a wan smile. "Her name is Cora and she isn't bashful when it comes to lecturing me about my nearly empty refrigerator, and lamenting the waste of good space in my loft apartment. She was busy ordering groceries when I left and warning me to put everything out of sight that might get broken. I've got to get her and the children out of there before they establish squatters' rights."

Kerri smiled back. "How old are the children?"

"The oldest is a boy, five or six years old and two little girls, a baby of about five months and a little girl of two."

"Wow," Kerri's eyes rounded. "That would be a challenge. How are they taking the absence of their mother?"

"Pretty well, I think. To tell you the truth, I've left everything up to Cora. They took over my bedroom and balcony couch. I slept in the den, and escaped as soon as possible this morning."

Kerri laughed at his harried expression. She was certain that three small children had succeeded in frightening him more than a roomful of hostile competitors. "Well, I would like to talk to the children. And the baby-sitter. She may be able to give us vital information."

"I could drive you to the apartment right now," Mark said, deliberately putting pressure on her. Under different circumstances, he would have related to this attractive, competent woman in an entirely different way. He was well aware of her feminine charms. As she relaxed in her chair, casually crossing her legs, he deliberately kept his eyes from traveling up the supple curves of her ankles, legs and rounded thighs. There was nothing provocative about the simple white shirt-waist blouse and navy skirt, but he was well aware of tiny pearl buttons pulled slightly across firm breasts. He liked her femininity and her manner. He was more than ready to rely upon her competency. "You could talk to Cora and the children this morning. I'll be glad to sign a contract and give you a check for your services."

"I haven't said I'd take the case, Mr. Richards," she said evenly.

"But you will, won't you?"

Without looking at him, she shifted the papers on her desk. She realized she should take time to think about this assignment, step back, and not let this man's attraction influence her. Her instincts warned her that she was courting an emotional involvement if she agreed to take this case. She knew what her Irish father would say. *Watch yerself, Kerri, my lass. Don't be mistaking yer heart for yer head.*

He waited, respecting her silence until she lifted her head and looked at him. "I'll talk to the children and then decide," she said, shutting out her father's warning voice.

Chapter Two

When Kerri came out of her office with Mark at her side, her secretary sent her a look of eager anticipation, silently asking, *Are you going to take the case?*

Ignoring her bright, questioning eyes, Kerri smiled and said, "Debbie, I'll be out of the office for a couple of hours. Is there anything on my calendar this afternoon?"

"You have an appointment at two," she reminded Kerri, as if trying to warn her that time could easily get out of hand in such handsome company.

"I'll be back before lunch."

Debbie nodded, but her grin almost shouted, *Wanna bet?*

The Crystal Loft Apartments were only a few blocks from Kerri's office, and they could have walked instead of taking Mark's luxury car. In that part of old Denver, numerous old buildings had been renovated into fashionable loft apartments, and the street was filled with businesses catering to nearby Coors Field, home of Denver's baseball team, the Rockies. Kerri knew the hefty price of real estate in this part of town, and suspected that Mark's loft had cost a pretty penny.

The entrance to the building was modest enough, and so was the foyer that was shut off from the rest of the lobby by two glass doors. Kerri noticed mailboxes and an intercom for each apartment mounted on one wall, but there was no sign of any kind of a doorman.

Mark used his key to open the inner glass doors, and they mounted three steps to a large open area that had a wide-planked floor that was softened with woven Indian throw rugs. A casual grouping of a leather couch, two matching chairs, lamps and a redwood coffee table added to a simple elegance that shouted interior decorator. Everything was coordinated, even the expensive wall hangings adorning the dark brick walls.

A modern elevator had been installed to replace the large, bulky freight elevators left in so many renovated old buildings. Mark shifted impatiently, as the elevator's signal light moved down from the fifth floor to the foyer. When the doors flew open, a slender, gray-haired man wearing a business suit and carrying a briefcase stepped out.

"How are you doing, Ted?" Mark's greeting was casual, but his neighbor's response was anything but benign.

"What in blazes is going on in your apartment, Mark?" he demanded.

"It's a long story," Mark said quickly, holding the elevator door open with one hand. "A family problem. But I've got a handle on it," Mark assured him.

"Glad to hear it. Some deliverymen were just up there moving in a bunch of baby furniture."

"What?" Mark blanched. Baby furniture! He'd told Cora to order in what she needed, but he meant food and the like, not furniture.

"Don't like to be unneighborly," Ted said, frowning, "but I'm telling you, Mark, I don't aim to put up with noisy kids all hours of the day and night."

"Don't worry. The kids aren't staying!"

"Good." As Ted turned around, he noticed Kerri for the first time. Glancing quickly at Mark, he deliberately waited for an introduction. When Mark missed the cue, Ted held out his hand. "I don't believe we've met. Ted Winters."

"Oh, I'm sorry," Mark said quickly, coming out of his fog. "This is Kerri Kincaid. Her agency is going to help me out of this...situation."

"Oh, what agency is that?" Ted asked, still smiling at Kerri.

"Finders, Inc.," she answered smoothly. "Nice to meet you, Mr. Winters. So, you have an apartment on the same floor as Mr. Richards?"

He nodded. "We bought the lofts at the same time. About two years ago. Nice place to live." He eyed Mark as if he hoped things weren't about to change.

Maybe the man had seen or heard something that would prove valuable, Kerri thought as she mentally added his name to that of the children and the babysitter. Seizing every stray bit of information for possible future reference was automatic for her.

"Finders, Inc.," Ted repeated thoughtfully. "Somebody lost? What gives, Mark?"

Mark put a guiding hand on Kerri's elbow and eased her into the elevator. "The children's mother appears to have deserted them. Talk to you later, Ted," he said, and gave a wave of his hand as the doors closed.

In the close quarters of the elevator, she was poignantly aware of Mark Richards's physical presence. The hand that had guided her into the elevator had been firm, and strangely disturbing. She wasn't used to relating to any client on a personal basis, but something about this man had already begun to breach her defenses. A faint whiff of spicy aftershave lotion teased her nostrils, and she idly pictured him standing in a shower, shaving as water droplets bounced off his naked body. *Stop it,* she ordered, wondering if she'd suddenly taken leave of her senses. He was a client, nothing more—and she'd better remember it.

She was conscious of his stiff posture and ashen face, and she wanted to blithely reassure him that things were going to work out. But she couldn't. Sometimes people disappeared for years. Some were never found. And some turned up dead. Kerri's gut feeling was that nothing about this case was going to be ordinary.

They stepped out of the elevator on the fifth floor, and Mark groaned as a cacophony of squeals, laughter and raised voices vibrated down the hall from his slightly open door.

"Listen to that! How can two small children and a baby possibly make that much noise?"

"You haven't been around kids, I gather," she said, smiling.

"No," he answered flatly.

"Well, you'd never survive the Kincaid family when all of us get together. I assure you, the uproar reaches deafening cycles. There are six of us and I'm the only one without a passel of kids."

His interested eyes settled on her. "Then you never married?"

"No, though I almost relented a couple of times," she surprised herself by admitting. "What about you?"

He shook his head. "Nope. I've been best man more times than you can count, but never made it to the altar myself."

"Ever get close enough to be thinking about it?" she asked with a smile.

He grinned back. "Not when I was stone sober."

Laughing, they shared a sudden intimacy that startled them both. Kerri immediately looked away, terribly conscious of Mark studying her as they walked down the hall.

"You must be hard to please," he said frankly. "What kind of a man would make you decide to take the plunge?"

"I don't know," she said. "I guess I haven't met him yet. But I know he'd be somebody that loved children."

"I see," he said with a shrug. "Well, to each his own."

A moment later, a physical shock of disbelief registered on his face as they entered his apartment. Even though he'd been warned, he couldn't believe his eyes.

The makings of a baby crib, sides, springs and mattress, leaned against the hall wall, waiting to be assembled and they could hear a woman's loud voice, the clatter of dishes and childish laughter coming from the open kitchen.

The place was a mess. A playpen sat in the middle of the beautiful Oriental rug, and his designer furniture was littered with pillows, toys and baby bottles. The baby was asleep in a swing, going back and forth in rhythm to some horrible tinkling melody.

Kerri ignored Mark's muttered swearing, and walked across the room to the beautiful baby girl whose tiny feet and legs stuck out of the holes in the swing's plastic seat. Her head lolled to one side as she slept. A soft tuft of golden hair and perfectly bowed lips made her a perfect little angel. Kerri's heart turned over just looking at the precious infant. She couldn't imagine any mother running off and leaving such a priceless baby girl with someone she didn't even know.

As Kerri stared at the beautiful child, she tried to glean some hint of the truth behind this strange situation. There was something terribly wrong with this whole picture of a missing mother.

But what?

Nothing about this case appeared straightforward, and she wondered if she should refuse to get involved before her own emotions became entangled. Now was the time to retreat. She had never been as tough as she pretended, and this case could tear out her heartstrings. She avoided looking at Mark's face as he led the way into an open kitchen, separated from the large room by a counter and some overhanging cupboards.

The size of the area astonished Kerri. For some reason, she'd expected a fairly small and compact kitchen suitable for bachelor living, not a spacious room with an island counter and every conceivable appliance suitable for gourmet cooking.

Two children perched on stools at a breakfast bar, were laughing and licking chocolate off dripping eggbeaters. A small plump woman with uncertain blond hair had finished pouring cake mix into two round pans and was running a finger around the edge of the mixing bowl, licking off a dabble of chocolate.

"Mmm-mmm, good." Her tongue came out and licked off a dab of cake mix at the corner of her mouth. When she saw Mark, she greeted him with a cheery, "So, you're back. I did what you said. I ordered in everything you'd need for the young'uns." She gave a deep chuckle. "I gave them yellow pages a workout, I'm telling you."

Mark opened his mouth to say something, and then

shut it. Kerri knew he was fighting an inward battle not to let the woman know how she'd completely overstepped her bounds. "I brought Ms. Kincaid to talk with you and the children," he said instead.

Cora shoved back her large plastic-rimmed glasses and smiled at Kerri. "So, you're going to be tending 'em? I'm glad he was able to find someone, quick-like, 'cause I got to get back to my regulars. Can't take a chance on the agency sending somebody else out. I—"

"Ms. Kincaid is not here to baby-sit," Mark interrupted, sending Kerri an apologetic look.

"Oh?" Cora said, puzzled. "I'm sorry. Is she your lady friend?"

Kerri smothered a chuckle as the exasperated look on Mark's face was quickly followed by a renewed effort to take control of the situation. "We need to find the children's mother and Ms. Kincaid is going to help. I'm sure she'll locate her in short order and get these children back where they belong."

Kerri opened her mouth to remind him that she had not committed herself to take the case but before any words came out, the small boy threw himself off the stool with such force that he turned it over with a crash.

"Timmy, come back here," Cora yelled at him, but he didn't pay any attention to her. As the little boy bounded out of the kitchen, his two-year-old sister nearly fell off her high stool trying to follow.

"No, you don't, Patti." Cora reached out and grabbed her. With flaying arms, the little girl became a wildcat, pounding Cora with her little fist, and screaming. "Me go! Me go."

Kerri left Cora and Mark to handle the screaming Patti and hurried out of the kitchen after the little boy.

She heard the bedroom door slam, so she knew where he had gone. Knocking firmly at the door, she said loudly, "Timmy, let's talk about this."

She turned the doorknob and found with relief that it was unlocked. Poking her head into the room, she saw his crumpled body in the middle of a king-size water bed. Quietly shutting the door behind her she walked over to the bed.

Child theatrics were not new to her. Her numerous nieces and nephews had all taken their turns acting out, but the causes of such tantrums had been minor and fleeting. She didn't know how to handle a child whose little fists were clutching the bed quilt in a deathlike grip. She guessed that the disappearance of his mother was sinking in, sending him into the throes of fear, and perhaps catching him up in a terror that she had abandoned him forever.

Quietly, Kerri sat on the edge of the bed, and put her hand on the water-filled mattress as she leaned toward him. "It's going to be all right, Timmy."

Drawing up his body into a tight ball, he kept his little back toward her, and his face nearly buried in the covers. He wasn't crying, Kerri decided, or he was swallowing his sobs so deeply in his chest that she couldn't hear him.

"I'm sorry. Really sorry." Her tone was gentle, and she resisted the temptation to reach out and stroke his tousled blond head. "I want to help. Make everything all right again. You'd like that, wouldn't you?" She waited, but didn't even hear a choked sound that might be yes.

Patience, she told herself. She wouldn't get anything out of him if she pushed too fast and too hard with her questions. She glanced around the spacious master bedroom, noting the harmony of white-brown-and-tan wallpaper, matching draw draperies and plush carpet of soft beige. An interior decorator's touch was evident in matching cherry wood furniture and balanced wall hangings, but the aesthetic effect of the room was spoiled by scattered books, shoes and toys littering the floor, half-opened suitcases and tote bags piled high on two bright green chairs and the round table placed by the window.

Purposefully, Kerri left the bed and walked over to the suitcases and tote bags. Very carefully she went through everything. Maybe, just maybe, she might find something that would be a clue to the mother's whereabouts. Delving to the bottom of each case, she found nothing but clothes. As she folded and replaced each garment, she noted that none of the children's clothes were new, and wondered if they'd been purchased at a thrift store.

As Kerri began picking up the stuff on the floor, her attention was caught by a book titled, *Are You My Mother?* that looked fairly new. On the inside cover was written, "To Timmy Lee on his fourth birthday. Love, Mother." As Kerri held the book in her hand, she glanced over at the bed and saw the boy watching her. Timmy had turned over so she could see his pinched face and tight little mouth.

"Is this yours?" she asked in all innocence as she held up the book.

When he didn't answer, she walked over to the bed, sat down on the edge, and began looking at the pictures. When he squirmed, she pretended not to notice, but when he moved close enough to peek at the pictures, she began reading the book aloud, and when she'd finished the last page, she handed the book to him.

"I'm glad your mother gave you that book," she

said with a smile. "What a nice birthday present. I didn't know your name was Timmy Lee."

He nodded.

"And what's your last name?" If she had the boy's surname name, things might go a lot faster tracking his mother. "Timmy Lee what?" she coaxed.

Setting his tiny jaw with childish stubbornness, the boy just glared at her. She wondered if Ardie had made an issue out of the kids using her newly married name, Richards. She decided it would be better not to push the matter. The way the child was glaring at her reminded her of a mongrel dog ready to sink in his teeth the moment the unwary looked away. He was going to take some gentle handling, but if she could get him to open up, he could provide some clues about his mother's background.

She was trying to decide what tactic to take with him next when Cora opened the door and bustled in. She was holding on to Patti's hand and Mark was right behind them, hauling in the crib frame.

"There's more room in here to set it up," Cora said as she gave one of the green chairs a hefty shove with an ample buttock. One of the tote bags went sailing off the chair, and would have emptied on the floor if Kerri hadn't closed it up earlier. Cora shoved it out of the way with her foot, and stood back as Mark put down the crib pieces.

He sent Kerri a questioning look, his eyes traveling from her to the boy. She gave a slight shake of her head and his exasperation was clearly visible in the tightening of his mouth.

Patti ran across the room and clamored up on the bed beside Timmy. She giggled as the water bed moved under her and her brother's belligerent expression eased.

"Can't keep the little one on a regular bed," Cora told Kerri as if she'd forgotten that Kerri wasn't going to take over the care of the children. "Scoots right off the edge. Last night I had her blocked in by pillows. Could have put her to bed in a playpen, if I'd had one." Then she smiled. "Should be easy to tend her now. The only thing I forgot was a high chair and I told the man to bring one by this afternoon. I signed for all the stuff, Mr. Richards, and they said they'd bill you." She looked a little apprehensive.

"I'll take care of it," Mark reassured her. "Now, I think Ms. Kincaid would like to talk to you, Cora. Why don't you two have a chat while I put this thing together."

"Okay," Cora answered, "but I have a cake to get out of the oven. I guess we can talk in the kitchen." She eyed Kerri as if trying to decide whether she had ever sat chatting in a kitchen.

Mark followed them into the hall, picked up the crib's mattress and springs, carried them back to the bedroom and dumped them on the floor beside the other pieces. A plastic sack held screws but no instructions. He'd never put a crib together in his life, but it couldn't be all that hard, he reassured himself.

Taking off his suit coat and loosening his tie, he was aware of four bright eyes on the bed watching his every move. That's all he needed, an audience. When he unsuccessfully tried to balance one end while he hooked it to a bottom brace, the whole thing fell. He swore under his breath and the kids laughed.

He was standing with his hands on his hips, trying to decide on a different course of action when Timmy slid off the bed and came over to him. The boy didn't say anything, just stood there, kind of waiting, his wide eyes looking up at Mark.

Mark wondered what the kid was thinking and reined in his impatience. "You want to help?"

Timmy nodded solemnly. "Patti had a crib. My daddy put it together. He let me hold the pieces."

"Good. I could use another pair of hands." Mark lifted up the end section that had fallen. "Can you steady this piece while I screw in the iron bar?"

Timmy nodded.

"I help, too," Patti scooted off the bed and tried to push Timmy out of the way.

Quickly, Mark handed her the sack of screws. "Hold this for me," he said as he gently moved her out of the way.

For a minute her little face scrunched up in disappointment, then as quickly as the sun coming out after a summer rain, she gave Mark a lopsided smile.

Mark let out a sigh of relief. "All right, gang, let's get to work."

In the kitchen, Cora busily removed hot cake pans from the oven, nodding in satisfaction at their rounded chocolate tops. "Some people turn up their noses at box cakes," she said, shooting a challenging glance at Kerri perched on one of the high kitchen stools.

"The only kind I bake," Kerri assured her. "Smells heavenly."

Cora set the pans on hot pads to cool. "I thought I'd leave the kids something to snack on. No telling how long their mom will be gone."

"She didn't give you an hint of how long that would be?" Kerri asked casually.

"Nope. I was just supposed to tend the kids 'til Mr. Richards got home. I figured he knew all about it." She frowned. "Funny that she'd take off without even telling him. Why do you suppose she did that?"

"Did she seem upset or worried?"

Cora thought for a minute. "Kinda preoccupied, you know what I mean? Like she had a lot on her mind."

"How did Timmy and Patti react to her leaving?"

"They didn't throw a fit the way some kids do. Maybe they're used to her going off."

"Did she mention the names of people or places? Did she say whether or not they just arrived in Denver? Or where they'd been before? Anything at all that might give us an idea where she's gone?"

Cora shook her head. "We didn't talk friendly-like. You know, just stuff about the kids that I'd need to know to take care of them for a few hours."

Kerri hid her disappointment. "I didn't find any pictures of her in the children's things. Could you describe her for me?"

Cora cocked her head to one side in a thoughtful manner. "She was a little taller than me—I'm five foot six. I bet she didn't tip the scales at more than a hundred and fifteen. Not carrying around this kind of lard." Cora playfully slapped her fanny. "No gusty wind's going to blow me away."

Kerri laughed appreciatively and then prodded, "What color was her hair and how did she wear it?"

"Light colored, real curly, but not like a perm. You know, natural-like, and shoulder length. She had some of it caught up in one of those newfangled clips." Cora touched her own bleached fuzzy locks. "I've been thinking about getting mine cut shorter. What do you think? They say short hair makes you look younger." She eyed the tapered, dusky waves framing Kerri's face. "You're pretty," she said with an envious sigh. "You could cut yours any old way and still look terrific."

"Thank you," Kerri said quickly. She didn't want

to spend precious time discussing hairstyles. "What color eyes?"

"I wasn't really paying that much attention."

"Would you say that she was a pretty woman?"

"Not *pretty* pretty. Not bad looking, though. Kinda okay."

Kerri groaned inwardly. *Great, that description should really narrow it down.* "Did she make any telephone calls?"

"I don't think so."

"Not even to call a taxi?" Kerri prodded.

"No." Cora thought a minute. "But now that you mention it, I remember she glanced at her watch several times, before she picked up her bag and said it was time to go, like someone was picking her up."

"Do you have any idea who that might have been?"

"Nope." Cora poured a couple of cups of coffee and slid one across the counter to Kerri. "I didn't pay much attention. She said Mr. Richards would pay me when he got home so I just took care of the kids and waited. When he didn't come until nearly seven, I wondered if there'd been a mix-up." She shoved back her glasses and locked eyes with Kerri. "Has there? Been a mix-up?"

"We don't know. But we'd like to talk to the mother, get a few answers. In the meantime, there's the problem of the children. Since you can't stay, and finding someone else suitable may be impossible, Mr. Richards may not have any choice but to contact Social Services to temporarily place the children until their mother comes back."

"No, he wouldn't do that! The poor little things need family. He's their uncle, after all," she said indignantly.

"I don't see him taking care of them all by himself in this bachelor apartment, do you?"

"No, but he can find somebody else to tend them."

"Are you sure? Reliable baby-sitters must be hard to find. Your agency wouldn't have sent you if there'd been somebody else, would they?" Kerri asked innocently.

"I can't give up my cleaning jobs." There was a pugnacious jut to her double chin. "If I don't show up, my ladies will find somebody else and I run the chance of losing my houses. Besides, the kids' ma may show up in a couple of days."

"True." Kerri nodded. "I bet Mr. Richards would make it well worth your while to stay at least that long. And that will give him time to figure out what he should do if their mother doesn't show up."

"Do you think she will?" Cora demanded.

"I haven't a clue," Kerri admitted honestly, as a dozen unanswered questions raced through her mind. Why would any mother choose to leave her children with a stranger? And why warn him not to try to find her? The loving inscription in the little boy's book seemed at odds with this callous treatment. Only painstaking detail work would give her the answers she needed, and Kerri knew better than to let her emotions guide her—or did she? Already, she was interfering, trying to talk the woman into staying with the children.

"Well, I guess I could tend them for a couple of days," Cora conceded. "Now that I've got things set up, it won't be such a headache. I don't think Mr. Richards likes me ordering in all this stuff and moving things around in his fancy rooms, but he better be getting used to it if he plans on keeping these young'uns around."

Kerri agreed.

In the bedroom, Mark surveyed his handiwork with satisfaction. The pieces of the crib were firmly put together, side rails moving smoothly up and down and locking in position, and springs and mattress in place. He smiled at the two children. "We did it."

While Mark had struggled with obstinate bolts and screws, Timmy's little hands were more in the way than a help, but as the crib went together, he'd lost his forlorn look, and now his lopsided grin showed as much satisfaction as Mark's.

Patti held up her little arms. "Me try. Me try."

For a moment Mark hesitated. Then he laughed. "Sure, why not?"

He lifted the little girl over the railing and sat her down in the middle of the crib. Patti clapped her hands with such innocent joy that Mark felt a strange tightening in his throat.

"My bed," she said happily. "My bed."

Mark silently groaned. Too late he realized that he'd made a big mistake. "No, it's the baby's bed."

He reached for the little girl, and tried to lift her out but Patti struck out with her arms and feet with such force that he couldn't get a good hold on her.

She started screaming at top of her lungs, and her piercing cries brought Cora and Kerri into the bedroom at a run.

"What on earth. Are you murdering the child?" Cora glared accusingly at Mark. "What's the matter with Patti?"

"Nothing's the matter with her," Mark answered shortly. "She just doesn't want to get out of the crib."

"She thinks it's hers," Timmy said scowling at Mark. "He put her in it."

Mark started to explain and then gave up. How was

he supposed to know the little girl would make such a fuss? Big tears were flowing down her cheeks and he felt like a perfect jerk.

"Poor baby," Cora soothed. "It's all right, darling. You don't have to get out right this minute. You just lay yourself down and have a nice little nap. Cora will get you a nice little blanket, and tuck you in real nice."

Mark turned and stalked out of the bedroom. Let the women handle the situation. Kids! Who understood them? In the living room, the baby was still asleep in the swing, and Mark gave the infant an apprehensive glance and fled to the sanctuary of his den.

Paperwork was piled up on his desk, and he had a dozen business calls to make, but before he could shift mental gears and take care of any of it, Kerri appeared at the door.

"May I come in?"

"Of course. Excuse the mess."

He got up quickly from his desk chair and scooted a blanket and pillow off the long leather couch so she could sit down. Last night, he'd unpacked his traveling bag in the den instead of his bedroom and been grateful for the small bathroom adjoining it, but as he touched the slight five o'clock shadow on his chin, he realized he hadn't taken time to shave that morning. He'd been too anxious to get someone working on finding the missing Ardie. This whole thing had put him off balance, and now he was conscious of his less than polished appearance. The clear, appraising eyes of Kerri Kincaid did nothing to boost his masculine ego.

"Did you find out anything from Cora?" he asked rather briskly, trying to make up for the unsettling feeling her steady gaze caused him. What was she thinking? That he was a world-class nincompoop when it came to kids? So, what else was new? He leaned back on the corner of his desk and folded his arms. "What did she have to say?"

"Not much, I'm afraid," she admitted. "I was hoping that the children's mother had chatted with her, but I guess there was little verbal exchange between them, except about the kids. Apparently Ardie didn't open up to her at all."

Mark's glower deepened. "Well, so much for getting anything helpful from the baby-sitter."

"Cora did make one interesting comment, though," Kerri added. "She said Ardie kept looking at her watch, and that she might have been picked up by someone. That means she probably didn't take a taxi, but we can check it out. See if any driver picked up a fare at this address."

Mark's face flushed angrily. "So, she ran off with somebody?"

"Could be. On the other hand, she might have been anxious to get away before someone found her and the kids. There could be lots of reasons why she kept checking the time."

"If she went off with someone in a private car, we'll have a hell of a time finding her."

"Maybe they just drove to the airport. We can do an artist's sketch that may jog somebody's memory if she took a bus or plane out of Denver. I don't suppose you have a photo of her, by any chance?"

He shook his head. "I didn't have any idea what she looked like until she came to the funeral."

"Can you describe her?" Kerri found it helpful to have more than one person's verbal picture of a client. People often noticed different things, but Mark's description was fairly close to Cora's. The absent mother had light blond curly hair, medium height, blue eyes, not pretty but not ugly.

"I really didn't notice a lot about her," Mark admitted. "Grief hits people in different ways and I was fighting my own loss when she was here. She didn't seem to need or want anything from me except information about what Jason had left her. Once that was taken care of, she left. I never expected to see her again." He gave a short laugh. "And now I'd pay a ransom just to have her walk through that door. It's a mystery to me how I got saddled with her kids."

"I'd like to take a look at the note she left," Kerri said.

"The note." Mark scrunched up his forehead. "I don't remember what I did with it. Everything was so confused."

"Did you throw it away?"

"I'm pretty sure I didn't," he said, but he picked up a small wastepaper basket, and carefully went through an assortment of envelopes, letters and papers. "Not here. I'll admit that the note made me so angry, I think I might have scrunched it up."

"Well, it might be helpful if you can find it. Even if you remember the exact wording, there might be something more that you're missing."

The telephone rang. When Mark heard his secretary's voice, he prepared himself for a problem. He had left word that he'd be out of the office all morning, and to hold all his calls. "Yes, Eleanor, what is it?"

"A personal telephone call that I think you ought to know about."

Mark could picture her sturdy body and the no-nonsense jut of her chin. Eleanor ran his office like the queen's frigate armed for battle. He rarely took issue with any decision the older woman made.

"A man called asking for you and when I told him you were out, he swore at me and demanded your telephone number. Of course, I refused and asked him to leave a message. He said to tell you that your sister-in-law was playing a dangerous game and you'd better make sure to keep your own nose clean."

Mark's hand tightened on the receiver. "And he didn't give a name?"

"No. Just said he would be keeping an eye on things, and then slammed the receiver down. Very strange, don't you think?"

"Yes, isn't it," Mark said sharply. "If he calls again, give him my number. Better still, give him my address."

"Yes, sir, if you think that's wise," Eleanor answered with a reprimand in her tone.

Mark hung up without replying and turned to Kerri. He repeated what his secretary had told him. "So, someone else may come around looking for Ardie." Mark set his jaw. "And if he does, I'll make sure he tells us what we need to know."

Kerri felt a spurt of apprehension. How, exactly would the caller go about keeping his eye on things?

Chapter Three

When Kerri returned to the office, she immediately began to initiate the search for Ardie Richards. There were many resources that could be tapped by contacting certain agencies and records. She was familiar enough with state and national archives to know which offices might provide her with statistics and personal data on every citizen in the United States.

"I thought you'd take the case," Debbie said with a smug smile.

"There are some unusual aspects to it," Kerri replied evenly.

"Yeah, sure. I knew that right off. The minute Mark Richards walked in the door, I said to myself, an interesting case, very interesting."

Kerri laughed. "You're impossible, Debbie. My taking the case has nothing to do with the client's sex appeal."

"Oh, so you did notice." Debbie grinned. "Well, I'd say that's some progress. For a good-looking gal, you sure keep the romantic burner on low. Since I've been here, there've been a half-dozen fellows trying to quiz me about your love life. I'm up-front with them and tell them, 'Love life? She doesn't have any.'"

Debbie cocked her head. "Maybe I'll have something different to tell them any day now."

"Debbie, you're an incurable romantic. Mr. Richards is a client who is depending upon us to find his sister-in-law and get him out of a difficult situation. I suggest we get started." Her voice became brisk and businesslike. We need to find out Ardie Richards's full name. We'll probably find it on a marriage license. I don't know where she and Jason Richards were married but I suspect California or Nevada. His office was in Los Angeles, and we know she met him in Reno. Check those states' marriage records first, and see what you come up with."

Debbie turned to her computer, and Kerri went into her office and pulled out a missing person's profile form. In addition to detailed questions concerning the missing person, this form also contained questions about any client seeking the missing person. It included relationship, circumstances of separation, and whether or not the search had been conducted before. Often a client had pertinent information about the missing person that he wasn't even aware of. It was possible that a client was deliberately holding back information that seemed too personal to share with anyone.

Kerri had warned Mark before she left the apartment, "If you're deliberately holding back anything pertaining to this case, I'll drop it faster than you can draw your next breath."

"I've told you everything," he had assured her.

"And if anyone shows up asking about Ardie, I want you to contact me immediately."

"All right, but if the guy knows anything, I'll get it out of him, one way or another."

"Don't try to handle this yourself," she warned him. "We haven't a clue as to who or what's involved in her disappearance. At this point, we need to go slowly and not close off any doors. Understand?"

He assured her that he did. When he walked with her to the elevator, she impulsively touched his arm. "I know you want this thing settled, but it may take time. Cora's willing to stay a few more days. Try to take it easy. You hired me to do a job, now let me do it."

She was surprised when he put a hand over hers and let it stay there. "Yes, boss. I understand." He gave her a wry smile. "I used to play football and I never second-guess the quarterback. You're calling the signals."

Sitting at her desk, Kerri felt a peculiar warmth creep up into her cheeks remembering the softness in those dark eyes of his. Debbie had been right about one thing. He had enough sex appeal to package.

Enough of that, she scolded herself. Keeping a detached perspective was essential for success in this business. She needed a clear head and steady nerves, neither of which matched the emotions she was beginning to entertain about three abandoned children and an engaging man who desperately needed her help.

She looked at the notes she'd made in Mark's study. He'd told her that the California office his brother had managed had a good staff, and for the moment, he was letting the office personnel stand as is. "Feel free to talk to Jeff Elders," Mark had said. "He's in charge now and he might have more information about Ardie than anyone."

Reaching for the phone she called the number of Fidelity Financial Investors in California. An efficient receptionist answered the phone, and asked a couple of questions before she put Kerri through to Mr. Elders. He had a pleasant voice and seemed eager to be of help when Kerri introduced herself, but when she told him that she was trying to locate Jason Richards's wife, he had little information to offer.

"Sorry. I never met Mrs. Richards. The lady wasn't from Los Angeles, you know. Jason met her in Reno, I believe. He did a lot of commuting to see her and we figured she had some kind of business she couldn't leave, but Jason never said what it was. I didn't get to fly to Denver for the funeral because things were kind of in a bind here," he offered in an apologetic tone. "Why are you trying to locate Mrs. Richards, may I ask?"

"There's a business matter to take care of." *Like two little abandoned kids and a baby.*

"Well, I'm afraid I can't help."

"Did Jason happen to mention anything about her background, like where she might have grown up, or gone to school?"

"Not that I remember. Of course, Jason never told us much about his private life, but, I confess, we were all a little startled when he told us he'd gotten married. He just announced that he had a new wife, and two months later he was dead. Kinda makes you wonder, doesn't it?"

"About what, Mr. Elders?"

"Oh, about life. You know, the way things turn out. Jason didn't live long enough to enjoy a decent honeymoon."

"Do you by chance know what Mrs. Richards's first name was?"

"Let me see…Ardie…that's what Jason called her."

"Any mention of a last name?"

"No, I don't think so. If he did, I don't remember what it was."

"Do you know if she was married before?"

"Jason never said. He never brought her to the office and it surprised us a little that he didn't seem to be in a hurry to find a place here in the city for the two of them. Of course, they'd only been married two months, you know."

"Well, thank you Mr. Elders. If you think of anything that might help us to locate Mrs. Richards, please call me at this number." She recited it to him.

"Doesn't Mark have her address?"

Would I be calling if he did? Kerri politely thanked Mr. Elders, hung up the phone and leaned back in her chair. Trying to access records without a full name was going to be tedious and frustrating. Her only hope was to find a thread that they could unravel and gather more clues as they went along. She sighed, knowing that this snail-pace approach demanded a lot of patience and time. She wasn't certain Mark Richards had a generous supply of either, although she really couldn't blame him. His well-ordered life had been turned upside down without a moment's warning. It was a mystery why Ardie had chosen him to take over the care of her kids.

MARK WAS HAVING the same kind of thoughts as he sat in his downtown office and stared unseeing at a stack of reports that needed his attention. He'd always prided himself on being the kind of guy who could size up a situation and take the appropriate action. He wanted to get things settled and back to normal. His mind searched for some immediate solution but none came.

He didn't know quite what he was feeling, but the word *trapped* came to mind. In less than twenty-four hours, three abandoned kids had taken over his life. Until their mother was found, there was no way he could avoid the responsibility of their welfare. He'd had to clean up a lot of messes for his brother, but Jason had outdone himself this time.

His secretary, Eleanor, came in with some letters for him to sign and Mark quizzed her again about the man who had called earlier.

"I told you everything. He wanted your telephone number. When I refused to give it to him, he swore at me." Eleanor's matronly nose rose an inch. She'd been an executive secretary too long to take any kind of verbal abuse, and Mark suspected she'd let the caller know it.

"Then what happened?"

"I agreed to give you a message. That's when he said your sister-in-law was playing a dangerous game and you'd better keep your own nose clean." She met Mark's eyes squarely. "What's going on?"

When Mark had finally arrived at the office, he'd hesitated to say anything to Eleanor about the abandoned kids. He'd been all business, concentrating on telephone calls to return, and attending to details from his business trip that needed prompt attention. He knew it was probably foolish, but he kept hoping that somehow the whole problem would be solved in quick order. Maybe the children's mother would show up at any moment. Mark set his jaw. Cora was supposed to call him immediately if she came back.

"You've been awfully closemouthed today." Eleanor prodded. "Want to talk about it?"

"You're not going to believe this." He managed a wry grin. "I still can't believe it myself. When I got back from my trip last night, I found three strange children and a baby-sitter encamped in my apartment. They'd moved in on me while I was gone."

"That's impossible!" Eleanor's usual composure gave way to an expression of utter disbelief.

"Jason's widow dumped them there. She took off. Left me a note saying she had to leave for while." Mark's mouth tightened. "She warned me not to try to find her, but I've hired Kerri Kincaid at Finders, Inc. to track her down."

"I didn't know Jason married a woman with children."

"Neither did I. She must have been widowed or divorced very recently when Jason married her, because she has a baby, a little girl about two, and a five-year-old boy. I'm guessing she married my brother for financial support, and when he died unexpectedly, she was on her own again. Instead of coming to me in an honest fashion, she just dumped the kids and took off."

"Good heavens. What are you going to do? A bachelor like yourself can't look after them. I've seen your loft. It's not set up for family living."

Mark laughed grimly. "It is now. My bedroom, bathroom and living room are filled with kids' stuff and rented furniture like cribs, a swing and a playpen. I'm trying to hold a beachhead in the den, but I fully expect to have lost that ground when I go home today."

"This must be awful for you. I know how much

you love your privacy. Why would the woman even think that you would be willing to keep them?''

Mark was saved from trying to answer by the buzz of the telephone. His secretary reached over, punched the right button on the intercom. "Fidelity Investors, Miss Donner speaking." She frowned and asked briskly, "May I say who's calling? Just a moment." She covered the receiver. "Somebody named Cora Dunbar. Says she has to talk to you right away. She sounds terribly upset.

Mark grabbed the phone. "Yes, Cora, what is it?"

"Oh, Mr. Richards, I don't know what to do. Dear God in heaven," her voice broke in a choked sob. "I've looked every place I can think of. One end of this place to the other. I didn't want to call but you said I should if I...if I needed to." She was weeping openly now. "I don't know how it happened."

Mark's mind raced in all directions, trying to make some sense out of her disjointed babble. Was Cora indulging in unwarranted hysterics or had something serious happened? He wanted to shake the truth out of the woman, but he managed a firm commanding tone. "Stop crying, Cora. I can't help if you don't tell me what's wrong."

"It's Timmy," she sobbed. "He's gone."

"Gone? What in blazes do you mean...gone?"

"I can't find him. I've looked in every hiding place I can think of, you know, thinking the little rascal was playing hide-and-seek, but he's not here. I know he isn't. He's gone."

"But he couldn't leave the apartment. The front door's locked, isn't it?"

Another choked sob. "The deliverymen brought another crib. Patti was making such a fuss over the first one that I decided to rent another one. I guess I didn't think about locking the door after them.''

"So, anyone could have walked in or out," Mark growled, knowing it was too late to indulge in recriminations now.

"What'll I do?" Cora pleaded.

"Nothing. Stay where you are. I'm coming home now." He slammed down the receiver and turned to Eleanor. "Call Kerri Kincaid at Finders, Inc. Tell her that Timmy can't be found and ask her to get right over to my place. She's only a few blocks away, and can walk it faster than I can drive from here." He swore. "There's a Rockies game this afternoon. The traffic will be horrendous."

"What could have happened to the boy?" Eleanor asked as she followed his strong stride into the outer office.

"Maybe nothing. He could be playing a game with Cora, stirring up a lot of attention for himself," Mark said crisply, but his tone denied the sudden churning in his stomach. This physical evidence of a protective streak took him by surprise. He wouldn't have believed that a little freckle-faced boy could get under his skin so fast. "I'm sure he's all right," he said as much to himself as to Eleanor.

"I hope so," his secretary said without much conviction in her voice. "There's a heck of lot about this whole situation that doesn't add up."

KERRI WAS ALREADY at the apartment when Mark arrived, still cursing the congested streets around Coors Field. He could hear the blare of the loudspeakers broadcasting the pregame warm-up. His fifth floor apartment had a good view of the brick stadium out of the large span of windows. Ordinarily, he would have been tempted to slip away and take in the afternoon game, but his thoughts were certainly not on baseball as he strode into the apartment.

"Any luck?" he asked Kerri, knowing her answer from the creased lines around her eyes. He could hear Cora in the kitchen, talking loudly above the demanding cries of the baby and Patti's high-pitched voice.

"The boy's not in the apartment. I've double-checked every place that Cora looked and a few more hiding places besides."

"You're sure?" He wanted the matter to be solved quickly and smoothly. He wanted to find the child playing a foolish game with them, because any other scenario held too many frightening connotations. At Kerri's firm nod, he put aside such hopes. This was no time for wishful thinking.

"All right then, what are the other possibilities?"

"Timmy slipped out of the apartment and decided to go exploring."

"On his own?" Mark looked skeptical.

"It's possible," Kerri assured him. "A five-year-old can have a false sense of confidence. When one of my nephews was about that age, he took off on his own for a bus trip. He had enough money to get downtown but he didn't even think about the fare back home. It's hard to get into a kid's mind about some of these things."

"Well, Timmy struck me as a stubborn little boy who might do something foolish."

"I called the furniture rental agency and talked to one of the deliverymen. They remembered seeing the boy when they came in with the crib."

"So, he must have left after they left?"

"Or while they were here. He could have slipped out then by himself...or with someone else."

Someone else?

They looked at each other in weighted silence. Neither one of them wanted to verbalize what was flashing through their minds. The possibility that the man looking for Ardie had found her children and taken Timmy was too frightening to contemplate. They had no evidence that such a bizarre thing had happened, but it was at the front of their minds anyway.

"Let's not get melodramatic," Mark said evenly. "The boy may have taken an elevator ride. He could be on one of the floors below. Most likely he'll end up in the foyer, or back here. Let's check out the building as best we can." He hoped he sounded more confident than he felt.

Twenty minutes later, they were back without having seen any sign of the child or gaining any information from anyone who might have run into him.

Cora was sitting in his recliner chair, giving the baby her bottle while Patti dressed and undressed a doll at her feet. The baby-sitter's round face fell like a high-altitude cake when they came back alone.

"I have a brother-in-law on the police force," Kerri said quietly. "He'll put the word out for us."

Mark paced the den while she made the call. All right, the boy wasn't in the building as far as they could tell. They'd have to expand the search to the crowded streets of downtown Denver. He blanched just thinking about the congested streets and sidewalks. He knew that today of all days, the area around Coors Field would be a moving mass of humanity, because as often as he could, he walked around the corner and took in an afternoon game. He'd been a

Rockies fan since their first game several years ago. As his eyes swung to the glass case holding his autographed baseball, he blinked and stared.

His prized ball was gone. He'd put it back under the glass case after he'd taken it away from Timmy. He remembered the bright gleam in the boy's eyes when he'd asked Mark, "Wanna play catch?"

Kerri hung up the phone. "Harry will put the word out. Then seeing a sudden flash of insight deepen Mark's eyes, she asked anxiously, "What is it?"

"I'm not sure." He spun on his heels and went into the living room where Cora was burping the baby. "What was Timmy doing the last time you remember seeing him?"

She thought for a moment. "Just wandering around, looking out the windows—"

"Which windows? The ones overlooking Coors Field?"

She nodded. "There was a lot of noise coming up from the street. Game day, I told him. He said that he liked baseball. I told him that maybe he could watch it on TV. I was going to check and see if the game was on channel two, but the baby needed changing and I forgot. When I came back into the room, he was gone." Her eyes rounded. "You don't think...? No, he's too little to be running off like that."

"If he loves baseball as much as I think he does, he could have gotten it into his head to go see the game," Mark reasoned. The unwanted responsibility for the kid weighed heavily on him. What he knew about kids that age could be put in a child's thimble.

"You think he went to the game?" Kerri frowned.

"It's a possibility."

"Let's check it out."

Even though Kerri thought Mark was really grasping at straws, she didn't have a better idea. She knew from her nieces and nephews that sometimes kids did crazy things. It was just like a five-year-old to take off, not thinking about tickets or anything else, like safety.

They rode down the elevator and hurried out to the busy street and crowded sidewalk. Mark took her hand as they moved quickly with the surging crowd toward Twentieth Street and the stadium fashioned of red brick with a large clock over the main entrance. Streams of people were lined up in front of the ticket gates.

Mark and Kerri craned their necks in every direction, searching for a small towheaded boy. Even if Timmy had gotten this far, the chances of finding him in the throng of people pressing toward the ticket gates looked nearly impossible.

"I can't believe he'd have enough courage to try to get into the game, but I don't see how we can question any of the ticket takers in this mob."

Kerri agreed, and wondered how soon the crowd would thin out—and if they'd find him when it did. There was always the possibility that he'd gotten frightened and never made it as far as the stadium, The little boy could have tried to backtrack, lost his bearings, and headed off in God knows what direction.

Mark tightened his handclasp and she knew he was having similar worries. "There's no way he could slip past the ticket takers, so if he came here, he has to still be outside."

"Maybe we could ask some of the vendors," she suggested, knowing it was foolhardy to expect anyone to notice a small boy in this bedlam.

What if someone had picked him up?

This fear stabbed Mark as they moved past the congestion at the front gates and walked a short distance in one direction and then turned back, passing the main gates, searching on the opposite side. At this end of the stadium, three mammoth baseball figures were mounted on a brick wall. The frescoes had been painted gold and stood out against the deep red brick. Mark was so used to seeing them that he paid them little attention, and was startled when Kerri suddenly threw out her arm and pointed at them.

Why was she excited about the figures? It wasn't until she gestured frantically that he realized she wasn't pointing at the figures, but at a little boy who had his head tipped back, and was looking up at the figures of the baseball players.

"Timmy! Timmy!" Kerri called.

The child turned around slowly, and grinned when he saw her and Mark. Then he waved at them with the autographed ball in his hand.

"Thank heaven," breathed Mark, admitting to himself that worry had stretched his nerves to the snapping point.

As they hurried toward him, Timmy's smile faded and his smile changed to an expression of fear. Kerri thought he was going to turn in the other direction and run away, but instead he ran as fast as he could toward them and threw himself into Mark's arms.

Kerri swung around to see what on earth had frightened the child. Something? Or someone? She couldn't tell. There was only the crowd, the noise and the retreating back of a man with a black ponytail who might have been following them.

Chapter Four

With Timmy walking between them, holding on tightly to their hands, they started back to the apartment. Several times the boy looked behind him with rounded eyes and a pinched look around his mouth.

Kerri and Mark exchanged glances. She could tell he was ready to sail into anyone who even looked the least bit threatening. No question about it, Timmy had found someone to look after him, and the way things were going, Mark was going to be a godsend. He was probably asking the same bewildering question as she. What had sent Timmy racing into Mark's arms? She knew Timmy was likely to clam up if they pushed too soon, and too hard, so her look warned Mark to be patient.

Smiling down at the child, she squeezed the sweaty little hand in hers. "Everything's okay, Timmy. Don't worry, we'll take care of you. Everything's okay."

Mark took his cue from her. "Sure thing, buddy," he said, even though one part of him wanted to light into the kid for leaving the apartment. The last hour had been hell, but he'd never forget the way the little boy had thrown himself into his arms and clung to

him. Timmy's first smile at seeing them had changed
to a look of childish terror in an instant. Why?

As they walked, Mark surveyed the sidewalk and
streets. Only a few stragglers hurried in the direction
of the ballpark, and no one was paying the trio any
attention.

When they reached the front door of the building,
Timmy darted into the foyer ahead of them, very much
like a young animal grateful for a safe burrow. Almost
immediately, he lost his haunted look. As they waited
for the elevator, he asked eagerly, "Can I push the
button? I know how."

"Sure, you can," Kerri agreed readily.

"Do you know what floor?" Mark demanded. He
wasn't in the mood to play games. He wanted to get
on with the business at hand—finding out what in the
hell was going on.

As Timmy hesitated, Kerri answered for him. "It's
five. Do you know your numbers, Timmy?"

He nodded, and as they stepped inside the elevator,
one of his little fingers thumped the number *five*. He
gave them a broad grin as he waited for their approval.
"See, I can run it all by myself."

"So we've noticed," Mark said dryly, biting back
a lecture about staying out of the elevator unless an
adult was with him. The kid had no business running
all over the place on his own. Now that they had found
him, his worry was changing into annoyance.

Kerri ignored Mark's frown and said smoothly,
"You're a big boy, all right, Timmy." She gave his
unruly curly hair an affectionate ruffle. "I think you're
going to be a big help to us. I bet we can find some
milk and cookies, and then we'll have a nice little talk.
Okay?"

"Okay," Timmy agreed.

As the elevator doors flew open, the little boy bounded down the hall ahead of them in a kind of childish half skip that made Mark shake his head. Kids. Who could outguess them? Such quicksilver moods left him feeling off balance. He gave Kerri an appreciative smile. "You're something else."

"What do you mean?"

"I would have lighted into the kid and clammed him up for good. Promising him milk and cookies disarmed him completely. Now, you've got him eating out of your hand."

"Maybe, maybe not. Kids are unpredictable."

"Well, if you're as good with adults as you are with kids, I've hired the best investigator around." He admitted to himself that he not only respected her professionalism, but he was beginning to enjoy her company for her own sake.

"Don't be handing me any bouquets yet. I haven't a clue as to what's going on." She lowered her voice. "I think Timmy saw something or someone who frightened him."

"Maybe he thought he was in trouble for running away and put on that little act to soften us up."

"I don't think a five-year-old is ingenious enough to change from glowing pleasure to sudden terror in a split second. His fear was genuine, all right."

"You think he recognized someone? What are the chances that someone he knows would turn up at Coors field?"

Kerri didn't answer. She wasn't ready to offer the possibility that there might be a connection between the man who had called Mark's office and whoever had spooked Timmy. There were too many what-ifs.

What if the caller found out where the children were? What if he somehow knew they were looking for Timmy? And what if he'd followed them to the stadium and saw the boy just about the same time they did?

She gave herself a mental shake. Too much speculation could be hazardous to clear thinking. She knew better than to try to connect too many things, too soon. Experience had taught her not to leap ahead of the facts, because once an investigation was headed in a wrong direction, valuable time was lost having to backtrack. And with the future of three children involved, it was more imperative than ever that she not make any mistakes.

When they entered the apartment, Cora came running from the kitchen. She gave a squeal of delight when she saw Timmy. Rushing forward, she enveloped the little boy in her round arms, and nearly hugged the breath out of him.

"Thank the Lord," she murmured. Then she drew back, frowned, and shaking a finger at him, she scolded him for being such a bad boy. "You need the seat of your pants warmed, that's what. Running off like that. Don't you ever take one step out of this apartment by yourself again. Do you understand? All kinds of bad things can happen to kids running around loose." At Timmy's sudden pallor, she hugged him again. "But you're back safe and sound. That's all that matters now."

"I promised Timmy some milk and cookies, Cora. Could you bring some into the den?" Kerri didn't want the baby-sitter influencing the boy's attitude before they had a chance to pump Timmy for information.

"Sure thing. I've got the little ones down for a nap."

Kerri took Timmy's hand and led the way into Mark's den.

"You want to put this back for me? I think you know where it belongs." Mark took the autographed ball out of his pocket.

Guilt brought a rise of color into Timmy's peaked face as Mark handed him the baseball. Longing was in the boy's every move as he carefully he put the ball back on its stand and replaced the glass cover.

"I'll get you another ball to play with, Timmy," Mark promised. "This one is kinda special to me." He made the admission with a slight sense of embarrassment because he didn't want Kerri to think he was one of those sport nuts who organized their whole life around some team. Baseball had always been his pick of sports, and he'd been financially involved in bringing Denver's first major league baseball team, the Rockies, here. When he'd been given the autographed ball as a gesture of appreciation after their first successful season, he'd been delighted. Supporting the Colorado team was a matter of pride and pleasure, and the ball meant something personal to him. He would have hated to lose it.

"A real ball?" Timmy prodded. "Not a baby rubber one."

"I promise you it will be a real baseball, Timmy."

The sudden joy in his childish grin brought a strange tightening in Mark's chest. He remembered the Christmas that his first baseball, bat and mitt had been under the Christmas tree. Even though there had been snow all over the ground, he'd insisted on going outdoors to play catch with his father and his younger brother. The three of them had had a wonderful time, yelling and running and falling down in the snow. The memory made him realize how different his upbringing must have been from this small boy's. How lucky he himself had been to have a stable and loving family. Mark couldn't imagine his mother abandoning him for even a moment. A protective anger surged through him and he had trouble keeping his thoughts about the kid's mother to himself. When they caught up with her, he'd have plenty to say.

Kerri made a quick call to her brother-in-law, the policeman. "The lost is found, Harry."

"Great. Where'd you find him?"

"Wandering around Coors Field. I'll fill you in tonight. Thanks."

"No problem. Glad to be of help."

Cora brought in a glass of milk for Timmy and a plate of cookies. Mark offered Kerri a drink from a small bar, but she refused. Sitting beside Timmy on the leather couch, she nibbled on a cookie while Mark plopped down in a nearby recliner and sipped his Scotch and water. She could tell that he was impatient to begin the questioning, but she took her time and waited until Timmy was nearly finished with his snack before she asked casually, "Timmy, did you see someone you know at the ballpark?"

He blinked at her, a white ring of milk around his mouth and a half-eaten cookie in his suddenly still hand. He swallowed hard and didn't answer.

"Who was it, Timmy?" she insisted, not giving him the chance to deny that he'd seen someone. "You can tell me."

His hand tightened over the cookie, crushing it into

pieces and he hunched down in the soft cushion as if trying to make himself smaller.

"It's all right, Timmy." Kerri tenderly put an arm around his fragile shoulders and drew the child closer. Resting her head against his, she coaxed softly. "What is his name? Who did you see?"

His pale lips moved and a strangled name came out in a whisper, too low for her to hear.

"Who?" She coaxed, gently stroking his tousled hair and holding her own breath.

"Dirk."

Not certain that she'd heard correctly, she repeated the name. "Dirk?"

He nodded. The child's slender shoulders stiffened, and he pressed closer to Kerri's side.

"You saw Dirk? At the ballpark?"

He nodded again, more vigorously this time.

"And you don't like Dirk," she said evenly, not as a question but as a statement. "Why not?"

The haunted look was back in his face, and his eyes fled to the doorway as if he expected the dreaded Dirk to appear any second.

"You can tell me, honey. Why are you frightened of this man, Dirk."

Timmy raised a pleading face to Kerri, "He thinks me and Patti and Pammy ought to be drowned in the river...like...like baby kittens." His lips quivered as he whimpered, "You won't let him, will you? You won't let him?"

Mark growled an oath, cursing the heartless man that had put such fear into the child. "Nobody's going to throw you in any river," Mark said angrily. "And if he shows up here, I'll take care of him in short order." His voice was strident and his face flushed.

"He's coming after me. I saw him. I saw him," Timmy wailed.

Mark scowled. Who in the hell was this guy, Dirk? And what was he doing sneaking around, frightening a little boy to death—if it really was the same guy? It was possible that Timmy had mistaken a perfect stranger for the man who had obviously put the fear of God in him.

When Kerri sent Mark a warning glance, he forced himself to shut up. He knew that he should let her handle the child, so he restrained himself from asking a legion of questions that needed answering. Nobody was going to hurt this kid. Nobody.

Kerri cuddled Timmy for several minutes, then she asked gently, "Is Dirk a friend of your mother's?"

Timmy choked, "No."

"Not a friend? Just someone she knows?"

An unreadable expression crossed his face, his mouth puckered as if trying to hold back tears.

"Can you tell us who knows Dirk?"

He nodded solemnly and stretched out his little arm, pointing to a picture on the wall of Mark standing with his brother. "Him."

For a weighted moment, neither Kerri nor Mark said anything. Utterly confused, they looked at Timmy, back at the picture, and then Mark left his chair, took the photograph down from the wall and handed it to the boy. He pointed at his brother, Jason. "This man knows Dirk?"

Timmy nodded.

Mark's astonishment was evident in his raised voice. "Are you sure?"

The child turned his head and buried his face against Kerri's chest, his tiny body clinging to hers.

Kerri bent her head and kissed his wet cheek. "It's all right, honey. No more questions." She sent a warning look at Mark.

He nodded, sorry that his raised voice had scared the boy. His impatience to know how his brother was connected to the man that held such terror for Timmy was so strong that it was a struggle to keep his mouth shut. Bewildering questions stabbed at him. Why had the boy connected the man with his brother? When in the two months that Jason had been married to Ardie, had Timmy been frightened by this man, Dirk? And why had he been close enough to the children to scare Timmy with the threat of drowning him?

Kerri tenderly cupped his little chin and raised up his tear-smeared face. "It's okay, Timmy. You've been a good boy. So good, I think I ought to read you a story. Would you like that?" At his slight nod, she said, "Good, let's go find a book."

After they left, Mark stood for a long moment, staring at the photograph in his hand. He hadn't really looked at it for a long time, but neither he nor his brother had changed much since it had been taken five years ago. The camera had always liked Jason, with his ready smile and relaxed stance that made him seem perfectly at ease. He was a head shorter than Mark, and usually thirty pounds heavier, but the family resemblance was there, same light brown hair, darker eyebrows, and firm mouth and chin. In looks, people might have taken them for brothers, but never in personality, Mark admitted. Jason had been easygoing, uncomplicated, and willing to let his older brother handle the nitty-gritty demands of their partnership. There had been times when Mark wished he was more like his brother—always going with the flow, and

never looking too far ahead. Jason's personal life was
always in a state of flux, and in the beginning Mark
had worried about his brother's fouled-up marriages
and romantic relationships, but he'd gotten over trying
to understand what was going on in his brother's personal life. Now he wished he'd kept in closer contact.
What was the connection between Jason and the callous man who made threats about a little boy like
Timmy?

Mark put the photograph back on the wall, fixed
himself a stronger drink and tried his best to put some
sense and order into the current tangle of kids, people
and dire questions.

When Kerri came back, she said, "He's asleep. I
don't think we ought to put any more pressure on him
for the moment. He's had enough trauma today for
one little boy." She glanced at her watch. "I need to
get back to the office and get some more wheels spinning."

Mark tried not to show his irritation. He'd been
waiting for her to come back so they could discuss
this latest complication, and here she was, ready to
take off without any attempt to clarify the situation.
His tone was brisk. "You're not even going to ask me
about Jason and why the kid pointed him out as a
friend of this bastard, Dirk?"

Her forehead creased in a slight frown. "From your
obvious astonishment, I assumed that you didn't have
the vaguest idea. I'm sorry, Mark. Have you thought
of something?"

"Not a damn thing!" he snapped.

A hint of a smile curved her lips. "Frustrating, isn't
it?"

"I don't know how you can be so...so blasé."

"If by blasé, you mean unconcerned, you're quite wrong. I don't know what this incident means, or how it fits into the picture of the children's mother disappearing, but I'm confident that in time we'll know."

"In time!" he sputtered. "We've got an impossible situation here. We need to do something now."

"Like what?"

"I don't know." He gave an impatient gesture with his hand. "Finding people is your business, not mine."

"Then why don't you let me handle it as I think best?"

He knew when he'd been checkmated. He backed off, mumbling, "Sorry. Didn't mean to come on so strong. I'm inclined to get a little aggressive when I'm worried. I just can't make heads or tails of this thing. Do you think the kids are in any danger?"

Kerri frowned. "We'd better make sure they're not left alone. If someone like Dirk is trying to find Ardie, who knows what could happen. We don't have enough of the puzzle to predict anything. I've warned Cora to keep the doors locked and not to let anyone in. I'll talk to my brother-in-law and see what he suggests. For the time being that's about all we can do."

"We could move them."

"Where?" She eyed him steadily. "Are you thinking of turning them over to someone else? Social Services, perhaps?"

"You think I'd do that?" he asked stiffly.

"No, of course not," she answered, instantly contrite. She had to give him credit. He'd given every indication that he'd do whatever was best for the children, and he'd rallied amazingly well for a man who was used to a smooth, well-ordered life-style. Not only had his fashionable bachelor pad been turned upside down, but his emotions as well. No telling what they would find out about his late brother. She feared that the worst was yet to come, and there was no way to protect him from any ugliness she might uncover.

"Just tell me what needs to be done," he said quietly, returning her contemplative gaze. "I'm teachable."

As their eyes caught, a peculiar fluttering of warmth went through her. His superbly fit body, his pervading masculine aura, and the way his strong mouth eased into a devastating smile was addictive. He moved closer to her, and for a moment she felt a longing to lean into him and experience his strong virility by being cradled in his arms. Fortunately the impulse was fleeting. Lowering her gaze, she took a step back, and thought, *I'm getting as bad as Debbie.*

As he walked with her into the spacious living area, the melodic chimes of the doorbell echoed through the loft. They exchanged startled expressions as if both of them had the same thought. Dirk?

Mark strode to the front door, quickly slipped the lock and jerked it open with a threatening expression that quickly faded when he saw who it was.

"Oh, Ted and Lisa," he said, surprised.

"Hey, have we come at a bad time?" his neighbor asked. "You look ready for bear."

The attractive blond woman at Ted's side smiled at Mark. A gold-colored dress, two inches above her knee, clung to her like Christmas wrapping. She had long legs, curvaceous hips and a bustline that could have been an ad for silicone implants. Kerri hated her on sight. "Ted was telling me you've got yourself a bit of a problem," she said as her gray-green eyes flickered to Kerri and then back to Mark.

"Come in," Mark invited with a wave of his hand, remembering his manners. Damn! He'd forgotten all about his promise to take Ted's niece to the traveling production of *Les Misérables*. He'd met Lisa a couple of weeks earlier when Ted had invited a few people in to meet his visting niece from Chicago. Mark had set up the date, told his secretary to get the tickets, and then completely forgotten that the performance was tonight. He'd taken Lisa out to dinner once and had enjoyed her company but he sure wasn't in any mood at the moment to play the gallant escort. Not with everything he had on his mind.

Ted greeted Kerri warmly. "Nice to see you again, Miss Kincaid," he said, as if it had been more than a few hours since Mark had introduced them. "Making any progress in tracking down the missing mother? I told Lisa that Mark had hired a professional. One of the best," Ted said in a flattering tone which did nothing to defuse Kerri's suspicions that he'd never heard of her or her company until today.

Kerri gave him a noncommittal smile and didn't answer. She wasn't about to discuss any details of the case. Finders, Inc. had a reputation for complete and strict confidentiality and she intended to keep it that way. If Mark wanted to share with his neighbor what was going on, that was his business. From the closed look on Mark's face, she doubted that he was going to satisfy Ted's curiosity.

"Just can't believe a woman would run off like that." Ted said, glancing around the disheveled room with it's baby swing, playpen, and scattered toys.

"She sure didn't do you any favors, guy. Dumping her kids on you like this."

"You're not going to keep them here, are you?" Lisa asked with a slight upturn of her pretty nose. "I mean, a man needs his privacy."

The hint of a secret smile in Lisa's eyes made Kerri wonder if the sexy niece and Mark had enjoyed some romantic trysts in his bachelor apartment. Obviously, three kids and a baby-sitter would put a crimp in any gal's style.

"At the moment there are no plans to move them," Mark answered evenly.

Ted groaned. "You mean, we have to put up with this racket for heaven knows how long? What if the woman doesn't come back after them? Or Miss Kincaid can't find her? What then?"

"We'll have to take it as it comes," Mark said shortly, cutting off any more discussion.

Kerri moved purposefully toward the door, and then, pausing with her hand on the doorknob, her frank, clear eyes met Mark's. "It's important that you let me know of any new developments here. Anything. Anything at all."

Mark nodded, and for a moment, Kerri though he might follow her out into the hall, but Lisa said something quietly to him and laughed softly. The laughter had an intimate tone to it.

Kerri closed the door with punctuating impatience. Some women really irked her, and Kerri readily admitted to a feminine bias against statuesque blondes who looked as if they belonged in a Lancôme ad. She wondered how much time Lisa had been spending in Mark's apartment, and then shoved the thought away into the Not Relevant compartment. Her own relation-

ship with Mark Richards was strictly business and she
intended to keep it that way.

WHEN KERRI GOT BACK to the office, she learned that
Debbie had drawn a blank on finding any marriage
records for Jason P. Richards in the two most likely
places for the wedding to have taken place, California
and Nevada. The Vital Statistics Department in Sac-
ramento had no record of the marriage and neither did
the Division of Health-Vital Statistics in Carson City,
Nevada. Kerri was disappointed because a marriage
license offered valuable information about each of the
parties: name, address, date and place of birth. It also
gave previous marital status—married or never married—whether the last marriage ended by death, di-
vorce or annulment and the number of previous marriages. Naturally, it also provided information about
the current marriage, such as where the ceremony took
place, name of the person performing the ceremony,
signatures of the bride and groom and names of witnesses.

A veritable gold mine if they could just hit the vein.

Without more than just the name, Ardie, they were
at a standstill in accessing other records. Once they
found a record of Jason Richards's marriage, they'd
have the name of his bride. Kerri prayed it had been
a legal marriage and not one of these modern live-
together arrangements. "Try all the states, if you have
to," Kerri told Debbie. "Maybe we'll get lucky."

Weary from so many unanswered questions, Kerri
finally called it a day and went home. She still lived
at home with her mother and grandmother, an arrangement that surprised most people. No one seemed to
understand why a successful businesswoman who

could afford to live anywhere in the city would be
happy in the same neighborhood, the same house, the
same bedroom; content with the same chaotic family
living that she'd had all her life. Kerri didn't understand it herself. It just felt right. She was happy living
at home. Not that she didn't want a home of her own,
she did, but she wanted a home, not a house. A fancy
address wouldn't create what she wanted from life,
which was family love, and a lot of sharing.

Her siblings, three brothers and two sisters, were
married with children. One of her sisters lived in the
neighborhood, the other in Colorado Springs, and her
brothers had settled their families back East. There
were times when Kerri wondered why she had never
made it to the altar herself.

"Too picky," her grandmother had said. "Too
much the career girl," her mother had decided. "It's
her father's fault for getting her into the damn business. She's married to it."

Maybe, they're right, Kerri admitted to herself as
she parked her car in a narrow driveway leading to an
ancient garage that nobody used, even in the dead of
winter. The house, a two-story white clapboard, was
cushioned in a nest of tall ponderosa pines and one
giant oak tree that brushed against Kerri's window at
the back of the house. Her father had bought the house
for his Irish bride, a lass of seventeen fresh from the
hills of Kilkenny in southern Ireland. Their marriage
was a happy one, and when Kerri's paternal grandmother was widowed, she came to live with them, and
helped raise Kerri and her brothers and sisters.

Kerri slipped out of the front seat, and grabbed a
briefcase that was filled with everything she needed to
put in a long evening at her home computer. She often

worked late into the night when the house was still, with the familiar sounds of creaking floorboards and groaning old plumbing keeping her company.

She hurried up the front steps to a porch that was weathered and needed a new coat of paint. Woodbines trailing along the eaves were harmonious with a porch swing and her grandmother's favorite rocker.

As soon as Kerri opened the front door, she knew her younger sister, Cathy, was visiting with her four-year-old twin girls. Squeals and laughter coming from the kitchen warned her that a clan gathering of four generations of Kincaid females was in progress. Cathy and her policeman husband, Harry, had bought a small house with a backyard directly behind the family home. For all intents and purposes, the alley separating the two properties didn't exist as the two families mingled.

Kerri smiled as she heard her grandmother's voice, raised above the hullabaloo. Grams was a feisty eighty-year-old who had no intention of turning her life over to anyone, including Saint Peter himself. Kerri doubted that heaven would ever be the same once her fiercely independent grandmother arrived. She'd have the whole place reorganized before they issued her wings.

"Look who's home," her spunky grandmother greeted Kerri warmly as she came through the kitchen door. The older lady's sharp eyes took in the dejected slump of Kerri's shoulders. "Just in time to join us in a snack of scones and honey. You look in need of a pick-me-up."

Amy, one of the twins, bolted from her chair and ran across the kitchen to Kerri. "Auntie! You have to help." An anxious expression scrunched up her little face and tears threatened to gush out of her round blue eyes.

Kerri bent down and gathered her into her arms. "What's the matter, honey? What's happened?"

Tearfully, the child croaked, "Bojo. I don't know where to look. He's lost. You'll find him for me, won't you?" She clung to Kerri and raised her pleading eyes. "You can find anybody. I know you can."

The little girl's childish confidence rang hollow in Kerri's ears. At the moment she wasn't sure she could find anything, including Bojo, a stuffed monkey that had become Amy's security blanket.

"Of course, I'll help," she told the child reassuringly. "Wherever he is, we'll find him."

"For heaven's sake, let Sis catch her breath a minute, Amy," Cathy chided her daughter. "She doesn't need to hunt for Bojo right this minute. Besides, we've looked every place we can think of."

Kerri took the little girl's hand and led her back to the table. "I bet Bojo hasn't wandered very far. He's probably just playing a game with you." *Not like a mother who had disappeared and doesn't want to be found.* The thought brought new feelings of compassion for three abandoned children who should be sitting around a family table, secure in a circle of loved ones.

Kerri's mother frowned as she wiped her hands on a dish towel. "You look tired, honey." She was a large woman with soft, warm arms and a round face that had smile lines around a generous mouth. Cathy and Kerri's older sister, Mary, took after their mother, struggling with their figures, while Kerri's slender body structure and metabolism came from her grandmother's genes—much to her sisters' disgust.

"Just another day," Kerri lied as she kissed her mother's pink cheek. In truth, there had been nothing ordinary about anything since the moment Mark Richards walked into her office.

"I called the office earlier this afternoon and Debbie said you were out." Her mother raised a questioning eyebrow. "She said you had a new client, one that could make a national Handsomest and Sexy Men list, hands down."

Cathy perked up. "Sis has a sexy, good-looking client for a change?"

"You know Debbie," Kerri said with a depreciating wave of her hand. "She's got radar out for any available male."

"Then he's not sexy? Not handsome?" her sister prodded.

"I didn't say that," Kerri answered as evenly as she could, hoping to heaven a betraying flush of color wasn't creeping up her neck.

Cathy smirked. "Then he definitely must be some hunk of man if you'll admit you even noticed. Is he married?"

"No, he's not married," she answered evenly. "He was referred by another client. He wants me to find someone for him."

"Who? Is he looking for a long lost sweetheart? Or a fiancée? What's his name?"

Kerri smiled patiently at her sister as she took the cup of tea her mother offered and sat down at the table. "You are a true romantic, Cathy. I'm running a business and that's all this is. His name is Mark Richards and he's looking for his late brother's wife. While he was out of town, she left her three kids at his place with a baby-sitter, and took off."

"I've been tempted to do something like that on occasion," Cathy quipped, winking at her girls to let them know she was kidding.

Kerri's grandmother snorted. "Some mother. She probably took off to kick up her heels. That's the way with some of these modern women. Don't want to grow up. It's a good thing she left them with family."

"Mark's not really family. The kids aren't his brother's so they're no relation to him. In fact, he didn't even know they existed until he came back from a business trip and found them camped out in his fashionable loft."

"That must have been a shock." Kerri's mother shook her head. "How small are the children?"

Kerri told her.

"Poor babies."

"The little boy, Timmy, is a handful." Kerri started to tell them about the afternoon's escapade and then changed her mind. She needed time to digest what had happened. Too many loose ends to talk about. Was Timmy mistaken about Jason's brother knowing the man the boy called, Dirk? And how would they ever get a handle on who the man might be? Everything had to fit together. But how?

"Didn't the mother leave any kind of a clue where she'd gone?" Cathy asked.

Kerri shook her head.

"Then how are you going to find her?"

"I don't know, but I will." Kerri knew that with one lucky break she'd be off. Once she hit full stride, she would successfully follow a trail until she had all the answers. She'd find the clue she needed somewhere. Maybe she'd find it if she went over everything again tonight. She'd love to have something positive to tell Mark in the morning, not that he wouldn't have more pleasant things on his mind after a hot date with Lisa. She felt a smug sense of feminine satisfaction that they wouldn't be coming back to his apartment after their date.

"Hey, come back, come back, wherever you are." Cathy waved a hand in front of her sister's face.

"Sorry." Kerri gave a sheepish grin.

"If you were thinking about your sexy, handsome new client you're excused. Were you?"

"In a way," she admitted.

"Aha! Do I detect more than just a business interest in this guy?"

"Leave her alone, Cathy. You're not going to find out anything pushing and pulling like a puppy worrying a shoe," her grandmother warned. "Don't you know that Kerri shuts up like a clam when it comes to her love life?"

"What love life? Whenever a fellow starts to get serious, she gives him the brush-off. She's had a dozen chances to get herself a husband but every time she hears the tinkle of wedding bells, she puts in earplugs."

"It's true," her mother agreed. "Not that I'd want her to marry just anyone."

Kerri winked at her grandmother. They both knew what was coming. Her mother kept an up-to-date roster of all the eligible men in the parish as well as any likely business or professional males who crossed her path.

As expected, her mother took a deep breath and launched sail. "Kerri, I was talking to Mrs. Teagarden, you know the florist, and she told me—"

"Mom, I really should look for Bojo before it gets

too dark,'' Kerri interrupted as she got up from her chair. ''Where did you last see your monkey, Amy?''

''In the backyard. Me and Emily were playing like we had a magic Aladdin's rug. It was fun. I was the princess and Emily was Aladdin. We flew high in the air—not really,'' she corrected, as if her aunt might take issue with such a claim. ''Just pretend. We went lots of places and Bojo went with us. But when Mom called us to come in the house, he wasn't on the magic rug anymore.'' Her eyes moistened and her lip trembled. ''He was gone. Emily said he went on a trip without us.''

''I see.'' Kerri noticed the way Emily was pointedly ignoring everything that her twin sister was saying. A telltale sign that Emily knew something she wasn't sharing. Although identical twins, the two girls were opposites in personality. Emily knew how to stir things up and Amy innocently played into her schemes. ''Well, I'm sure Bojo's back from his trip by now. You stay here, Amy. Emily and I will go look for him.''

Ignoring Emily's protesting scowl, Kerri took the twin's hand and led her out the back door. The backyard was a child's paradise with wonderful trees to climb, a deep green carpet to roll on, and even a log fort that Kerri's brothers had built when they were young. The rug the girls had been playing with still lay under a white trunked maple spreading its branches over a grassy corner of the yard. A lingering sun sent a wash of soft light across the green grass and tipped the high branches of the tree with gold.

As they walked across the yard, Kerri felt Emily's hand tighten in hers, and when they stood beside the rumpled rug, the little girl kept her head lowered, assuring Kerri that she'd guessed right. Emily knew more about the whereabouts of Bojo than she'd admitted.

Kerri dropped down on the rug and motioned Emily down beside her. "So this is Aladdin's magic rug? Your mother and I used to play all kinds of pretend games when we were your age. We had lots of fun together, and were good friends. That's what sisters should be, good friends looking out for each other. Don't you think so, Emily?"

The little girl squirmed.

"I know you were sorry when Bojo turned up missing. Was he playing the Aladdin game with you? And then he just disappeared?"

Emily nodded.

"What do you think happened?"

Her little jaw worked for a moment without any words coming out, then she said in a weak voice, "He just left."

"Left? Where did he go?"

Emily's voice grew stronger. "Bojo didn't want to stop playing, and when Mom called us in, he just flew away."

"Bojo just flew away," Kerri repeated. "Where?"

Emily bent back her head and pointed up in the tree. "Up there."

Kerri had spied the stuffed monkey half hidden in the tree branch above them when they first sat down, but she wanted Emily to own up to what had happened.

"He just flew up there, Auntie," Emily said with a rush. "He didn't want to quit playing. So...so...he just flew up there."

"And why didn't you tell your sister that's where he was?"

"I was going to tell her but she got so upset and everybody was looking all over and...and..." she stammered. "I didn't want them mad at me." Her face scrunched up with tears. "Amy's such a baby."

Kerri smothered a smile and hugged the child. "Games are not fun when someone gets hurt. I know you were just playing, but you should have told Amy right away that you threw Bojo up in the tree. That's what happened, isn't it?"

Emily nodded.

"I'll get a rake and get Bojo down. Then we'll go in the house and you'll tell Amy you're sorry for making her worry. Okay?"

When they returned to the house, Emily's mother scolded her soundly.

"It was just a prank that got out of hand." Kerri said, coming to the little girl's defense. "She wants to tell her sister that she's sorry."

Amy's reunion with her beloved monkey brought smiles all around, and Kerri wished to heaven that the mystery of Ardie's disappearance could be solved just as easily as the stuffed monkey's whereabouts. When she thought about Mark, she wondered what he'd make of all this family commotion over a child's missing plaything. She knew he was trying to adjust to the unwanted father role that had been thrust upon him, but he'd never understand the give-and-take of a large family like hers. She sighed, realizing how far apart their worlds were.

"We're staying for dinner," Cathy announced, which was no surprise. When her policeman husband was going to be delayed getting home, she and the girls often had their evening meal with the family. "Harry called and said he'll be along in a couple of hours, hopefully," she said, crossing her fingers.

Kerri liked her brother-in-law. Harry was a wonderful husband and father, and as honest and conscientious as you'd want any officer of the law to be. They were just finishing their meal when he came in and pulled up an extra chair at the table. Kerri's mother rushed to get him a warm serving of her Irish stew and sourdough bread.

"I'm glad you found the kid," he told Kerri. "You say he wandered over to Coors Field?"

She nodded. "He heard all the ruckus coming from the nearby stadium, and slipped out of the apartment building."

"Well, you were damned lucky to find him in that crowd. That place is a zoo on a game day. As usual, there was plenty of excitement going on all over the place. We had to break up a fight or two before I went off duty. Good thing the kid's safe."

"It certainly is," Kerri said with prayerful thankfulness.

"By the way, on my last run, there was an ambulance pulled up to the front entrance of the Crystal Lofts building. Couldn't see who they were taking out on a gurney."

Chapter Five

The kitchen floor under Kerri's feet dipped. "What? You saw an ambulance at that building?"

"Yeah. Just caught a glimpse of white uniforms and flashing lights as we went by. They were loading somebody up."

Kerri's stomach muscles jerked as she pushed to her feet. "I have to make a call."

"What is it, honey?" her mother asked anxiously. "Is that the place where the children are?"

Kerri shot a look at Harry. "You're talking about the Crystal Lofts, aren't you?"

"That's the place all right," he said.

Her feet barely touched the floor as she flew to the telephone stand in the center hall. Her hands were moist as dialed the number she'd already memorized. It rang four times before the answering machine kicked in and Mark's deep vibrant voice advised her to leave a message.

Her voice was urgent as she said, "It's Kerri. Is everything all right? Mark? Cora? Someone call me back. Right away." She left her number and then stared at phone. Who was going to take the time to listen to telephone messages if there was a crisis? It could be hours before she found out what was going on. Then, again, she schooled herself, maybe nothing was going on. There were other residents in the building who could have called for an ambulance. Mark was probably out on a date with Lisa, and Cora had the kids bedded down for the night, and all was well. Maybe.

And maybe not.

Kerri went back to the kitchen. "No one's answering the phone. I think I'll check and make sure it's not my client who called the ambulance."

"Oh dear, I hope that one of the children isn't sick," said her grandmother, shaking her head. "That's the way kids are. One minute they can be jumping all over the place and the next laid low with a burning-up fever. I remember the time—"

Kerri cut Grams off with a quick kiss on her cheek. Then she gave one to her mother and promised, "I'll call, Mom, if I'm going to be delayed."

Her mother hurried after her to the door, delivering her usual monologue about driving carefully and keeping her doors locked. Kerri took the front steps two at a time as her mother watched from the doorway. When she backed her car out the narrow driveway at a speed that nearly laid rubber tracks on the cement, her mother shook a warning finger at her.

Once out of the residential area, Kerri took Sixth Avenue, one of the main arteries from Lakewood into downtown Denver. With difficulty, she forced herself to stay with the traffic flow, already going five miles over the speed limit. *Don't jump to conclusions,* she mentally lectured herself, but the words made little impact on the coil of anxiety tightening her chest.

The area around Coors Field was still humming

with postgame revelry. She idly wondered if the Rockies had won, not that it made any difference to the
merrymaking crowd of sports enthusiasts. She was
surprised and grateful when she swung the car into a
parking place just a half a block away from Mark's
apartment.

Out of breath, she made it to the front door of the
building before she had a horrible thought. She might
be exactly on time to meet Mark and Lisa leaving on
their date. What a total embarrassment that would be.
Disheveled, out of breath, babbling about an ambulance, she'd look like a perfect fool. And what was
worse, this kind of impetuous behavior wasn't like her
at all. She cursed herself for giving in to an emotional
involvement that had so quickly sent her into such
devastating turmoil.

Well, no matter, some stern inner voice reminded
her. She was here, and the need to satisfy herself that
all was well outweighed any chance of embarrassment.
If Cora was trying to cope with an emergency, and
Mark had already left with his lady friend, Kerri would
be needed.

Armed with this rationalization, she went inside the
building. The doors that opened to the foyer and elevator were locked but she turned to the row of intercoms lining one wall in the outer vestibule, and jabbed
the button with Mark's name on it. After waiting for
a short minute that seemed like an eternity, she laid
on the button again.

Come on. Come on. Maybe Mark hadn't shown
Cora how to work the intercom. Suddenly she heard
a click and Mark's voice saying, "Who is it?"

From his curt tone, she guessed she'd interrupted
something. In her mind, she had already sent him off

on his date with Lisa, but the curvaceous siren might still be there with him.

"It's Kerri," she managed to reply, now feeling the utter fool, wondering how to make a graceful retreat. "If you're busy—"

Instead of answering, he buzzed her in. Now, she had no choice but to face him and try to explain her melodramatic dash back to his apartment.

His door was already open when she stepped out of the elevator, but she didn't hear any sounds from the baby or the other children. Were they still there? Had he changed his mind and made other arrangements for them? This possibility brought a spurt of anger, instantly followed by a lurch of fear as another thought hit her. *Maybe they'd been hurt and the ambulance had taken them all to the hospital.*

With quickened heartbeat, she stepped into the foyer, and a hushed silence that was eerie greeted her. The loft was dimly lit, but she could see Mark was standing at the far end of the room with his back to her. Choking back the impulse to call out to him, she started across the open area, and he must have sensed her presence because he turned around slowly with studied stiffness.

What on earth was the matter with him? He was as rigid as a ramrod. Shocks of unruly hair drifted forward around his face as he looked down at something in his arms as if it were a time bomb about to go off.

The she saw what he was holding—the baby. He took a couple of cautious steps toward her like a desperate man who saw deliverance within his reach.

"Take her," he ordered in a hoarse whisper.

Kerri had to bite her lip to keep the smile off her

face. No warrior in battle looked any more apprehensive than Mark Richards did at that moment.

"And don't wake her up," he warned, acting as if he were about to hand her a bundle of spun glass.

Kerri slipped her hands under the sleeping baby, lifted her into her arms and put Pammy gently up to her shoulder. The baby's head lolled to one side in contented sleep. Kerri didn't know what her given name was, but Timmy had referred to the baby as Pammy, which Kerri decided might be a diminutive of Pamela.

As Kerri patted the baby's back, Mark collapsed in his lounge chair and closed his eyes, as if all strength had flowed out of him. Then he leaned his head back on the chair as if he'd gone through an ordeal that had sapped all his strength.

"Shhh," he warned, when Kerri asked, "Where's Cora?"

Kerri decided to put the baby down before she asked any more questions. She quietly opened the door to the bedroom and peeked in. Timmy was curled up in the middle of Mark's bed, sound asleep, and Patti was asleep in the crib that Mark had put together.

She came back into the living area, glanced up at the balcony. Cora must have decided to set the second crib for the baby up there beside the Hide-A-Bed. Cautiously Kerri made her way up the circular staircase and gently laid the baby down on her tummy in the crib.

As Kerri tenderly covered her up, the baby girl continued to sleep contentedly, her head to one side, and her tiny rosebud mouth slightly open. Chubby arms and tiny hands lay in a relaxed position next to her fair head, and a fringe of delicate eyelashes brushed her cheeks. A swell of protective love filled Kerri's chest as she looked down at her. How could any mother willingly leave this precious baby in the hands of strangers? What circumstances could be so dire that there was no other choice?

An urgency that Kerri had never felt about any case before swept over her. She stiffened her resolve to find Ardie Richards and bring her back to these children as quickly as was humanly possible. Her steps were quick and purposeful as she came back down the stairs and walked to the end of the room where Mark was sitting. So, the children were all here and safely asleep, thank God. But where was the baby-sitter?

Sitting down on the couch across from Mark's chair, she demanded, "All right, what happened? Where's Cora?"

He raised his head from the chair rest. "At the hospital."

"So, the ambulance was for her."

He frowned. "How'd you know about the ambo?"

Kerri told him about Harry seeing the ambulance. "That's why I came. Just to check."

"Thank God you did," he breathed with pure thankfulness. The last two hours had been a trip to hell. Even now his head was spinning from the most recent catastrophe.

Seeing his troubled expression, she didn't know what to think. Had someone tried to take the children and Cora been hurt defending them? Something had put her in the hospital. Had she been assaulted, shot or knifed?

"What happened?" Kerri asked, bracing for the worst scenario.

"She fell down the balcony stairs." He nodded toward the circular wrought-iron staircase. "I knew she was on edge about everything that's been happening. She told me that she'd answered the phone several times today, but nobody's been on the line." He ran a hand through his hair. "She'd put the baby to sleep, and was coming down the staircase when she missed her footing. Fell down a half-dozen steps. I heard her scream and came running."

"How badly was she hurt?"

"I'm not sure. She broke something. Hip or a leg. Don't know which. I called 911 right away. They took charge and whisked her away." Mark leaned forward in his chair. "Before I could decide what to do, all the ruckus with the paramedics woke the baby. She started screaming her head off."

Once again Kerri smothered a smile. She knew it wasn't the least bit funny to Mark, but a big strong man like himself humbled by less than fifteen pounds of fury had an edge of humor to it. "So, what did you do?"

He looked pained. "I wasn't sure what was the matter with her, so I did the diaper bit. Bless the person who designed a recognizable front and back with those stick-em tabs. I got the darn thing on even though she was jabbing her feet and legs out in every direction. I was afraid I was going to wake the other two up."

"How'd you get her back to sleep?" Kerri didn't know why she was enjoying this so much. Maybe she was guilty of a little feminism, secretly glad that at least one man was learning about the trials of baby tending. She had loved her father, God bless him, but it was her mother who'd carried the full load of caring for their six children. She doubted that Patrick Kincaid had changed one diaper in his whole life.

"I figured if I stuck a bottle in her mouth, she'd shut up. I managed to warm up one of the ones that Cora had fixed and left in the fridge."

"How'd you warm it?" Kerri asked innocently.

"In the microwave. How else?"

She blinked. "Did you know how much time? I mean, weren't you afraid of getting it too hot?"

He looked abashed. "That's what happened the first time. So I just took another bottle out of the fridge and put it in the oven for half the time. The second one was still too hot, but I got one lukewarm on the third try." A hint of satisfaction curved his mouth. "The little tyke slurped the milk down like a half-starved kitten. Maybe I'm not too bad at this after all."

Kerrie smiled. "It's a good thing you were still here when Cora fell. You could have been gone on your date with Lisa."

"Oh, that." He gave a dismissive wave of his hand. "I backed out of going. No way I could leave the way things were here. Who knows whether that guy, Dirk, is really hanging around."

Kerri stiffened. "You haven't seen any sign of him, have you?"

"No, but I couldn't take a chance on leaving the kids and Cora alone." He massaged his chin in a worrying fashion. "Who knows what in the hell is going on. After Timmy's bombshell this afternoon about my brother knowing this guy, Dirk, I was trying to figure out what to do with the kids. This is no setup for them. Besides, they'd be safer somewhere else."

"And out of your hair," she added, not too charitably.

He raised an eyebrow. "Do I detect a little gravel in that remark?"

"Perhaps," she admitted.

"Well, what in blazes do you expect me to do? Cora was threatening to leave, and beating the bushes for another nanny could take time. I was trying to plan ahead. What do you expect me to do? Play Dad and stay home with three kids I don't even know?"

"That prospect is intriguing. Do you take vacation time?" she asked with a teasing smile.

"That isn't funny," he said but she laughed aloud anyway.

He got up from his chair. "I'd better call the hospital." He felt bad about the accident, and putting Cora through such a painful ordeal. She'd been a life-saver. He vowed to make it up to her as best he could.

And when he finally reached someone with information, his worst fear was realized. She'd fractured her pelvis. Mark gave the hospital his name, made arrangements to pay all the bills, and told them to call him if she needed anything at all. Then he called a florist and ordered flowers.

"Well, I guess that's that," he said when he turned away from the phone. "Damn, I feel responsible. She was a good soul trying to help out."

"Accidents happen," Kerri said quietly. She knew that Mark would make sure Cora didn't lose financially. In fact, the cleaning lady would probably come out ahead moneywise, but that didn't help either Cora or Mark at the moment.

"I could use a drink." He disappeared into the den and came back with a couple of glasses of ice and a bottle of Scotch. "Will you join me?"

At her nod, he handed her a glass, poured a heavy shot of Scotch into it, and then poured the same amount for his own drink. He set the bottle down on the coffee table and eased down on the couch beside her. ''What toast shall we make?''

''How about to the quickest successful search on record?'' she suggested.

''And to the wonderful lady who's going to make it happen,'' he added.

''And to a happy ending for all concerned.''

They clicked glasses. *''Salud.''*

As Kerri sipped her drink, she was painfully aware of his physical nearness. Her betraying senses bombarded her with arousing stimuli. She was close enough to feel the brush of his strong legs and thighs as he turned toward her and bathed her face with his warm breath. A spicy masculine scent teased her nostrils and her fingers were tempted to thread through a wave of his hair that lazily drifted down on his forehead. She almost gave in to a protective urge to get to her feet and walk away from him as fast as she could.

''What's the matter?'' He frowned as he leaned closer and touched her arm.

The hot contact made her ease away from him. ''Nothing.''

''Nothing? You're suddenly taut as a bowstring ready to snap.''

She felt utterly foolish and juvenile. In her business, having a drink with a client was almost routine. Why, then, did she suddenly feel so vulnerable? What had happened to the cool, always-in-control Kerri Kincaid, who could deflect any sexual overtones with utter confidence? Not that Mark Richards had made any advances. Fixing her a drink and sitting beside her on a couch didn't add up to any kind of a romantic come-on. Her own feelings were the ones in question. She felt a strong sexual attraction to the man sitting beside her. Admitting it to herself only made matters worse. The challenges of her business were demanding enough without letting personal emotions interfere. Warning signs flashed inside her head. She knew darn well she couldn't compromise this case by letting some absurd romantic feelings for her client get in the way.

She drew in a deep breath. "Just concerned about the way things are going."

"Are you holding something back?" He searched her face. "Have you made some discoveries that you haven't shared with me?"

"About the case? No." Grateful to slip into her role as investigator, she brought him up to date on the results of the futile search for a marriage license in California and Nevada.

"Do you have any idea where your brother's wedding might have taken place besides Reno?" When he shook his head, she sighed. "It will take time to cover all the states. Of course, there's always Mexico. Did you perhaps get a postcard from him from anywhere in or out of the states about the time he was married?"

He shook his head. "No. He was in California, at the office, when he called me and told he was already married. I guess I didn't invite any of the details. Knowing Jason's record with women, I wasn't overly optimistic about his latest marital foray."

"Once we get a full name for Ardie, we'll have all kinds of trails to follow." Giving him this assurance, Kerri set down her glass and stood up. "Well, I guess I'd better be going."

"What?" He was on his feet in an instant. "You

can't go. You can't leave me here with these kids,'' he protested vehemently.

''You'll manage just fine,'' she assured him. He looked for all the world like a man who'd just been informed that he'd be shot at dawn.

''What if the baby wakes up in the night? And what about in the morning? They'll need to be dressed and fed, and heaven knows what else.''

Kerri had never seen a grown man look so panic-stricken.

She was certain Mark would have been less apprehensive facing an advancing enemy legion.

''Kids are adaptable,'' she assured him. ''You just have to give them what they want, when they want it.''

''Terrific. That solves everything.''

She laughed. ''I think it would be a great experience for you. Everyone starts out as a beginner when it comes to child care.''

''Please, Kerri,'' he coaxed, smoothly changing tactics. ''If you won't take pity on me, what about the kids? They'll need some reassurance with Cora gone. You don't want to turn them over to an untrained recruit when they need someone who knows how to soothe their fears, now do you?''

''You're not playing fair,'' she accused him.

''I know.'' His persuasive mouth softened. ''But it's a fact. The children know you. If you're here when they wake up, things will go a lot smoother. You can't just abandon them, can you?''

She wanted to reply in a firm tone that the children were not her responsibility, but even as he waited for her answer, she knew he had hit the right chord. She couldn't just ignore the way those little innocent lives had been completely turned upside down. She thought about her nieces and nephews and how devastated they would be to be abandoned and left with strangers.

"You will stay, won't you?" He put his hands on her shoulders and gave them a slight squeeze. "Please?"

Later, she wondered if something more than the children's welfare was really under the surface of her decision to stay. She avoided his eyes. "All right, for the children's sake."

"On behalf of the children, I thank you." He smiled and resisted the temptation to draw her close for a grateful hug. He'd never invited a woman to spend the night under these circumstances, and for a fleeting moment, he wished the situation was different. What would it be like to have her body yielding soft and supple, blending with his? He quickly shoved the fantasy aside before his thoughts betrayed him. Something in her expression told him that she'd drawn a line and he'd best not step across it.

"I'll call home and arrange for an overnight bag," Kerri said, turning away.

She went into the den and silently groaned as she dialed the number, knowing that she'd have to endure the third degree from her mother. In a way she was glad when her sister answered.

"Oh, Cathy, I didn't know you and Harry would still be there. I need you to do me a favor."

"Sure, Sis, what's up?"

"Will you pack me an overnight bag and a fresh blouse for tomorrow? Something's come up. I'll be spending the night at Richards loft."

"You're going to spend the night where?"

Kerri could picture her sister's eyes rounding. "It's

not what you think. I need to stay here with the children. Their baby-sitter fell down some stairs and is in the hospital. Mark will need some help with the children.''

"Oh, I'm sure he will," Cathy agreed pointedly. "The two of you could be up half the night."

"Pack my flannel pj's and robe," Kerri ordered. She didn't trust her sister not to send the sexiest nightclothes she could find. Parading around in a negligee in front of Mark wasn't the message she wanted to broadcast. "This is strictly a business operation. Nothing more."

"Sure it is," her sister mocked. "Maybe I should pack for a couple of nights? You know, just in case there's another emergency?"

Kerri ignored the teasing, and arranged for Harry to run the bag over for her. "Let me speak to Mom."

"Good luck convincing her that spending a night with a handsome client is part of your job description." Kerri heard her laughing as she put down the phone.

When her mother came on the line, Kerri explained the situation and then took the tack that Mark had used on her. "The children need to have a familiar face here in the morning, and some reassurance that everything's going to be all right."

"Poor little tykes. Lost babes in the woods, they be, for sure."

"Of course, Mark will have to try to find help the first thing, or he'll have to send them someplace else."

"Not to one of them child care agencies!"

"I don't know, Mom. I guess it depends upon how quickly I can locate their mother. Anyway, I'll be home tomorrow when things are under control here.

I've got a pile of work to do at the office first, but I'll give you a call.''

"You're going to be all right, aren't you? I mean, spending the night in some man's apartment? He's not the kind to take advantage, is he?''

"No, Mom. I'm perfectly safe.''

When she went back into the living room, he was standing at a window, looking out at the Denver skyline. She came up beside him and he gave her a questioning look. "Everything set?''

"Yes, my brother-in-law will drop off the bag. You have a live-in nanny 'til tomorrow morning,'' she said briskly. "After that, whatever arrangements you make for the children will be your decision.''

"I don't know what the hell to do.'' He ran a worried hand along his chin. "This loft is no place for kids even if I get a lucky break and can hire another satisfactory baby-sitter. And I worry about how safe they'll be here if someone wants to get to them. Can we believe Timmy? Was this guy, Dirk, really in the crowd, or just part of a little boy's paranoia? I've racked my brain and I don't remember my brother ever mentioning someone by that name. If Jason knew the guy, I haven't a clue whether it was business or pleasure.''

"Maybe neither.''

"None of this makes one damn bit of sense.''

Kerri had to agree with him. Be careful what you wish for, she reminded herself. She'd been bored with her usual clientele, but she hadn't expected anything as bizarre as this case. "If the children's mother doesn't want to be found, it could take weeks, even months to get a hot trail.''

"And what happens to the kids in the meantime?''

That was the jackpot question. Kerri didn't have an answer.

When Harry arrived with her overnight case, they exchanged a few words at the door, and he said in a low tone, "If this guy gets out of hand, call me."

"I will," she whispered back. She appreciated the big-brother concern, but she knew Mark only wanted her volunteer help with the children. He didn't have designs on her romantically, and she was glad, she told herself. She ignored a spurt of feminine vanity that mocked her overnight stay in his bachelor pad, so different from how it might be if she were, say, Ted's neice, Lisa.

When she returned to the living room, she bid him good-night, even though she still hadn't finished her drink. She was afraid that if she lingered any longer, the conversation would get personal, and he might get the wrong idea.

"I'll carry your case up." He motioned for her to mount the circular stairs in front of him, which was a mistake, he soon realized. The view of her rounded bottom and graceful legs was tantalizing enough for any red-blooded man's hormones. He was totally aware of her on a sexual level that took him by surprise. As a confirmed bachelor, he'd been content with casual relationships that demanded little from him except a good time. He knew all the warning signals when a woman was beginning to get too serious, and he made a quick exit before any commitments were made. Maybe he was a coward, but he wasn't good husband material, and he knew it.

He quickly set the case down at the top of the stairs. If Kerri were anyone else, he might have lightly kissed her good-night and thought nothing of it, but in truth, he didn't know how to relate to a woman whose deep reservoirs of strength, integrity and loyalty would, undoubtedly, demand the same from the man who loved her. After a moment of awkward hesitation, he said lamely, ''I hope you sleep well.''

''I'm sure I will,'' she said rather primly. Why was he standing there, looking at her like that?

''Thanks for being here,'' he murmured and he knew he wasn't only referring to her help with the children. Strangely enough, there was more than just gratitude in his emotions at that moment.

''Good night, then,'' she said quickly, conscious of some undefined energy radiating between them. ''If I know kids, we'll all be up bright and early in the morning. I'll give the baby a bottle if she wakes in the night.''

He smiled wryly. ''I'd volunteer, but I don't think the baby deserves a repeat of my first attempt. If there's anything else, I'll do my best.''

''If I need you, I'll wake you up,'' she promised.

''Who's going to be asleep?'' he muttered under his breath. With all he had on his mind, he'd be lucky to close his eyes before the sun came up.

He turned away abruptly, and went down the stairs before he made some kind of fool of himself. In the den, he slumped in his lounge chair. Tomorrow he would have to make some decisions. He tried to marshal his thoughts in the same way he would if he were handling a business crisis, but the strategy wouldn't work. It wasn't dollars and cents that were involved, but three little human beings who couldn't be put in debit and credit columns.

He spent restless hours, going over everything, again and again. The children were no kin of his, but

they were under his protection, and he wanted to do
what was best for them. His brother had acquired them
with his recent marriage, and there must be family
members somewhere. All he had to do was find them.
Once they located some relatives of the children, his
responsibility would end. He wondered why the
thought brought him no comfort.

THE BABY SLEPT through the night, and so did Kerri,
but Mark had dark rings under his eyes when he joined
her in the kitchen the next morning. He eyed Kerri's
tousled wavy dark hair, her pink robe, slightly open
at the neck, and her lovely face, devoid of makeup.
She looked appealing and beautiful, and her bright
smile mocked his disheveled, disgruntled appearance.

He glowered at her as he made his way to the cof-
feemaker, grumbling, "Morning."

"No need to ask how you slept," she chided, putting down an empty nursing bottle and shifting the
baby over her shoulder.

He didn't answer. He'd have to admit to her soon
enough that his sleepless night had netted him exactly
zero when it came to any feasible plan for handling
the crisis.

Kerri read his silence loud and clear. An idea had
been surfacing at the edge of her consciousness like a
sea creature poking his nose above the water's surface,
and she had begun to recognize it as the answer to a
prayer. She decided to make a telephone call and test
the feasibility of her idea.

"I'll put the baby in her swing and see about some
breakfast before the other two wake up."

After depositing the baby in her swing, she went

into the den and made her call. In a few minutes she was back in the kitchen with a smile on her face.

"Well, it's all arranged," she told Mark smugly. "I've found the perfect place for the children."

He blinked, staring at her with heavy eyes, and an expression that betrayed his disbelief. How could she blithely announce the problem was solved when he'd looked at it from every angle and came up short? He wanted to believe her but was afraid to give in to the relief that was beginning to seep through him. "Are you sure?"

"Positive."

"Where can they go?"

"I called my mother and she thinks it's a grand idea that the children stay at our home until their mother comes back. They'll be properly taken care of and spoiled rotten by her and my grandmother." She grinned broadly. "Don't you see? It's a perfect solution."

With an explosive laugh, he threw down the measuring spoon, spilling coffee grounds all over the counter. He couldn't believe the flood of relief that flowed through him. His spirits soared like someone who had just received an unbelievable, wonderful gift. He didn't understand his own feelings. It was a mystery to him how three little children had suddenly made everything else in his life seem insignificant. Now he knew that Timmy, Patti and the baby would be safe, and just as important, they would be loved and pampered. Being honest with himself, he knew he never could have turned them over to some uncaring, professional hands. "Hallelujah! You're an angel!" he said, laughing.

"Shhh, you'll wake up the children," she protested

as he grabbed her around the waist and swung her in a mad whirl.

"I don't care, you wonderful angel, you," he replied laughing.

"Stop, you're making me dizzy."

He set her down but didn't immediately release the clasp of his arms around her small waist. As she lifted her laughing face to his, he kissed her. The contact was light, only a brush of his mouth on hers, but the sweet taste of her lips instantly fired his desire. He tightened his embrace, and would have kissed her again, ardently fueled with a lover's touch, but she quickly put her hands against his chest, and pushed her body away from his.

One look at her questioning face and he knew that the kiss had startled her as much as it had him. The spontaneous, carefree moment was gone, and he cursed himself for having ruined it.

THEY MANAGED TO TRANSFER the children to Kerri's home without a great deal of fuss. They left behind the baby paraphernalia that Cora had rented. Kerri knew that there were enough things stored in the old house to meet the needs of a half-dozen children of all ages. Besides, anything they didn't have could be borrowed.

Cathy had been alerted to the new arrivals and was on the spot when Kerri arrived in her car with the baby and Patti, and Mark in his with Timmy. Kerri's sister gave Mark a frank measuring once-over as he got out of his Buick Regal, and she whispered approvingly to Kerri. "Way to go, Sis."

Kerri was in no mood to play games with her sister. Mark Richards was completely out of her league. This morning's incident had proved that. She was still trying to handle the intimacy of his kiss, which had threatened to level her defenses like those of any giddy adolescent. The playful twirling had turned into something else, and the sexual desire suddenly flaring between them had been as sharp as summer lightning. No telling what would have happened if she'd invited another kiss.

"What happened?" Cathy prodded, seeing the frown on her sister's forehead.

"Nothing. Now, let's get the kids settled," she said shortly and plopped the baby in Cathy's arms.

"What a darling," Cathy cooed and was rewarded by Pammy's toothless grin.

As Kerri lifted Patti out of the car, she murmured reassurance to the little girl, who had her thumb stuck in her mouth and was fiercely clutching Kerri's hand. "It's all right, darling. See, there's Timmy. He's going to stay here, too."

Mark had kept his promise and bought the boy a baseball and bat. When Amy and Emily ran up to greet him, Timmy clutched his new possessions as if ready to defend them against all forces.

"We'll play ball with you," Amy offered, ever the sweet outgoing soul that she was. "We like to play catch, don't we, Emily?"

A faint smile crossed Timmy's narrow freckled face. The little girl's welcome had hit a home run.

Kerri's mother bustled out of the house, wiping her hands on her apron. She greeted Mark with a broad smile and waved away his thanks. "'Tis better that they be here while Kerri looks for their mama. A man's apartment is no place for a baby and young'uns like these. Most men are all thumbs when it comes to child tending.''

''I couldn't agree with you more, Mrs. Kincaid.'' He grinned and gave Kerri a wink that said he liked her mother.

''Well, then, let's get them settled,'' Mrs. Kincaid said briskly. Like a mother hen, she picked up Patti, held her hand out to Timmy and shooed Cathy and the baby ahead of her into the house.

Kerri lingered with Mark on the sidewalk. ''Thank heavens, the problem is settled for the moment,'' he said. Then he shifted a little uneasily. ''But I'm wondering how long I can impose upon your family. I hired you to find their mother, not take over the responsibility of her kids. If we don't find her soon, what then?''

''Let's don't jump hurdles until we get to them. This could have a successful ending within a few days. And, of course, there's always the possibility that Ardie will show up again to pick up her kids, full of apologies and explanations.''

''That doesn't seem likely,'' he said with frank pessimism. ''If we only knew why she left, we'd have some clue to when she's coming back.''

''True. And I'm not going to find anything out standing here chatting. Now that the children are settled you can get your life back on track. I'll keep you updated on what progress we're making.'' She started to turn away.

''Kerri?''

She paused, and waited. ''Yes?''

He hesitated. A shadow flickered in his eyes and then was gone. ''It's not important,'' he said briskly. ''We'll talk later.''

All the way back to the office, she wondered what he was going to say. Was he wanting to dismiss what had happened in the kitchen, and assure her that a light kiss was not his invitation to a passionate affair? She felt like an idiot for having reacted so strongly, but he needed to know that she wasn't open to the kind of dallying that he obviously enjoyed with Lisa. She wondered if good-morning kisses were routine with his overnight female companions. *Cut it out,* she told herself. *Green is definitely not your color.*

Kerri's mood was less than harmonious when she reached the office and had to put up with Debbie's eager curiosity.

"Tell me all," she bubbled. "I called your house early this morning and your mother said you spent the night at Mark Richards's place."

Kerri silently groaned.

"Did you really spend the night in that hunk's apartment?"

"The baby-sitter fell down some stairs and ended up in the hospital. Someone had to help out with the kids."

"Where did he sleep? Where did you sleep?" Her sparkling eyes added, *Together?*

"Sorry to disappoint you, Debbie, but there was absolutely no undercurrent of romance." Thinking back, she was almost certain she had misinterpreted the tightening of his embrace and the near capture of her lips for a different kind of kiss. She certainly wasn't going to toss Debbie any romantic bones to chew on. "Strictly business. Now, let's see what you've got?"

"Not much. I did obtain Jason Richards's driving record and a copy of the California report about his fatal accident. It's on your desk. I'm still working the marriage bureaus. If we only had the woman's given name, we'd be off and running."

Kerri sighed. "I know. Ardie is most likely a nickname. I checked a name book and found Ardith, Ardella, Ardene, Ardin, Ardine, Ardis, Ardel, Arda and several more. We'll have to keep on Jason Richards's records until we can get a more complete name for the missing woman."

Kerri went into her office, and carefully looked over Jason Richards's accident report, which listed address, location of accident, time and verification of a single-car accident and death at the scene. On an impulse, Kerri called the California Highway Patrol and was put in touch with the officer who made out the report. She identified herself and refreshed his memory about the accident report.

"Yeah, I remember that one. Why the interest?"

"I'm trying to locate his widow. There wasn't a name or address for her in the report you sent me."

"There wasn't? Well, I guess next of kin was notified through his business office. I'm sure they can help you."

Not according to Jeff Elders, Kerri thought. "I was just wondering if there was something more you might know about the accident that wasn't in the report," she persisted.

"Sorry I can't think of anything. He was alone. The car went right off an embankment on Highway 101. Could have been going too fast, lost control of his car." The officer was abruptly silent, and Kerri felt that he was holding something back.

"Anything else?" she prodded.

He hesitated a second longer and then admitted, "I remember now. At the time I wondered if some car had forced him off, but we didn't have anything to go on. Without any evidence, we had to close the file."

Chapter Six

Kerri stared at the phone a long time after she'd hung up from talking to Officer Rossi. The policeman's words brought a cold prickling at the nape of her neck like one caused by an unseen draft.

I wondered if some car had forced him off the road.

Until that moment she'd only been interested in Jason Richards's accident as a possible means of locating his widow. Now her mind began to whirl with other stabbing questions that might very well hold the answer to the disappearance of the children's mother. If Jason had been a victim of foul play, was Ardie Richards in the same danger? Or was there another side to the coin? Maybe the woman had somehow been responsible for what happened to her new husband and was on the run. Had she abandoned the children to save them, or to save herself? And if she was on the run, who was threatening her? If Timmy's remarks could be trusted, there was a connection between the man, Dirk, and Mark's brother. Did that fit in with Ardie's disappearance somehow?

Kerri leaned back in her chair and stared at the ceiling until she was satisfied with what her next move should be. Then she pushed the intercom. "Debbie, book me on a late afternoon flight to Los Angeles. And make hotel reservations at the Windhaven Hotel for a couple of nights.''

"Single or double?''

Kerri laughed. "You never give up, do you?''

"Nope. Someday you'll prove me right.''

Kerri debated calling Mark and telling him what she'd learned about his brother's death, but decided against it. At this point, there was nothing to be gained by stirring him up. The police had not found any evidence to prove anything amiss. As far as they were concerned the matter was finished, and she had no intention of second-guessing the police. That wasn't why she had decided to go to Los Angeles. She wanted to talk to Jason's co-workers and see if she could uncover some kind of lead to the woman he had married.

Kerri worked through the noon hour, making arrangements for other investigative services to do some research for her. For a fee, there were many agencies who would comb existing files and records for data that might prove helpful. After she'd done as much as she could, she went home and packed a bag.

Everything was under control at the house, just as she had expected it to be. Patti was sitting on Gram's lap, sucking her thumb while being rocked, Timmy and the twins were running around the yard in some wild game of follow-the-leader, and the baby was asleep in a small bedroom off the kitchen.

Kerri's mother immediately started lecturing her on the perils of the big city. "Don't be going out alone at night, you hear? And mind you watch out for purse snatchers. Always keep your door locked. Don't open it for anyone you don't know.'' She sighed. "I'll never forgive your father for leaving the business to you. I do wish you'd stop traipsing all over the country by yourself.''

Kerri gave her an affectionate hug. "I'll call you tonight when I'm tucked in bed, safe and sound, I promise. Have a good time with the kids."

"No problem. They're good little tykes. I guess your handsome Mr. Richards told Timmy to call him Uncle Mark. It's easy to see the little fellow's really taken with his new uncle. I guess Mr. Richards's got a way with kids and adults."

Kerri ignored the inuendo as she started toward the door. "Well, if he calls to check on the children, you could tell him I'm going to be out of town for a few days."

"Shouldn't you be calling him yourself?" her grandmother asked with her usual bluntness.

"When I have something to report, I'll get in touch with him."

The old lady just snorted. "You don't fool me none, Kerri, girl. I may not see as good as I used to, but I'm not blind. There was some sparkin' going on between the two of you."

"You're imagining things, Grams. There's nothing but business between me and Mark Richards. He's not my type." She thought about sexy, curvaceous Lisa. "And I'm definitely not his."

THE FLIGHT TO THE West Coast was routine. Kerri liked flying, and was perfectly relaxed thirty thousand feet above the earth, reading, dozing, or catching up on paperwork. She preferred not to engage in conversation and thankfully other first-class passengers usually felt the same, leaving her to her own thoughts.

Idly, she wondered what it would be like to have a traveling companion like Mark Richards. She could all too easily imagine his long legs stretched comfortably out in front of him, an amber glass of Scotch in his well-formed hand, and the brush of his sleeve on the armrest between them. For a moment, a remembered masculine scent teased her nostrils. She closed her eyes, and the sensation of his presence was so strong that she was almost afraid to turn her head and look at the passenger sitting beside her. Then she chided herself for indulging in such absurd fantasies, and gave a weak smile to the older gentleman who occupied the aisle seat.

The plane landed without incident, and she took a taxi to the Windhaven, a fashionable downtown hotel. When she checked in, a young desk clerk handed her a note that was waiting for her.

"Have a pleasant stay, Ms. Kincaid," he told her with practiced friendliness, but there was a shine in his eyes that said he meant it.

She didn't look at the note until she reached her room, a pleasant single bedroom on the twelfth floor. Then, sitting on the bed, she read the message from her secretary. "Just finished contacting marriage bureaus in all fifty states. No luck."

Kerri crumpled the note. Maybe there had been no marriage. But why would Jason lie to his brother and everybody else? None of it made sense. She was getting nowhere fast, and complications kept piling up.

Moving around the room, she felt like swearing and throwing something. As a child, she'd never handled frustration well, and her father had warned her more than once, "Keep a leash on your temper, lass, or you'll be dragged into a cow pie." Through the years she'd tried to heed his warning, but at the moment, she felt as if she were definitely being dragged into something smelly.

The feeling stayed with her when she entered the office of Fidelity Investments the next morning, and asked to see Mr. Elders.

"Do you have an appointment?" asked a rather plain young woman working at a computer in a small outer office. A brass name tag identified her as Elsie Jones.

"No, I don't."

"May I ask what this is about?" She shoved back a pair of gold-rimmed glasses.

"Here's my card. Will you kindly give it to Mr. Elders?"

The receptionist raised an eyebrow as she read the card. "You find people?" she asked with open curiosity. "People who are missing?"

Kerri nodded.

"Who are you looking for?"

Kerri had learned not to pass up any avenue for gaining information, so she said a confidential tone, "Jason Richards's widow. Do you have any idea where I might contact her?"

"Is she missing?"

"Not really," Kerri lied. "We just need a current address."

"Oh," said Elsie, losing interest. She obviously was conditioned by television to expect some hair-raising tale like those on "Unsolved Mysteries."

"Did you ever meet Mrs. Richards?" Kerri prodded.

"Nope, Jason never brought her to the office. He was funny like that. Never mixed business with his personal life. I got the impression that it was one of those open-ended marriages. You know the kind, you go your way and I'll go mine and we'll hit the sack whenever we're together.'' She had the grace to blush slightly. ''I didn't mean to gossip about the dead and all.''

''Did you by any chance make any telephone calls to her for him? Or post any mail to her?''

Elsie cocked her head for a moment, and Kerri's hopes vaulted sky-high, but came plummeting down with a crash when she said, ''Not that I remember. Like I told you, he was real private about his personal life.''

''But he told you what his bride's name was, didn't he?''

''Ardie.''

''Just, Ardie? No last name?'' Once again Kerri's hope rose as the woman's forehead furrowed in deep thought.

''Let me see.'' Her face brightened. ''Once he called her Mrs. Ardie Richards.''

Kerri mentally groaned but managed to keep a smile on her face. ''Thanks for your help. Now, if you'll tell Mr. Elders that I'm here…''

She nodded and went down a short hall. In a moment she was back, saying, ''He said to come right in.''

Mr. Jeff Elders, a tall, slender man with a precise mustache, greeted her when she came into his office, smiling as he made a quick assessment of her trim figure from neck down to her ankles. He obviously approved of her fawn-colored linen suit and buttercup-yellow blouse. There was a slightly flirtatious overtone in his manner that had been absent on the phone. He wasn't *elderly* at all, probably only in his early forties.

"What a nice surprise, Ms. Kincaid." He put out his hand and held hers just a fraction too long to be all business. "I didn't know I was going to have the pleasure of your company."

"Thank you for seeing me without an appointment. My decision to come to California was rather sudden."

"Please sit down." He waved to a conversational setting of a chairs around a low table. "May I get you some coffee?"

"Yes, thank you," she said as she eased into a chair that curled around her with deceptive softness.

When Elsie had settled a tray on the table in front of them, he deftly poured two cups from a silver percolator. As he handed a cup and saucer to Kerri, a diamond ring on his pinkie finger flashed in the air like a twinkling star.

"Cream and sugar?"

"No, black." She'd already noted his expensive silk suit and hand-painted tie. His attire was such a contrast to Mark's conservative appearance that she had difficulty believing that Mark was the boss and Jeff Elders the employee. "As I told you on the phone, I'm interested in speaking with Jason Richards's widow," Kerri said smoothly.

"Well, I've told you just about everything I know. I never met the lady, and frankly, Jason wasn't in the office very much after he hooked up with her." He smoothed his tie in a preening fashion. "I've been the one to keep this office going. Things have been much easier since Mark put me fully in charge." The smug satisfaction in his tone was obvious. "He should have done it a long time ago. Our client list has appreciated considerably. I tried to make Mark see that Jason was nothing but a liability, but you know how it goes. Family loyalty is blind.''

Obviously, Jason's fatal accident had not been a cause for mourning as far as Jeff Elders was concerned. In fact, he had benefitted from the death. The question came from out of nowhere, and Kerri was startled to find it on her lips. ''Was Jason a careless driver?''

''Maybe not careless, but fast. He used to brag about what good time he could make going from here to Reno and Carson City. He had a gambling problem, you know.''

''No, I didn't.''

Jeff Elders nodded. ''I'm surprised Mark didn't tell you. He was always pulling his brother out of one scrape or another. If it wasn't women and bad marriages, it was debts. The sad part was that Jason was a nice guy, and everybody liked him. Mark tried his best to protect his brother, and keep him on the right path, but I know Mark washed his hands of this last marriage.''

''Do you happen to know if Jason knew a man named Dirk?''

''Dirk? Who's that?''

''We don't know, but we have reason to believe Jason knew him.''

Jeff shrugged. ''Jason knew a lot of people, but not many of them were clients.'' The sarcasm was thick. ''Mostly racehorse people or gamblers. I know he bet heavily on the ponies.''

''Did the police interview you after Jason's accident?''

He looked surprised. "No, why should they?"

Kerri shrugged. "Just asking. Did anything happen out of the way that day? I mean, did he seem himself? Did he leave the office at his usual time?"

Jeff frowned. "He worked in his office, saw a few clients, and took off a half an hour early. I remember that because someone called just a couple of minutes after he left. I told them they could probably catch him in the parking garage."

"But you don't know who it was?" *Like someone who wanted to follow Jason in his car and force him off the road?*

"No, I don't," Jeff answered readily.

"I suppose someone has already cleaned out Jason's desk?"

"Elsie took care of it and boxed up all his personal things. We've refurnished the whole office. Mark has asked me to interview another associate to take Jason's place. I have several good prospects for the job." Then he looked at his watch, as if remembering an appointment. "I'm sorry, but I have someone coming in a few minutes. Is there anything else?"

"Would it be all right if I looked through Jason's personal effects? Maybe there will be some clue to his wife's full name." *Maybe even a picture,* Kerri silently hoped. She was due for some kind of a break.

"Sure, go ahead. I don't think he kept much personal stuff here, and Elsie may have already sent it to Mark." He stood up and walked her to the door. "How long are you planning on staying in Los Angeles?"

"I'm not sure."

"Why don't you leave your hotel number with Elsie, in case I think of something that would help. I'm busy tonight but perhaps you'd like to have dinner, and continue our conversation another time?''

She gave him a noncommittal smile. ''I'll let you know.''

Elsie frowned when Kerri asked her about Jason's things. She looked uncomfortable, and twisted slightly in her chair.

''Mr. Elders said you cleaned out his desk. I'd like to look at any pictures, telephone and address books, mail, notes or anything else of that kind.''

''There wasn't anything like that. The drawers were almost clean. I think Jason was moving out and already clearing out his desk. He left one sweater and a pair of shoes in the closet. There was only one other thing and I gave it to Mark.''

''And what was that?''

Elsie swallowed hard. ''A gun.''

Kerri knew she'd heard correctly, but echoed anyway, ''A gun?''

Elsie nodded. ''Mark told me not to say anything to Mr. Elders about it. I think he wanted to keep it quiet. I hope he won't be upset that I told you.''

''I'm sure telling me about the gun just slipped his mind,'' Kerri said with a Christian charity she didn't feel. Blast it all, why did she have to dig up all this information the hard way when Mark could have told her plenty about his brother that might have saved her a lot of time? She hadn't learned much about Ardie, but she'd learned a heck of a lot about Jason Richards. Of course, whether any of it would help track down the missing mother remained to be seen. That was the trouble with the sleuthing business, you never knew when you were pulling on a loose thread or one that would unravel the exact information you needed.

"Will you give me the address where Jason lived?" Kerri asked on impulse. Maybe the landlord would be more helpful than Jason's office personnel.

"He rented one of the Palisades Bungalows, near Huntington Beach," Elsie said as she wrote down the address. "Don't know what good going there will do."

"You never know," Kerri said with more confidence in her voice than she felt, and in the end, she had to admit it was pretty much a waste of time.

The manager of the half-dozen cottages that were almost obscured by thick stands of palm trees only shook his bald head to most of Kerri's questions. No, he'd never met a Mrs. Richards, didn't even know there was one, and didn't care one way or the other. The cottages were built for privacy, and as long as the rent was paid on time, he admitted to little interest in renters' private lives.

"What about Mr. Richards's private belongings? After his death, who cleared out his cottage?"

"His brother."

So that was that. On the way back to the hotel in her rented car, she wondered if Mark could have overlooked something like a telephone bill that might contain a frequently called number to his absentee wife. If Mark paid the last bill, he might have a copy from the telephone company, or request another one. She made a mental note to follow up on this possibility.

She spent the rest of the afternoon collecting more information on Jason's fatal accident. The autopsy showed no signs of drugs, and only a modest trace of alcohol. That meant Mark's brother had been sober when he ran his car off the cliff and crashed to his death on the rocks below. If speed wasn't the factor,

then it could have been something else more insidious.
Why did Jason Richards keep a gun in his desk?

At the moment, the best bet on finding the missing
widow seemed to be collecting as much information
on Jason as she could. Somebody in his acquaintance
must know something about the woman he'd married.

Kerri returned to the hotel late in the afternoon, intent upon making some telephone calls before she
typed up the day's report on her laptop computer. As
soon as she entered her room, she checked her phone
for any voice messages. None. That meant Debbie
hadn't had any luck to report.

She called home and her mother's cheery voice
eased away some of her fatigue. "How are things going, Mom? Are the kids settling in okay?"

"Like little angels, they be. The baby's eating and
sleeping contentedly. Timmy and the girls are playing
in the tree house." Her mother gave a deep laugh. "It
sure does my heart good to see him leaping up and
down the tree like a monkey. And remember all those
cloth books that you and Cathy used to love so much?
They've been stored all these years, but your grandmother found them easily enough and is reading them
to Patti. I heard her laugh for the first time just a few
minutes ago, and my heart got in a twist, I'll tell you.
What have you found out about their mother?"

"Not much," Kerri said instead of the truth which
was zero.

"Lordy, you must have some idea why she left
them the way she did," her mother insisted. "From
what I'm seeing, they don't act like neglected children.
Anybody in their right mind can tell that they're ready
to love you back if you give them half a chance. But,
Lordy, they need their mama. You know that picture

in the living room, the one of the mother holding a child on her lap? When Timmy saw it, his little mouth quivered, and he sobbed, 'My mommy went away.'

"I hugged him, and said, 'I know she did, honey, but she's coming back. Kerri's going to see to that.'"

"I'll do my best, Mom," Kerri promised, then hung up with a heavy heart. She only knew one reason a loving mother would not want to be found—fear. What had frightened Ardie so much that she'd left her children with a man she didn't even know?

Sighing, Kerri kicked off her shoes, slipped out of her linen suit and headed for the shower. She hated the city grime, and felt dirty from head to toe, but before she could step into the shower, there was a brisk knock on her door.

Grabbing the white terry-cloth robe that the hotel provided, she pattered to the door and looked through the peephole. Then she slipped the lock and opened the door. "What are you doing here?"

Mark's eyes slid over the soft robe, down her bare legs to her slender feet and lightly painted pink toenails. He grinned as he leaned casually against the door frame. "I guess I should have called up from the desk."

"I was just getting into the shower."

"So I see. Do you need somebody to scrub your back?"

She was not amused. She'd never faced a client with only a thin piece of white material between her and nudity. Her determination to maintain a strictly business demeanor with this man was suddenly as firm as a soap bubble.

"May I come in?" he asked. "We could leave the door open if you like."

"Don't be juvenile," she snapped, walking away from the door with as much dignity as she could manage.

Mark appreciatively eyed the rear view of her fanny wiggling under the tightly clutched robe. As she moved away from him, he thoroughly enjoyed the long sweep of her back, her small waist, and rounded buttocks, so soft and naked under the robe. In his mind's eye, he let the robe drop to the floor and— He caught himself, and jerked back from the fantasy, but not in time to deny the truth. He'd never wanted to make love to a woman more in his life.

Ever since Mark had learned from her secretary that Kerri'd gone to Los Angeles, he'd rationalized that he needed to check on the Los Angeles office anyway. It was bad enough that he'd followed her, but instead of going to his usual hotel, he'd made a reservation at the Windhaven where Debbie said Kerri was staying, asking for a room on the same floor. Now he asked himself if he were some kind of idiot, chasing a woman who had made it clear he was only her client and nothing more.

"I'll just stay a moment," he promised, realizing he should make his apologies and leave before his firing hormones made it clear what was going through his mind as he looked at her in that skimpy robe. "I was just anxious to know if you'd made any progress," he said lamely.

"I usually type up a daily report for my clients," she replied as she straightened her back and her eyes met his. "I really prefer to get everything down on paper so I can see exactly what we have. Unfortunately, I decided to shower before booting up my laptop, so I don't have one ready for you, but if you'll give me a couple of hours…''

"Of course, but just this once couldn't you make an oral report? Say, over dinner?"

She worked her mouth as if to make a caustic retort, and then, much to his surprise, she broke into a laugh. "You're impossible! I don't think you even realize how embarrassed I am at this moment, standing here, conducting this business conversation in near nudity."

"Oh, I didn't notice," he lied. "But now that you mention it, I guess I should leave and let you get dressed. What time do you want to go to dinner?" He glanced at his watch. "It's nearly six now. Say, an hour? We could have drinks here at the hotel and decide what we're in the mood to eat."

"I really had planned on room service and—"

"But that was before I showed up. Right? Now, you won't have to eat in your room nor write a report that you can give me in person." As she hesitated, his voice deepened. "Please, have dinner with me, Kerri. I admit I'm pushing you, but it would really mean a lot to me."

"All right, you win. I really do have some things I need to talk over with you. Seven o'clock, it is. Where are you staying?"

"Down the hall."

"You booked a room here?" A flare like a Roman candle sent a warning through Kerri. She couldn't help but wonder if he was manipulating her and the whole situation. Certainly, creating this kind of cozy proximity was suspect. He was way off base if he thought she'd be delighted with this arrangement, and behave accordingly. "This isn't your usual hotel, is it?"

"No, but I knew that you'd want a conference with me during your investigation here," he said smoothly.

"And we couldn't have done that at your office?"

He had the grace to color slightly. "I thought it might be more convenient if I stayed here. Don't you agree?"

She shrugged as if it really didn't matter one way or the other. "I really don't plan to be here more than one more day."

"Then you didn't find out anything pertinent?"

"I'll tell you at dinner. Now if you'll let yourself out, I'll get back to my shower." She gave him a wave of her hand, went into the bathroom and shut the door.

WHEN HE RETURNED an hour later, Mark decided that the simple black sheath wasn't nearly enough covering to dispel the kind of provocative vision the skimpy robe had provoked. She was one sexy woman.

They went downstairs to the lounge for drinks. The hotel bar was small, and tastefully cozy. The hostess seated them at a half-moon table set against one floral wall. After their drinks arrived, Kerri pulled a small notebook and a pen out of her clutch bag. "I need to ask you some questions."

Mark's eyebrows rose. "Now?" Surprise mingled with a flush of irritation. He put down his glass so quickly some of the liquid spilled over the side. He'd been appreciating the lovely contours of her face and neck, and the way the simple sheath enhanced her bustline. As she had lifted her glass and sipped her drink, his eyes had rested on the graceful curve of her arm and smooth, delicate fingers. So totally aware of her, her utter femininity had completely charmed him, and he'd been vain enough to think that she had been sexually aware of him at the same time. Now, he realized, her mind was centered on something more than his company. "Can't we wait until after dinner?"

She gave him an infuriating smile that only made him more aware than ever of her pink-glossed lips. "We could, but now is a good time to tend to business, don't you think?"

How deftly she had dispelled any idea he might have had that this was a romantic date. He was only a client. She was here to work on the case. He took a big slug of his Scotch before answering curtly. "Ask away."

His strident tone took her back for a moment. Surely he wanted her to conduct the investigation as speedily as possible. She couldn't understand his attitude—unless there were things that he didn't want her to bring to light. Maybe he didn't like this focus on his brother's affairs. Was he reluctant to have her uncover something he would prefer to keep hidden?

She sighed as she opened her notebook to an empty page. The problem with delving into other peoples' lives the way she did was that she often turned over some stones that her clients would have preferred left forgotten.

"What happened to Jason's personal effects from the office and from his home? Address books, letters, personal papers, bills, receipts and the like?"

"I disposed of them."

"All of them?"

"Why would I keep them?" He leaned back against the soft cushion of the booth. "I had no idea that anyone would ever want to go through the stuff."

"Any photos or anything like that?"

"No. Don't you think I would have told you? There wasn't anything of value."

"Except a gun?" *You didn't tell me about that.*

He frowned as he his eyes squarely met hers. "Elsie told you, I suppose?"

She nodded.

"Well, if you're going to ask me why my brother had a loaded gun in his desk, you can save your breath. I don't know. Jason didn't like guns," he said flatly. "Never did. I went duck hunting a few times with our dad, but Jason refused to go with us. He was the last person I'd expect to own a gun."

"Do you know if he had a permit for it?"

He shook his head. "I sold the damn thing, and then put it out of my mind. I suppose I could have asked Ardie about it at the funeral, but it never crossed my mind to quiz her about anything. I didn't know she was going to waltz back into my life and dump her kids on me."

"As Jason's wife, why didn't she see to Jason's personal effects?"

"Don't ask me. She told Jeff to take care of everything, and I ended up collecting Jason's personal stuff at the office and his cottage. She never showed her face around here, as far as I know."

"Do you think Jeff Elders might have some information he's holding back? Maybe he knows more about Jason's wife than he's willing to admit. Your brother's death was obviously a boost up for him."

"Just in title. Jeff's earnings have always been more than Jason's, and my brother took directions from him. I guess Jeff's glad that it's now official that he's in charge. I think he and Jason got along fine, but they weren't close friends."

"Did your brother have any close friends? Maybe we could find someone who knew Jason and Ardie socially. Do you have any idea where he might have spent his leisure time?"

"Besides the racetrack, you mean?" As if he might be tempted to say something more, he turned his attention to finishing his drink. Then, as he set down the empty glass, he said, "There was a pretty big unpaid tab at the Dolphin Club. Kind of a fancy country club, famous for its stuffed lobster and other things."

"What other things?"

"I'm not sure. I guess we could have dinner there and find out." Then he grinned and added, "All in the name of business, of course."

"That sounds like a good idea," she responded as evenly as she could. His devastating grin threatened to send all her defenses into limbo. How could she maintain the proper emotional distance between them when he seemed intent upon challenging her professionalism?

THE DOLPHIN CLUB overlooked the city, and its expansive facilities included a restaurant, lounge, game room, swimming pool and spa. Valet parking was required for all guests, and the exclusive, well-heeled clientele were carefully scrutinized as they made their way up broad steps under a columned portico.

"Will they let us in?" Kerri asked anxiously, grateful for Mark's guiding hand on her arm as they approached the entrance.

"They damn well better. I'm the one who paid the membership fee."

As they stepped into a brilliantly lighted foyer with white marble floors and alabaster statuary, an impec-

cably groomed man in evening attire stepped forward
to greet them with a welcoming smile.

"Good evening," he said with a slight bow. "Nice
to see you, Mr—?" His pause was a very polite, unspoken demand, *And who are you?*

"Mark Richards. My firm has a membership here.
You may remember my brother, Jason Richards. I believe he was a frequent guest of the club?"

"Of course, of course. My condolences on his passing. We have missed his company."

Kerri sent Mark a satisfied glance. Good. His
brother was known here. She was ready to ask the man
whether or not Mrs. Richards had also enjoyed the
pleasures of the club, but Mark guided her smoothly
forward, forcing her to control her eagerness to start
her interrogation.

The lighting in the dining room was more subdued
and a maître d' with a foreign accent quickly seated
them near windows that gave a spectacular view of
the valley below. Mark smoothly handled the rituals
of ordering, selecting the proper wine to go with
stuffed lobster tail. A pianist sat at a baby grand piano
on a small elevated platform that moved slowly in a
circle so that in time his offerings reached every corner
of the room.

Kerri let out a breath that said *Wow.* The cost of
membership in this club must be unbelievable. As she
looked around at the opulent luxury, she was suddenly
ill at ease, but not because she felt her appearance or
conduct wasn't as presentable as any of the other
women. No, her sudden discomfort was something
else entirely, she admitted to herself. Mark Richards
must have money, plenty of it. If this club was any
indication of the life-style he and his brother enjoyed,

the world of the wealthy was commonplace in their lives. Usually the financial status of her clients didn't register with her, but she was suddenly conscious of the old rambling house that she called home as a contrast to the kind of luxury that he obviously took for granted.

Well, no matter, she thought, as she gave herself a mental shake. Once this case was finished, it was unlikely that their paths would cross again. For the moment, she'd enjoy this peek into a pampered life-style she'd only viewed in movies and on television. She smiled as a favorite saying of her father came to mind, "'Tis a foolish soul who refuses a pint when someone else is laying his sixpence on the bar."

"What are you smiling about? Your eyes give you away, you know," he said as he studied them. "Right now they're soft and misty, like an early morning sky, but when you're angry, they deepen to a cold blue like Arctic ice." His voice softened. "Sometimes I can see clearly into their depths, but other times they're tightly shuttered against me, and I don't know why."

Kerri wasn't quite certain how to respond to the invitation in his unspoken question. The conversation was veering off in a direction that was full of emotional hazards. Surely he must realize that even under these bizarre circumstances, she had to keep focused and avoid any distractions that might interfere with the job he'd hired her to do.

"What is it about me that you don't like?" he asked, deliberately holding her eyes with a probing gaze of his own.

Her hand tightened on her wine goblet. If he could read her eyes so well, he ought to know that she liked him more than was prudent. Admitting that she was attracted to him would only invite the intimacy that she was trying to avoid. She managed a light laugh. "Would you like a list now, or later?"

He didn't smile back, and she was grateful that the waiter arrived at that moment. Turning the conversation to an appreciation of the beautifully prepared food, the disquieting moment passed as Mark slipped into his role as the congenial host.

I could get used to this, she mused, as she enjoyed the luxurious dining opulence, but the thought was fleeting, because to be honest, she'd never trade the warm bustle of her mother's kitchen for this kind of fancy culinary artistry.

"I called home to see how the kids were doing," she said, trying to keep the conversation general as they ate. "Both mom and my grandmother are spoiling them in good fashion. Ardie may have three rotten kids on her hands when she gets them back."

"I can't thank you and your family enough. I honestly don't know what I would have done with them."

She waved away his thanks. "Things aren't moving as fast as I'd like." Then she lifted her chin in a determined fashion. "Once we have Ardie's full name we'll be able to track her past movements and have some chance of determining where she might be now. If Jason brought her here, someone might remember her. At this point in the investigation, I'd be happy with any personal data we might turn up, like a mutual friend of Jason and Ardie's. Can you give me the names of people he saw outside the office?"

"I'm afraid I can't. Jason didn't like his big brother knowing too much about his private affairs. The only time he let me in on what was happening was when he needed my help to get out of another mess. He knew that I loved him and would always be there for him." Mark's jaw tightened. "Jason must have said as much to Ardie and that's why she saddled me with her kids."

Kerri nodded. "She knew they'd be safe with you."

"Safe from what? And from whom?"

She wasn't ready to venture an opinion. Not yet. Some suspicions were building, but she wasn't ready to share them. She'd learned that Jason gambled, kept a revolver, and had a history of getting into trouble. There was even a possibility that someone had deliberately forced him off the road, but until she had some supportive evidence, she'd keep her suspicions to herself. Where the missing Ardie fitted in with all of this was another missing piece of the puzzle.

"I think it's time to chat with some of the staff, and even some of the club members," she said, putting down her napkin after coffee and some sinful chocolate dessert. "I'll start with the ladies' room, and see if the attendant remembers a Mrs. Jason Richards. There's always a chance that the maid eavesdropped on a conversation that might prove helpful. Why don't you take the maître d' and any of the waiters that might remember your brother?"

"What about the guy at the door?"

"I'd like to question him myself. I think I might be able to get a little more out of him than you can." She smiled to soften her frankness. "This is my turf, remember?"

"No argument." He spread out his hands in a gesture of surrender. "I'd much rather handle a volatile stock market than try to do your job." He nodded toward open French doors. "Shall we meet on the patio later? I think I hear dance music coming from that direction.''

"Good idea. We'll have an opportunity to mingle, and talk with some of the guests.''

He got the message—they were sticking to business, and dancing with him under the stars wasn't part of the agenda. *We'll see about that,* he thought as they left the table and went their separate ways. If luck was with them, maybe they'd have something to celebrate.

Thirty minutes later, they met on the patio with nothing to share but frustration. Kerri had struck out with the ladies' attendant. The older woman was obviously hard-of-hearing and paid little attention to the parade of women in and out of the ultramodern restroom.

Kerri had a little better luck with the doorman. He admitted that Jason Richards had brought several women to the club, one of them could have been slender and fair-haired, but no names were exchanged.

"I didn't know that he had gotten married.'' He gave Kerri a conspirator's wink. "But then, our members don't always show up with their wives, you know.''

Kerri ignored the wink. "Was Mr. Richards ever a member of a party that came to the club in a group?'' She hoped for a name that she might contact for more information about Jason and his bride.

He thought for a moment. "No, Mr. Richards was always alone or with a lady.''

Mark had the same kind of information to share as they sat at the far end of the patio near a fragrant planting of roses and trailing vines. He reported to Kerri that several of the staff remembered his brother, but no one recalled him introducing any woman as his wife.

Kerri stared at Mark for a long moment. "Maybe he never married her."

This took Mark back for a bit. "Of course, he married her. Jason called and told me so."

Kerri spoke slowly, thinking aloud. "Maybe your brother was just testing the ground. You know, trying to find out what your reaction would be before the act. Maybe they hadn't tied the knot yet when he called. Is that possible?"

Mark was silent. For a long moment, he stared unseeing into the flickering lights of the city below. Then he nodded. "That would be just like Jason. He always wanted to share a bad decision with someone."

"Your reaction to the news might have made him decide not to go through with the marriage." *And maybe that's the reason Debbie has been unsuccessful in finding a record of the ceremony.*

"But the woman came to the funeral as his wife," Mark protested.

"And yet, Jason made no financial provision for her. You said the only insurance he had was partnership insurance. She might have taken a calculated risk, pretending to be his wife in the hopes that you would come through with some kind of a settlement."

"So I may have no obligation to her kids at all. She's just using me as a patsy." His eyes flashed angrily. "Surely she would know that I'd find out the truth eventually?"

"Maybe she's buying time."

Kerri watched pain deepen the lines in his face as he fell silent. This must be terribly hard for him, she thought. Mark obviously had cared deeply for his brother, tried hard to keep him on the right track, wanted the best for him, but always ended up carrying the burden of Jason's mistakes. This last one was enough to break anybody's heart.

She reached over and touched his hand. "Give me a little time and we'll have some answers."

He sighed. "Yes, of course. In time we'll know everything. I don't know about you, but I've had enough questions for one day. Let's dance."

Later when she thought about it, she was surprised to realize that she hadn't even thought about refusing. He led her to the dance floor and she cradled into the graceful length of his body with perfect ease. He was a polished dancer, guiding her with slight pressure, and holding his head so close to hers that laying her cheek against his was a given.

They didn't talk. There wasn't any need. The harmonious movement of their bodies was communication enough. Each dance created a suspended detachment from the cares of the day, and when she let her hand move slowly around his neck, he whispered, "I like what I see in your eyes now."

His words instantly dispelled the harmony between them. She came to herself with a jolt and missed a beat of the music. What kind of signals had she been giving out? It didn't take a genius to know where this kind of romancing on the dance floor was leading. Her sister Cathy would have said, "So what? Go for it!" But she wasn't her sister, and she wasn't the kind of career woman who slept with her clients.

Avoiding his direct gaze, she gave a light laugh. "Sorry about the stumble. I think it's time to call it an evening. It's been fun, but that's enough dancing for one night." She eased away from him, and walked quickly back to their table.

As he paid the tab, she knew he was baffled by her mercurial change in mood, but she didn't care. He had to share the blame for turning the evening into something that she had promised herself wouldn't happen. If he hadn't drawn her out on the dance floor, she wouldn't have been mesmerized by the wonderful feel of their bodies moving together in such tantalizing nearness.

As they left the club, Mark politely kept his distance, all the time cursing himself for not leaving well enough alone on the dance floor. Why did he have to open his big mouth and spoil everything? With any other woman, he would have danced and wined her, and kept any references to her beguiling eyes to himself. He'd never been one for poetic utterances and he couldn't believe he'd acted like some adolescent Romeo.

As they drove back to Windhaven, Kerri made certain that she didn't give her client any more wrong signals. She stayed on her side of the car seat.

They rode the elevator in silence and as she paused in the doorway of her hotel room, she made eye contact with him for the first time since they left the dance floor.

Before she could say anything, he held up a hand and stopped her. "I know. You've made it clear enough. Either I fire you so I'm not your client, or I keep my distance? Is that about it?"

"I think it's better that way."

"Well, I can hardly blame you if you've already begun to hate the name, Richards. By now, you know that I wasn't the brother I should have been." He looked grim. "I failed Jason when he needed me the most."

"Maybe the situation was beyond your help from the very beginning," she countered. "Don't flay yourself until we know a lot more. I'll keep poking around, and usually something turns up unexpectedly when the trail seems cold." Even as she admitted to herself that the remark was a prayer as much as anything else, she gave him a reassuring smile, and bid him good-night. "We could meet for breakfast, if you're up about eight. I'll have a written report ready for you by then."

"You're going to work tonight? It's after midnight."

"I know, but it always takes me time to settle down after an evening out." *Especially when my emotions have been taken on a roller-coaster ride.*

"Maybe I could help?"

"Good night. I'll see you in the morning." She impulsively touched his cheek with her hand, and then quickly shut the door. As she heard his muffled footsteps retreating down the hall, she fought an impulse to call him back. They were two adults occupying rooms a short distance from each other. Why not admit how much she wanted to be with him? Her father's voice echoed in her head: *Ye know why, Kerri, lass. Keep your feet on firm ground. Ye can't be tending to business when your mind's up in the clouds.*

Kerri tossed her evening bag on the bed and kicked off her shoes. A blinking light on her telephone told her she had a voice message.

"I've been trying to call you all evening," Debbie said excitedly. "This afternoon, on a hunch, I contacted the Office of Civil Marriages in Mexico City. Are you ready for this?"

Kerri's heartbeat quickened, and her fingers tightened on the receiver.

"Yep. Jason Richards was married in Acapulco, six months ago. He married Ardella L. Browski."

Bingo!

don't remember how he's ... and then remembered he
used to the service."

Kree-lo-koe? . . . was reunited in . . . few of six
months ago. He shared Ardella's last wish-
finger? . . .

Chapter Seven

Kerri told Mark the good news over breakfast. "Now
that we have a name, things should move a lot faster."

An instant wave of relief crossed his face. "Ardella
Browski," he said thoughtfully. "It's certainly not a
common name that one would forget. What does the
L stand for?"

"Maybe a middle name, or maybe one from a previous marriage. Somewhere along the line, we'll tag
into her full name. I've already talked to Debbie this
morning. By the time I get back to Denver, she should
have more data for me."

"Then you're going back today?"

She nodded. "I have a noon flight. There's really
nothing more I can do here. You'll find everything in
this written report." As she handed it to him, she said
hesitantly, "There's something in it that I haven't
mentioned before."

"Oh?" He raised one eyebrow. "Why do I have
the feeling you'd rather not mention it now?"

"Because I wasn't successful in turning up anything."

"All right, tell me about it." He leaned back in his
chair, waiting.

"I spent some time at the police station, looking into your brother's accident. Jason's lab tests didn't show any alcohol or drug impairment. Speed or falling asleep at the wheel could have caused him to lose control. There's no way to know."

"I don't follow. What's this all about?"

Kerri saw him stiffen, and she chose her words carefully. "One of the officers who was at the scene mentioned to me that it was possible that someone might have run him off the road. It's just a possibility," she repeated quickly. "There's no evidence to go on."

Kerri could tell that Mark's acute mind was searching for some support or denial of what she'd just said. Finally he shook his head. "I don't know. I just don't know. From time to time, Jason was in with some pretty tough company, but I thought he'd pulled back, had gotten his act together. I haven't had to pay any big gambling debts for more than a year, but maybe Jason was afraid to ask me for any more help. I didn't mince words the last time. I warned him I was through bailing him out. Maybe he reneged on a debt and...and..." Mark's mouth worked but the words were lost in his throat.

Sometimes I hate this job, Kerri thought, seeing the pain reflected in his eyes. She believed in being honest with her clients, and sometimes that wasn't easy, like now, when she wanted to reassure Mark that his brother had reformed and his death was just an untimely accident.

He stared at some point beyond her for a long time. Then he came back, and asked, "What do we do now?"

"Once we find Ardie, she'll be able to tell us what

was going on in your brother's life. Until then, we'll just have to live with some unanswered questions."

"Even though we know the woman's name, we still don't know where the hell she is," he countered gruffly.

"A lot of the mystery will clear up once we start compiling a personal history through records like social security, driving licenses, state and county records, health records and the like. We'll get a composite of her background, and maybe even a trail of activities that brings us up to the moment she left her children with you and disappeared."

"You sound pretty sure of yourself."

"I am. Most people who disappear can be found with time and effort. I just hope that finding Ardie doesn't jeopardize her well-being in some way."

"What are you saying?" He frowned and searched her face.

"Since we don't know why the woman disappeared, there's the possibility that our search for her might somehow put her in danger."

"I'm more inclined to think she acted on a purely selfish level," Mark answered shortly. "Besides, if she had a legitimate reason, why wasn't she up-front with it?"

"Would you have been receptive to accepting the temporary care of her children?" When he readily shook his head, she nodded knowingly. "That's what I thought. Maybe that's why she didn't stick around. Anyway, let's not waste time on speculation. I'll spend a few days in the office and see what I can come up with. How long will you be staying in Los Angeles?"

"I don't know. Jeff seems to have the office under

control, but we have to hire another consultant. Probably I'll be able to get away in a day or two."

"If anything jells before then, I'll let you know," she promised.

They walked out of the hotel restaurant together and paused in the lobby to say goodbye. As they stood together in the swirl of hotel activity, he moved closer, and she remembered how it had felt to be in his arms, her cheek pressed against his. For a moment, a total awareness of his presence swamped her senses.

As he looked down at her and saw the sudden softness in her eyes, he was tempted to forget all about her insistence on maintaining a professional decorum between them. And yet, he knew she was right. He certainly knew better than to complicate his life with a romantic relationship. He'd remained a bachelor because that was the life-style he preferred. Although he enjoyed the company of women, he'd never found himself mesmerized by one. Not until now. It was not a vulnerability that he liked and he cursed the whole blasted situation that had thrown him off balance. He'd spent a night plagued with a restless desire that had flared again the moment he saw her that morning.

"Goodbye then," he said, wanting to throw good sense to the winds and take her in his arms and kiss her soundly.

"I'll be in touch," she promised.

For a fraction of a minute longer than necessary, they stood looking at each other, then he turned and walked away.

Kerri's gaze followed his strong masculine figure as he weaved through the mingling crowd and disappeared out the revolving doors. For a moment, she entertained inventing a pretense of having to go with him to his office, but quickly chided herself for such foolishness. She reined in her emotions, and went back to her room to complete some office work she'd brought with her.

KERRI'S TWO-HOUR FLIGHT back to Denver was uneventful, and she decided to see how things were going at the home front before going to the office.

"I'm back," she called out, as she shut the front door and dropped her traveling bag in the hall. No answer. The house was unnaturally quiet.

Kerri's chest tightened. Where was everyone? She expected to be greeted with a cacophony of childish noise, not the creaking silence of an old house.

The kitchen was deserted. No sign of anyone in the backyard. Maybe they were over at Cathy's house. Letting the back screen door bang loudly behind her, she crossed the yard and alley, and then let herself in through the back gate to her sister's yard. There was a hushed stillness about the house that told her even before she tried the back door, that everything was locked up. Nobody was home.

"Looking for your sister?" Mrs. Tipton called across the wire fence separating her backyard from Cathy's. The woman was the neighborhood gossip, always tugging and pulling at any strand of gossip that might be raveled into a good story for her bridge club, but even gossips have their uses, Kerri thought as she nodded and smiled brightly. "Do you know where she is?"

"Gone to the park. You must have some family with kids visiting? I don't remember seeing them around before?"

Kerri only gave her a noncommittal nod. She wasn't

about to feed the neighbor's avaricious curiosity, and
could just imagine Mrs. Tipton's near apoplexy if she
told her the whole story. What a delicious tale to
spread about abandoned children staying in her own
neighborhood, and the search for their mother. Kerri
gave the neighbor a wave of thanks and quickly made
her escape.

A small residential park was only a couple of blocks
away, and recently new equipment had been purchased
by the city to upgrade the playground. Kerri had been
too busy to pay much attention to the improvements,
but as she crossed a wide span of grass which bordered
the playground, she was pleasantly surprised to see a
small merry-go-round, several different-size swings, a
slide that looked like a space ship, and some gaily
painted teeter-totters.

There were only a few children and adults enjoying
the park. As Kerri came closer, she saw that Cathy
was pushing Patti in one of the toddler's swings. The
twin girls and Timmy were playing on the merry-go-
round. Squealing, they hopped on for a whirling ride
until they had to jump off and push again.

Kerri's mother and grandmother sat at one of the
picnic tables, the remains of snacks and drinks still
littering the table. A double baby carriage that Kerri
hadn't seen since the twins were infants was parked
at her grandmother's knee.

"Well, Lordy, look who's here," her mother
greeted Kerri with a big hug. "Sit yourself down,
honey. There's still some brownies and a spot of tea
left in the thermos. I guess you figured out where we'd
be, most likely."

"With the help of Mrs. Tipton," Kerri admitted

with a wry smile. "I was a little baffled when I found all of you gone."

"Worried, were you?" her sharp grandmother asked, peering at her through spectacles resting low on her nose.

"Well, not really. Just a little anxious to know if everything was all right."

"Well, now, did you find something out in California that ain't to your liking?" the elderly lady prodded.

Kerri was tempted to admit that unanswered questions about Jason's accident weren't to her liking, but decided against mentioning it. No use spending time on idle speculation; better to stick to known facts. "Debbie called me with some good news. We now know the name of the children's mother."

"Ardella?" her mother echoed when Kerri told them the name. "There aren't many of those around. Lordy, I'm glad she didn't saddle her girls with a name like that. They're really sweet, and that Timmy's a real charmer. Now that he's settling in, he's showing a bit of spunk. Took his mother's running off really hard. Poor thing. Just the mention the word, *mother,* and his little eyes looked sadder than a lost dog's."

Kerri felt her heart tighten a little as she watched the little boy throw back his head and laugh as the merry-go-round whipped him around in a circle.

Cathy waved at Kerri from the swing set where she was pushing Patti, and motioned her over. "Your turn, Sis. She won't get off." Patti had her little hands fastened around the swing's chains as if she'd defy Hercules himself to remove her from it. "She's all yours for another hundred swings," Cathy said, heading back to the picnic table.

At that moment the merry-go-round wound down to a slow stop. "Come push us, Auntie," yelled Amy, waving her arms madly.

"Push us. Push us," Timmy and Emily took up the cry.

"Okay, okay," Kerri yelled back. Then she turned to Patti, and ignoring the belligerent pout of her little lips, said, "It's time to play on the merry-go-round now, and show Timmy what a big girl you are."

The operative word was *Timmy,* and Kerri could see the little girl's stubbornness wavering. Kerri just smiled and waited. Slowly, Patti held out her little arms to be lifted out of the swing. A small victory, but Kerri flashed a triumphant smile at her sister, as she and Patti joined the other children on the merry-go-round. Maybe she wasn't so bad at this child-rearing business, after all, she thought with a tinge of smugness as she pushed the merry-go-round, and hopped on for a ride herself.

She laughed and played with the children in a carefree mood she wouldn't have thought possible a few hours before. Their innocent joy renewed and strengthened her and made her laugh, but another emotion brought tears to her eyes as Patti gave her a hug and sloppy kiss. What if these kids were hers—hers and Mark's?

Finally, thoroughly worn-out, and ignoring the children's pleas for "More, more," Kerri decided it was time to call it quits. The other women agreed.

As they prepared to leave the park, amid the squealing and scrambling children, Kerri became aware of a solitary man sitting on a nearby bench watching them with solemn intensity.

Instantly alert, she tightened her clasp on Timmy's

hand as they walked. Cathy was pushing Patti in the double stroller with the baby, and the twins were bouncing along beside her grandmother. There was no way someone could get to the children without confronting an adult, Kerri reasoned, but her heart had quickened and she was suddenly tense.

She stiffened when Timmy glanced in the direction of the man, prepared for the boy to react with the same emotional recognition as he had in the Dirk incident. When Timmy suddenly pointed and squealed, Kerri heart lost a beat.

"See! Up there."

She realized then the boy wasn't pointing at the man but at a bright blue Steller's jay flitting through the branches of an evergreen spruce tree. All she could do was nod, and stiffen her knees that had gone weak.

As Timmy skipped happily beside her, she chided herself for letting her imagination run away with her, but a flicker of apprehension stayed with her. When they got home, she made a point of impressing upon her mother the need to keep the children under the watchful eye of an adult at all times.

WHEN KERRI GOT TO the office, Debbie was as ecstatic as a bridesmaid who'd caught the wedding bouquet. "What's in a name that doesn't smell sweet, sweet, sweet," she said, mangling the quote from Shakespeare.

Kerri laughed, "I gather you've had some luck checking the records I suggested."

"You bet you're sweet patooties, I did." Debbie shashayed over to Kerri's desk, and laid down some papers with a flourish. "I zeroed in on California and Nevada driver's license bureaus as you said."

"And—?"

"*Voilà!* A driver's license issued to Ardella Browski, two years ago, Reno, Nevada. I'm expecting a fax any minute."

"Good work, that will give us a photo, plus our mystery lady's height, weight, color of eyes and her age. And more important, an address." There was no reason to think that Ardie had returned to Reno after leaving the kids, but picking up her trail, even if it was two years old, was a place to start. "What else?"

"No telephone currently listed for Ardella Browski, but five years ago, she was in the Reno directory, and I got that address."

"All right, let's go through the marriage records again. This time for an Ardella L. Browski. If her ex-husband is still alive, we may pick up her trail from him. And if he's dead, we still may get some information from him that will help us."

"If he's dead, he's dead," Debbie countered. "Even if we get a death certificate, I don't see what you can learn from a dead man."

"Every person's life is a mesh of people and happenings," Kerri explained. "Everything that happens in life is interwoven, and is in some way connected to everything else. Every choice is a link to something in the past, the present or the future. In order to find Ardie, we have to follow those links. Along the way, we'll discover things about her life that don't seem related to finding her, but they are." Kerri paused. "I have a feeling we're going to run into a lot of things that won't make sense, but somehow they'll add up to an answer that explains why a mother took off and left her kids with strangers."

"How are the kids doing?"

"Great. Thanks to my family, they're responding to all the love around them, and loosening up. If we can just keep them safe…" Kerri's voice trailed off.

"What do you mean, safe? That Dirk guy hasn't shown up again, has he?"

"Not that we've seen, but I'll admit I'm just a little uneasy about this whole situation."

"Did you find out what the connection was between him and Mr. Richards's brother?"

"No. I struck out finding out much of anything about Jason." Then Kerri told her about the time she spent looking into Jason's accident. "I wrote it up for the files, but I don't know if his death is connected to anything at all. Everything is pure speculation at this point."

Debbie let out a slow whistle. "You mean we could be dealing with a murderer? And that's why the woman took off? Oh, my gosh, she's afraid for her own life and is on the run from someone who wants to kill her! Maybe, she's tied up with the mob and—"

"Slow down, Debbie," Kerri ordered. "Don't go all melodramatic on me."

"But what if someone is trying to kill her?" she protested, her eyes rounded with anxiety.

"We don't know anything at this point that even points to her life being in jeopardy," Kerri cautioned. "Mark is convinced the woman saw a chance to make him responsible for her kids. He has money, he can support them and give them all the advantages. Not a bad motivation for a mother who wants more for her children than she can give, wouldn't you agree?"

"Yes, but—"

"Debbie, we have to tie down some firm facts before we have any idea about the real reason she decided to disappear. We're beginning to move on the case, but we can't get ahead of the evidence. Right now, we have a name, and we're beginning to build a background that may answer some of our questions.''

"But even if we find out why she wanted to disappear, we still won't know where she is."

"No, but we may have some idea how to find her. Even people who don't want to be found are trapped by their own patterns. They repeat themselves once too often. Unable to completely change a life-style, they unwittingly hold to old habits, interests, weaknesses and ways of thinking. Once we get to know Ardie, we'll have clues to where she might be, and answers to why she ran away.''

"I don't know how you can be so patient." Debbie sighed. "I want things to happen fast."

"So I've noticed."

"Which brings to mind the handsome Mark Richards. You said on the phone that he followed you to Los Angeles.''

"I didn't say he followed me. I said he flew out to Los Angeles.''

"Same difference." Debbie smiled knowingly. "And you went out with him, didn't you? Level with me. You had a date. Where did he take you?"

"It wasn't a date. We were trying to find someone at this exclusive club who knew his brother. So we had dinner and talked."

"And...?" she prodded.

"That's all. It was all strictly business."

Debbie leaned over the desk, and grinned right in Kerri's face. "You're going to have to lie to yourself better than that. You're like a kid caught with a chocolate bar melting in his hand, swearing he doesn't like candy.''

Kerri couldn't help but smile back at her. "You may be right, but I have great willpower when it comes to sweets that aren't good for me.''

"We'll see." Debbie winked and laughed softly as she returned to the outer office. The telephone rang almost the moment she was back at her desk, and she chuckled to herself as she buzzed Kerri. "Mr. Mark Richards is on line one. He's inquiring if you are in the office. Shall I tell him you're busy?''

Kerri sat forward in her chair with an eagerness she would have readily denied. "I'll take it.''

She glanced at her watch. Four o'clock in California. It had only been seven hours since they had breakfast together. Why did it seem like forever?

"I hope I didn't interrupt anything." His voice was as deep and resonant as if he were sitting beside her, and an olfactory memory brought his scent back to her. "I checked at the telephone company and got a copy of Jason's final bill. There's a Reno number that is listed several times. I called it, but it's been disconnected. I'm working on getting the name of the party who had that number.''

"Terrific. That will help. We found a telephone listing for Ardella Browski, but it's five years old. The number you have may be a more current listing. We've made progress on another front," she told him. "Ardie has a Nevada driver's license, and once we have a copy of it, we'll have a photo, a description, and an address from the time she got the license two years ago.''

"So, we're making progress?" He sounded doubtful.

She knew he was asking the same question that Debbie had. *How is all this old data going to tell us where the missing woman is today?* "Slow but sure progress," she answered, hoping she wasn't misleading him. She knew that they could run into a brick wall at any time, and with the future of three children involved, there was an urgency that could not be denied. Pressure was building with every passing day. She'd never had a case where the time clock was ticking at such a frantic rate.

"I should be able to finish up here tomorrow," he said hopefully. "And catch a flight home tomorrow evening. Oh, I almost forgot. I may know where I put that note from Ardie."

"Terrific. Where?"

"In the telephone stand by the door. It seems to me I had the folded note when I thumbed through the yellow pages looking for a delivery service to pick up Cora's overnight bag at her house and bring it to the loft. Maybe I left the note in the drawer with the directory."

"Is there any way I could stop by your place on the way home and check? I'd really like to get a handwriting analysis as soon as possible. I could take it over to the graphologist tonight and let her get started."

"Sure. I'll call my secretary and have someone bring you the extra key to the loft that I keep at the office, but I'm not positive it's worth your trouble."

"Well, it's worth a try." She wasn't going to pass up any faint possibility of getting another clue to the missing Ardie. Any glimpse into her personality traits might be a big help. "I'll stop by your place on the way home."

"I'll call you the minute I get anything on the disconnected number," he promised. After a moment's hesitation, his businesslike tone softened. "And Kerri, I really did enjoy last night. Could I persuade you to have another business dinner date when I get back?"

"We'll see," she answered evasively. How could she admit she was afraid that she'd lose all sense of balance if she allowed herself to view him as anything but a client? There were too many things she didn't know about him—and about herself. Her body remembered the compelling attraction she'd felt as they danced, the total awareness of his hands drawing her close, the light caress of his cheek against hers. She'd never felt such physical harmony with a man. Even now she regretted closing the hotel door against him with only a crisp good-night. Mixing business with pleasure definitely was not a good idea.

They exchanged a few more casual comments. Kerri stared at the phone for a long minute after they hung up. A dissatisfied feeling mocked the things she might have said to him and didn't. *Get it together, girl,* she lectured herself, and with determined effort managed to put Mark Richards out of her mind long enough to catch up with some of her other work.

She worked past the dinner hour, alone in the office after Debbie left, a habit of hers when she got behind on her reports. Muscles in her neck and back were protesting when she finally called it quits. A copy of Ardie's driver's license had come in with its empirical data. Hair: blond. Height: five feet six inches. Weight: 112 pounds. Address: 2712 Moana Lane, Reno, Nevada. Kerri feared that the woman's photo wasn't sharp enough to assure ready recognition, but it was better than nothing. At least they had a place to start.

Taking the key that a messenger had brought over from Mark's office, she decided to leave her car in the garage and walk over to his apartment building. The streets of lower downtown Denver were aglow, and bustling with people enjoying restaurants, bookstores and art shops. If Kerri hadn't been so preoccupied, she might have lingered in front of the some of the enticing windows, and window-shopped as she walked the few blocks to the Crystal Lofts building. Instead, her steps were quick and purposeful, her thoughts centered on finding the note and taking it to the woman graphologist that she had used in other cases to get a personality profile on a missing person.

No one was in the foyer as she quickly walked to the elevator and punched the fifth-floor button. The cage hummed reassuringly as it lifted upward. When the doors flew open on that level, Kerri was startled to find herself face-to-face with Lisa.

The blonde's precisely plucked eyebrows rose as Kerri stepped out. She glanced down at the key that Kerri had taken out of her purse, and held ready in her hand. Then she said sweetly, "I thought Mark probably told you he's in California. He left yesterday."

Kerri smiled just as sweetly. "Yes, I know. I just got back myself this afternoon. In fact, I just talked to Mark a little while ago." Something about the woman's proprietary air brought out the worst in her, and Kerri was ashamed of herself for the spurt of feminine cattiness.

"Oh, I see. Mark was kind of vague about how long he would be gone," she said with markedly less cordiality. "I guess you sent the children away, thank heavens for that. He didn't say where they'd gone?"

She made a question out of the statement, and her eyes were sharply inquisitive.

Kerri ignored her open curiosity. The fewer people who knew where the children were the better. Giving Lisa a vague smile, she started away from the elevator.

"I'd be glad to help if Mark has asked you to pick up something for him," Lisa offered. "I'm pretty familiar with Mark's things."

"I'll remember that—if I need any help," Kerri answered in the same tone. Then she turned her back on the woman and walked down the hall, telling herself that Mark's playmates were no concern of hers. In a way, she was glad there was someone like Lisa to remind her of her client's life-style.

As Kerri opened the door and stepped inside the shadowy loft, she was aware of its high ceilings, brick walls and heavy draperies that had been drawn across the windows. Only a small kitchen light shining across the open counter into the living room gave faint illumination to the open-space room.

A lingering aura of bodily warmth struck her with such force that she couldn't even reach for a light switch. Either someone was still in the loft or had just left it. She was positive of it. An intuitive awareness of human scent was undeniable, and all of her senses reached out into the large darkened area, trying to see any shadowed form, any movement or sound of quickened breathing.

She held her breath. Nothing. After a long moment, she moved quickly to the nearest light switch and sent a blaze of overhead lights into every corner of the living room and kitchen area. Then she forced herself to turn on the den, bedroom and bathroom lights.

The loft was empty, and if anyone had been there earlier, they were gone now.

She felt slightly foolish as she quickly located the small telephone stand. Two deep drawers contained bulky metropolitan telephone directories. Kerri looked carefully for any small paper that might be caught in the drawers, but didn't find anything but some advertising flyers. If Mark had the note in his hand when he looked up a telephone number, he hadn't left it in the drawer.

She began flipping through the regular directory and came up empty. Then she picked up the yellow pages directory. She remembered that Mark had said he thought he'd had the note when he was calling about someone to pick up Cora's things at her house and bring them to the loft. She quickly turned to the section listing delivery services, and there it was, a folded piece of paper stuck between the pages.

Kerri's cry of joy echoed through the empty apartment. She read through the note carefully, searching for something that Mark might have missed telling her, but it was as short and concise as he had said. "Have to leave for a while. Don't try to find me. Ardie."

As Kerri read this concrete link to a woman who had deserted her children, her determination to find her was renewed. She stuck the note in her purse, determined to drop it off at the graphologist before she went home.

As she lingered a few moments in the loft, she quietly embraced the essence of the man who lived there. Everything had been put neatly back in order by some unseen hands, probably by a housecleaning service, she guessed. Without the children and their clutter, she saw Mark's home as a place of contentment and refuge from the business world. She could picture him relaxing in his chair, listening to fine music pouring from an elaborate entertainment center. A John Grisham novel lay on a coffee table next to a book on Colorado history and a thick volume on Wall Street investments. His strong personality was everywhere she looked, and she was acutely aware of the many facets of this man who'd come to dominate her thoughts and emotions.

For the first time, she realized how shattering the invasion of his home must have been for him. He'd spent too many years living alone to be prepared for the sudden assault of noise and confusion that erupted into his life. He had created a personal sanctuary for himself, and there was a quiet dignity about everything in the loft. She was aware of the sharp contrast between these surroundings and the bustling old house she called home.

Kerri turned off the lights and left the apartment, making sure she locked the door behind her. When she stepped out of the elevator on the first floor, she was surprised to see someone outside the double glass doors. A woman stood near the bank of intercoms and had her head bent as if about to buzz one of the apartments. Then, suddenly, she turned away quickly and hurried out of the building.

An alarm like a fire bell went off in Kerri's head. *A fair-haired woman, about five feet six inches tall, weight about 112 pounds.*

Kerri dashed to the glass doors, let herself out and bolted down the steps and out of the building.

Where did she go?

Kerri sent frantic glances down the sidewalk in both directions. The woman couldn't have gone far. There hadn't been time. But where—?

Before she finished the thought, she sensed a presence behind her. Even as she swung around, her head exploded into a thousand shattered pieces. A man's oath roared in her ears, and the sidewalk sank beneath her feet as she lost consciousness.

But as she turned to face the sunlight, she spotted a man approaching her. Even as she swung around, he lunged, exploding into the unexpected, shattered blows. A bright pain flashed in her forehead, and sidewalks spun beneath her feet as she fell unconscious.

Chapter Eight

Kerri floated up through thinning layers of gray mist. A painful throbbing at the back of her head kept rhythm with a loud ringing in her ears. Her skull seemed filled to bursting. As she tried to lift her weighted eyelids, a woman's demanding voice assaulted her.

"Can you hear me? Open your eyes. That's it. Good." The disembodied voice told her, "You're in an ambulance. We'll have you at Saint Joe's in a few more minutes."

Ambulance? Saint Joe's? The words floated around in Kerri's consciousness like foreign particles, detached and incomprehensible. She tried to raise her hand to touch the tube in her nose but couldn't. Either the message didn't get through to her arms, or something was holding them down. And she couldn't move her head, either. Something stiff like a collar around her neck held it firmly in place.

She was aware of the swaying action of the ambulance and muffled voices that came and went like echoes in a tunnel. After she felt the vehicle braking to a stop, someone propelled her on a fast-moving gurney into the building. Different voices assaulted her.

"A mugging."

"Bring her over here!"

"Head injury."

"Call Dr. Vanderfelt."

Blurred faces hung over her, and every part of her body seemed to be compressed, constrained or restricted. She felt like a doll whose stuffing was being pulled out by uncaring hands.

"Can you hear me?" A man asked as he pulled back her eyelids and shone a bright pinpoint of light in her eyes.

She managed a croak that he must have taken to mean, yes.

"Good. Looks like someone gave you a good wallop on the back of the head. I'm checking your eye reflexes and visual fields. Can you tell me your name?"

She wanted to ignore him, but he kept prodding her, so she mumbled, "Kerri Kincaid."

"Do you remember what happened, Ms. Kincaid?" he asked as he tested her limbs for loss of sensation, and checked on her muscle strength.

Kerri's memory was like an old strip of movie film, broken and frayed. As pain ricocheted through her head, some scenes came clear, others blurred and fuzzy. She'd been in Mark's apartment, she remembered that. Looking for something. Yes, the note. She latched onto the memory as if it were a rescue line, but she couldn't quite recall what happened next. Her memory jumped and she was running out of the building. Even now, a sense of urgency remained with her but she couldn't pin down the reason.

"Do you know who hit you?"

Once again she croaked a sound that caught in her throat.

"All right, Ms. Kincaid, the cranial nerves seem intact. We're going to take some pictures and see what we have."

With a wave of his hand, the stretcher was moving again. She closed her eyes against the dizzying patterns of lights flashing by on the ceiling above her. Various hands lifted, tugged and pulled, and crisp voices ordered her to hold her breath.

By the time they'd finished with X rays and checked her into a patient room on the ninth floor, she was ready to shut out the world and go to sleep. But they wouldn't let her.

"We have to monitor your vital signs," a pleasant woman advised her as she took Kerri's blood pressure, pulse and respiratory rate, yet again.

"Can't you go pester somebody else for a while?" she grumbled.

The nurse just laughed. "So, we're getting better, are we?"

When the doctor came in, Kerri had a good look at Dr. Vanderfelt for the first time. A small, dapper man in a white coat, he sailed around the side of the bed and gave her a cheery smile. "How's the head?"

"Thumping like a bongo drum."

"Well, we can give you a little something for that. And we'll remove your neck collar. You're lucky, Ms. Kincaid. No sign of a skull fracture. Looks like head trauma, with a transitory loss of consciousness. Of course, we'll have to keep you a while to observe for subdural hemorrhage or brain injury."

"Great," she muttered. "How long is 'a while'?"

"We'll know more tomorrow." He patted her arm.

"Just relax." He murmured some instructions to the nurse and disappeared.

A few minutes later a nurse came in with her pain pill. "A policeman is here to see you. Do you feel like talking? He says he's your brother-in-law."

"Oh, yes, let him in."

Tears swelled up in Kerri's eyes as Harry came in. *Harry. Blessed Harry.* Still in uniform, he bent his sturdy frame over her bed, wrinkles of concern in his round face. "What happened, Kerri?" he asked softly.

"I...I don't know for sure."

"The report came in as a mugging. A woman driving by in her car saw you slumped on the sidewalk and called it in. Your purse with your wallet was still on you, so identification was immediate. As soon as the report came in, I came right over."

"I'm glad," she said, more foolish tears springing to her eyes.

He bent over her. "Kerri, if you can give us any clue at all who did it, we'll put out a net."

"I wish I could, but nothing's very clear." She bit her lower lip. "The doctor says my mind will clear as the trauma to my head lessens but I'm having trouble remembering."

He nodded, and patted her hand. "It's okay. When you think of something, let me know. We usually don't have muggings in that area. It's too well patrolled and there's good security in buildings like the Crystal Lofts. The attack on you must have been an impulsive one."

Impulsive? Maybe so, but she couldn't help but ask, "Why would someone mug me and then leave my purse and wallet?"

"Maybe they were scared off," Harry offered. "So

far no witnesses have come forward, but we might get lucky. Anyway, we'll keep a lookout and see what we can dig up." He patted her hand again. "Rest while you can, hon. Your mother and sister will be here shortly to smother you with attention. Grandma and I will watch over the kids while they tend to you."

Harry gave her an avuncular kiss on the cheek and told her not to worry. "Everything's going to work out."

After he'd gone, she felt guilty about causing her family even more trouble. What in the world would she do without them? She'd really pulled them into a mess this time. How could she do her job of tracing anyone when she couldn't think straight? And what would be Mark's reaction when he heard what had happened?

HE NEARLY DROPPED the phone. "What?" Mark gasped when he called Kerri's office the next morning from Los Angeles, and Debbie informed him that Kerri had been mugged the night before and was still in the hospital.

"Why in the hell didn't you call me?" he roared.

"I didn't know anything about it myself until a few minutes ago," Debbie retorted defensively. "Kerri called me from the hospital herself, and she didn't say anything about notifying you."

Damn stubborn woman. He swore. "How badly is she hurt?"

"She's hoping they're going to release her later to-day."

Some of the tightness in his chest lessened. "Then she's going to be okay?"

"She sounded a little out of it on the phone," Debbie admitted. ''I mean, her voice was all wavery, and I could tell she was in pain. Real pain.'' Debbie sighed. ''It's so sad. Her being all alone like that. And she shouldn't be worrying about business, but I guess it'll take more than a crushed skull to slow her down.''

''A crushed skull! Is that what she has? Why would they be releasing her with a severe injury like that?''

''Oh, you know hospitals these days,'' Debbie said with a meaningful sigh. ''And Kerri's so stubborn. I was surprised she didn't want me to bring some work over to the hospital. She's determined to find your sister-in-law at all costs.'' Debbie sighed again. ''If she hadn't gone to your place, she wouldn't have been mugged.''

''*What?* She was mugged in my apartment?''

''Not *in* your apartment. But right in front of the building.'' There was a slight accusing edge to Debbie's tone. ''Kerri doesn't remember exactly what happened. The police are trying to find a witness.''

Mark couldn't believe what he was hearing. Never in the world would he have thought her in any danger stopping by the loft to look for the note. And yet, somehow, he felt responsible. ''Which hospital?''

''Saint Joseph's. Would you like the number?'' Debbie asked sweetly. ''She's in room 912. I know she'd love to hear from you.''

Mark wasn't so sure. Maybe she rued the day she'd ever met him. With a driving need to reassure himself that she was all right, he quickly dialed the number, but didn't get past the front desk. ''I'm sorry sir, we have a temporary hold on that number. I am unable to connect you.''

''Why? What's happened?''

''I have no information, sir, but there's no need to

be alarmed. It may be that the doctor has ordered complete rest, no visitors, no telephone calls.''

"But she was hoping to go home today.''

"That would be up to her physician.''

"Who is her physician?''

"I'm not authorized to give out that information. I'm sorry.''

"So am I,'' Mark snapped and hung up the phone. Then he dialed information and got Kerri's home number. After several rings, a sweet old lady's voice answered very politely, "Kincaid residence. To whom am I speaking?''

Kerri's grandmother. Mark didn't want to alarm the old lady by questioning her about what was going on at the hospital, but he had to know. "It's Mark Richards,'' he said and tried to identify himself by adding, "I brought the children to your home the other day and—''

"Oh, Mr. Richards. I remember you very well. I was telling Kerri you were a fine strapping figure of a man.'' Her voice suddenly became muffled and he realized she had put her hand over the receiver and was talking to someone in the room. He thought he heard his name, and then there was a silence before Kerri's mother with her Irish lilt came on the line.

"Oh, Mr. Richards, how nice of you to be calling. Kerri was saying that you were in California. Are you back then?''

"No, I'm calling from the Los Angeles office. I just learned this morning about Kerri's accident. I tried to talk to her at the hospital but they wouldn't put my call through.''

"Doctor's orders. That girl of mine is as stubborn as a goose laying eggs. Doesn't know the meaning of rest when there's a phone within reach. She was hoping to come home today, but the doctor wants her to stay quiet for another twenty-four hours. That means no visitors, and no phones. If you're wondering how soon she'll be back to work on finding the children's mother, I really don't know.''

Mark hadn't even thought about the delay this might cause in finding Ardie. ''We'll worry about that later. If Kerri's okay, and they let her out of the hospital tomorrow, that's all that matters. I can't fly back to Denver until tomorrow afternoon. I'll check with you as soon as I get back.''

''I rather suspect she'd be willing to give you a minute or two,'' Mrs. Kincaid answered dryly.

He asked how the children were doing, and listened to a glowing monologue about every cute thing they'd said or done. No doubt about it, the kids had hit the lotto when Kerri took them home to be with her family. Mark found himself wishing he'd seen their antics himself.

THE NEXT TWENTY-FOUR hours were the longest Mark had ever spent as he tried to keep his mind on hiring a new consultant. He knew there was nothing he could do to ensure Kerri's well-being, but that didn't keep him from wanting to pick up the telephone and begin issuing some orders. Instead, he'd sent flowers and a note that promised he'd see her as soon as he got back to Denver.

When he was finally in the air, counting the minutes of the two-hour flight, his anxiety rose to a new peak. Maybe Kerri hadn't been released from the hospital as planned. What if her condition had worsened since he'd talked to her mother the day before? Would someone have called him? He doubted it. He wasn't family, just a client. Reaching for the cellular phone on the plane, he silently cursed himself for not keeping in touch with Debbie or the family every few hours. He dialed Finders, Inc., and received a recorded message for his efforts.

Where in blazes was Debbie? Glancing at his watch for the hundredth time, he saw that it was only two-thirty Denver time. Was she taking a long lunch hour? Or had she gone to the hospital? He quickly dialed the number for Saint Joseph's Hospital. A repeated busy signal fueled his frustration to an explosive flash point. When he finally had the receptionist on the line, he was ready to do battle, but was left without a target when she said, "Miss Kincaid was released this morning."

Weakly, he hung up the phone, leaned back in his first-class seat, and motioned the stewardess to bring him a strong Scotch and soda. As soon as they landed, he picked up his car, and went straight from the airport to the house.

Cathy answered the door and gave him an appraising smile as she invited him in. "What a nice surprise, Mr. Richards."

"I called the hospital and they said Kerri had been released."

"Yes, we brought her home a couple of hours ago."

"How's she doing? Is she up to company? I know she needs to rest, and I wouldn't want to tire her. If she's sleeping, I could come back. I guess I should have called first, but I was anxious about her so I came straight from the airport. I really would like to see her." He knew he was talking too fast, but his nervousness, pent up for too many hours, demanded some release, and he wasn't even embarrassed by this plea to see for himself that she was all right.

Cathy's smile broadened. "I think your visit would be good medicine. Come on, let's go upstairs and take a peek into her bedroom. If she's awake, you can say hi."

He followed Kerri's sister up an old-fashioned staircase with a beautiful banister, topped by a polished mahogany newel post. Wide steps creaked under his weight, and a grandfather clock that dominated the landing welcomed him with a deep bonging that boldly declared the hour. He could hear muffled noises somewhere deep in the old house, but on the second floor, there was a hushed quietness that promised soothing tranquility to frayed spirits and a hurting body. Thick walls had weathered storms raging against roof and rafters, standing firm, and protecting those inside. He could almost feel the presence of all those who had lived within these walls, as if something of their loving spirits remained. For the first time, he understood why Kerri loved this house so much that she chose it over any modern condominium.

Kerri's bedroom door was open. Mark hesitated in the hall while Cathy poked her head inside the room. Then she turned back to Mark. "She's awake and decent. Go on in." With a knowing chuckle, she disappeared back down the stairs.

"Hi. It's me," he said from the doorway.

Kerri sat up against some pillows in the middle of a large brass bed. A late afternoon sun coming through lightly curtained west windows lent a muted golden glow to the room. If the situation had been different, Mark would have laughed because she looked very much like a little girl pretending to be grown-up enough to sleep in the monstrous bed.

"Come in," she said with a welcoming smile.

"How're you doing?"

"Fine. Just playing lazy." Shadows darkened her deep-set eyes, but he was relieved to see that she seemed as spunky as ever.

"I should have known you were too hardheaded to come to any harm," he said lightly, even as his heart tightened just looking at her. He hadn't been able to think about anything but how important she was to him, and how devastated he was that something like this had happened to her.

"You don't look so hot yourself," she chided, eyeing his tired, worried expression and the deep lines around his mouth.

"Thanks, I make the trip from California like a bat out of hell, and all you can do is insult me." He sat down on the edge of the bed beside her. "I worried about you the whole trip back. I didn't know whether you'd been released from the hospital, or if something had happened to keep you there. I tried calling your office from the plane but only got a recording."

"I sent Debbie over to the graphologist's with Ardie's note. No use everyone lying around taking a holiday," she said, smiling at him. "Thanks for the bouquet of roses. I think five dozen is overdoing it a bit," she chided. "I wasn't *that* sick."

"Really?" He searched her face, and fought the need to take her in his arms and hold her close. "I was under the impression that you got carted off to the hospital in an ambulance."

"I just got bopped on the head." A slight tremble of her lower lip defied the bravado in her voice. "I don't know who or why. The police think it was a mugging, but…'' Her voice trailed off.

He took one of her hands in his, lightly caressing it with his thumb. "Don't talk about it if it upsets you."

"I need to understand what happened. My purse wasn't taken and nothing I had in it is missing. It just doesn't add up." She drew in a shaky breath. "I've had trouble remembering everything that happened. I know I went to your apartment and found the note just where you thought it would be." Moistening her dry lips, she said, "And last night, I woke up from a dream and remembered something else." Her hand tightened in his. "I think I saw Ardie when I was leaving your building."

His eyes widened. "Are you sure?"

"No," she admitted reluctantly. "I told you my memory is a little faulty. Until last night I didn't re-member seeing anyone in the foyer. Then it came back to me as clearly as anything. There was a light-haired woman, Ardie's height and weight, on the other side of the glass doors. I had just come out of the elevator when she saw me and hurried away. I remember run-ning outside."

"And did you see her?"

"No, but that's when someone hit me on the head."

"Could she have been the one that did it?"

"I don't think so."

"Why not?"

"Because just a second after I was hit, I know I heard a man swear."

Mark was silent, trying to make some sense out of what Kerri was saying. If Ardie had returned to his place, why wouldn't she come out in the open about getting her kids back? Mark knew Kerri could easily be hallucinating about having seen her. The impression that she saw Ardie could have been a subconscious illusion. And her conviction that it was a man who struck her could be a part of the same faulty memory.

"You don't believe me, do you?" Kerri drew her hand away from his. "Well, to tell the truth, I don't believe me, either. There're too darn many pieces of this puzzle that don't fit anywhere." She brushed a hand across her eyes as tears of frustration threatened to well up in the corners. "Maybe I'm not the one to solve this thing."

As she tried to turn her face away from him, he gently brought it back, and lowering his head, brushed soft kisses on her moist eyelids.

She knew she should resist this show of tenderness, but she couldn't. As he trailed butterfly kisses from her eyelids, down to the corner of her mouth, she parted her lips in welcome expectation, ready for the passionate kiss that every fiber of her being welcomed.

It never came.

She was confused when he touched her lips lightly with a kiss as feathery as the ones on her eyelids, and then drew back. Had she misread all the signs? If that kiss was the height of his ardor, her struggle to keep him at arm's length was ridiculous.

As if he read her thoughts, he gently stroked her cheek. "Think of that kiss as a promissory note, 'To be redeemed at some more appropriate time—with interest.'"

Only pride kept her from demanding payment right then and there. He drew back as Mrs. Kincaid bustled into the room, like a mother hen, ready to flap her feathers and take care of her chick.

"Doctor says Kerri's not to get too tired," she warned Mark. "She's had quite a shock, you know."

"Mom, no need for melodrama," Kerri chided. "I feel fine."

"Your mother's right," Mark said, smiling at Mrs. Kincaid. "I was just leaving."

"Oh, you'll be wanting to see how the children are faring, won't you?" she protested. "I was thinking it would be nice if you'd stay for supper...so we can all get acquainted a little better."

Kerri silently groaned. How obvious could her mother get? Poor Mark. She knew what happened when the Kincaid clan swung into high gear, checking out suitable males. He'd have to run a gauntlet of personal and professional questions that would put an FBI inquiry to shame.

"Thank you. I'd love to stay."

"We'll be having stuffed roast chicken. Not that store-bought stuffing," she assured him. "I have my own recipe made with apples, raisins and my own special sausage. I suspect, being a bachelor and all, you could use a good home-cooked meal."

"I sure could," Mark agreed. Kerri knew he was smothering a smile.

Mrs. Kincaid removed the pillows from behind Kerri's back, and settled her under the covers. "We'll bring you up a tray, dear. Now, you take a nice nap."

"Quit fussing, Mom. You're wearing me out with all this coddling. Tomorrow, I'm up and out of here."

"Can't you talk some sense into her, Mr. Richards? She's been pushing herself like there's no tomorrow, and I don't see why. The children are fine, and she'll find their mother soon enough. I don't know what all the panic is about."

"That reminds me, Mark," said Kerri, ignoring her mother. "Did you find out who was listed at that Reno telephone number on your brother's bill?"

He nodded, wishing he had better news, but Kerri was waiting for an answer so he couldn't sidestep the question. "My brother had a condo in Reno, and the disconnected number was his. I'm guessing Ardie was staying there and he made the calls to her. Sorry."

"Enough of that." Mrs. Kincaid gave Mark a purposeful nudge toward the door.

He paused in the doorway, resisting a need to go back to the bed and kiss her the way she should be kissed. In spite of her protests that she felt fine, she looked wan and tired. "I'll see you tomorrow," he promised.

She nodded, and gave him a wry smile. "Beware of the mating traps downstairs."

He laughed. "I'll do my best."

Downstairs, everything seemed in purposeful chaos. Mrs. Kincaid resembled Mission Control as she sent adults and children scurrying here and there in the last phases of dinner preparation and the setting of a long table in the dining room.

Timmy hung on to Mark as if his new uncle might take off again at any minute. When the little boy looked at him with such guileless, trusting eyes, something in Mark's chest tightened with a strange emotion. He didn't know how to respond to such open affection. When Timmy asked him to help with an airplane kit he'd been trying to put together, Mark said "sure."

The twin girls competed with Timmy for Mark's attention, and even little Patti scrambled up on Mark's lap without waiting for an invitation. Before Mark knew what was happening, he was put in charge of the children's "wash up." He discovered that this meant herding four reluctant, dirty-faced kids into a bathroom for more than a slight swish of water over their grimy hands.

Timmy and the twins' caked fingernails were a tell-tale sign of the clay dirt they'd been using to make mud pots. Mark did the best he could to get rid of most of the grime, but he hoped none of the women would do a merit inspection. When he held Patti over the sink to wash her hands, she decided it was play-time and swished the water all over him and the floor.

Timmy was ready to join his sister in a water fight, but Mark managed to get him and the girls out of the door before he lost complete control of the situation.

Cathy's husband, Harry, had arrived while Mark was in the bathroom with the children. After a quick introduction, the two men escaped to the living room for a few moments of private conversation. Mark pumped the policeman as much as he could about the attack on Kerri, but the officer admitted there wasn't much to tell.

"We haven't turned up any witnesses. There isn't much more that we can do. Kerri can't give us a description."

"Did she tell you she thought she saw the children's mother just before she ran out of the building?"

"No." Harry raised a bushy eyebrow. "She didn't say a thing about someone else being there."

"I think she just remembered it last night—if it really happened. She might be imagining the whole thing, but then again, she might really have seen her. Could the police put out Ardie's description and see if someone comes up with an ID? If she's wandering around lower downtown, we might get a clue where to find her. What a relief it would be to locate her here in Denver, right under our noses."

"I'll talk to the captain," Harry promised. "He knows Kerri's trying to find the kids' mother. Sure is going to be hard on everyone when the kids leave," Harry said with a shake of his head. "My girls are going to throw a fit. They don't understand that all children should be with their mother, even if she acts like a boob sometimes."

When they were called to dinner, Mark sat between Timmy and one of the twins. He found himself buttering rolls and pouring milk, and engaging in a nodding conversation with the two of them about the "ugh" taste of broccoli. Patti's preference for using fingers instead of a fork seemed quite acceptable, and he couldn't remember when he'd felt so much at ease.

The food was as good as he had expected, and he wished that Kerri could have been sitting at the table with them. The conversation was general, except for some very pointed questions that he managed to answer or deflect. Not knowing how Kerri felt about him made him cautious, but all in all, he felt that he had come through the interrogation unscathed.

The evening was a pleasant one, but as Mark drove home, he tried to convince himself that a family like Kerri's could smother a person. The boisterous giving and taking that seemed so natural to this Irish family was foreign to him. It wasn't a life-style that he could readily accept. How could anyone maintain his individuality when being pulled in all directions in the name of family love? He'd always protected his privacy, his space, and most of all, his independence.

He let himself into his loft with what he thought

was a sigh of gratitude, but later, as he stood at his window, listening to the rumbling traffic below and looking across the lighted impersonal city, he admitted to a bone deep loneliness that had never been there before. With painful honestly, he asked himself if he was falling in love with a woman whose life was steeped in traditions that he could never understand or share—and three children who didn't belong to him.

Chapter Nine

Kerri spent one day at home and then went back to the office. Her motivation for finding the missing mother had grown more intense. She was getting too attached to the children. Having spent more time with them, Kerri was captivated by the baby's toothless smiles, by Timmy's eagerness to play and Patti's innocent sweet affection. If the mother of these wonderful children was in jeopardy and needed help, finding her quickly was of primary importance. Kerri put all her other cases on hold and went after every lead with the tenacity of a pit bull.

"What are you trying to do, kill yourself?" Debbie demanded when, on the first day Kerri was back, she never left her desk and computer.

"I have a gut feeling that today's the day."

"The day for what? That you're going to end up back in the hospital because of exhaustion?"

Kerri ignored her. "Check with the graphologist and see if she's got anything for me. And here's a list of telephone calls I want you to make." After giving her secretary enough work for three people, Kerri went back to her computer and began checking every conceivable resource that might provide any information

on the name Ardella L. Browski. The pile of data on
her desk began to build.

Mark wandered into the office at closing time, and
through a half-opened door, Kerri could hear Debbie
unloading on him. "Thank heavens, maybe you can
do something with her. She hasn't taken a break all
day, and the lunch I brought in is almost untouched.
She's like a soul possessed. I've never seen her like
this." Debbie reached for the intercom to announce
him but he shook his head.

He gave a polite knock on the half-opened door, but
didn't wait for a response. As he came in, he was
surprised to see her standing at a window, staring
down at the street below. She looked small and fragile
against the wide expanse of glass.

"Hi," she said, without turning around.

"Hi, yourself. Whatcha doing?"

"Thinking."

"Too much of that can be harmful to your health,"
he said lightly. "Why don't you give those brain cells
a rest and go to dinner with me?"

"I can't. I've got to go home and pack." She turned
away from him, went back to her desk, and picked up
a sheaf of folders. "Sit down. I have a report to make
to you. And it's not one that you're going to like."
She sighed wearily. "In fact, it's a real bummer."

Clammy sweat suddenly beaded on his palms as she
sat down on the couch beside him. He couldn't imagine what those papers in her hands were going to tell
him. Whatever the news, her strained face told him
that she was paying an emotional price for her involvement. He wanted to take the burden on himself, and
make it as easy on her as he could.

"It can't be as bad as all that. Is Ardie an escaped

convict?'' He'd thought he'd bring a smile to her face, but her expression was as solemn as ever. ''She isn't, is she?'' he demanded quickly. At the shake of her head, he breathed, ''Thank God for that. Then what is it?''

''We know now that Ardie was married to Buddy Browski.'' She waited for his reaction. When she didn't get any, she asked, ''The name doesn't ring a bell?''

''No, should it?''

''I suppose not. Apparently he was a well-known racketeer in gambling circles. He had an extensive criminal record and was charged with running an illegal con game. The case never went to trial.''

''Why not?''

''Because he was murdered.''

Murdered. For a suspended moment, the ugly word had no meaning, but when she handed him copies of newspaper clippings, police reports and county records, a cold prickling traveled up his spine. ''Who killed him?''

''The case is still open.'' She took a deep breath. ''His wife, Ardella, was suspected as being one of the ring, but no charges of any kind were brought against her.''

He was afraid to ask, but he had to know. ''Does my brother fit into all of this?''

''Not that I've discovered so far,'' she told him with obvious relief, ''but Jason married Ardella about two months after Buddy Browski was ambushed and killed on a road between Reno and Carson City.''

Mark felt as if he'd taken a fierce punch in his stomach. He sat there, staring at the sculptured carpet, unable to organize his thoughts in any constructive manner. How could he have been so ignorant about what was going on? Had he been so distant with Jason that the only line of communication they had was around business? He knew the answer to that. His brother's history of getting into trouble had made Mark jaded about Jason's personal life. As long as there wasn't a crisis of some kind, like a debt to be paid or a marriage to be dissolved, Mark had looked the other way. Now his guarded interest in his brother's affairs had come home full force. He leaned forward and put his head in his hands.

Kerri put a hand on his arm. "I'm sorry, Mark. I wish I didn't have to turn up all this unpleasantness, but it's necessary if we're going to solve this thing."

When he straightened up after moment, he asked wearily, "Well, what do we do now?"

"The focus of the investigation is the same. We have to find Ardella."

"Those poor kids. They deserve better."

"Whatever else the woman's failings may be, I think she's a good mother."

He scoffed. "How in blazes can you say that when she dumped them the way she did?"

"Maybe leaving them with you is evidence of her conscientious mothering. The kids are safe. She must have known you'd take care of them."

"I turned them over to you fast enough. Without your family in the picture, no telling what I would have done."

"You would have done the right thing," she assured him. "Don't be so hard on yourself. None of this is your fault."

"Jason was my younger brother. I should have known what was going on."

"He was an adult, living his own life, and making his own choices." *And reaping the consequences of those choices?* Kerri shoved the disturbing thought away. She had enough on her mind without debating whether Jason's death had been accidental or deliberately caused. Her first priority was finding Ardella Browski Richards.

"Okay, so you dug up all this garbage. What next? What happens now?"

"My next step is to try to retrace the woman's actions before she showed up in Denver with her kids. To do that I need to make a trip to Reno, and maybe, Carson City. Since Ardella Browski has been in the newspapers and people will recognize the name, it should be easy to pick up some helpful information about her."

"Why take all the trouble of going to Reno? If you really did see her at my place a few days ago, why look someplace else?"

"Because if she's still hanging around Denver, there must be a reason, and maybe that reason will tell us where we can find her. Besides, I can't be positive that I really saw her that night. Maybe wishful thinking planted the fantasy. There's nothing sharp and clear about the memory."

"If you suffered that much of a head trauma, you shouldn't be putting in god-awful hours working, and flying all over the country." He put a masterful arm around her shoulders and drew her to him so that her head rested in the crook of his arm. "You should be home in bed, dressed in those fuzzy pajamas, with someone bringing you hot toddy nightcaps."

She closed her eyes, her cheek against his chest, lulled by the steady rhythm of his heartbeat and the warmth of his embrace. For a suspended moment, she almost believed that love could be simple, lovely and filled with contented moments like this one. She was tempted to let her defenses down and open herself to loving this man who could make her feel that there was no other woman in the whole world. If Debbie hadn't come in at that moment, breaking the spell, she might have bought into the fantasy.

"Oh, excuse me," Debbie apologized, her eyes avidly taking in the way Mark was holding her. "I was just leaving, and wondered if there was anything else you wanted me to do."

Kerri straightened up, the moment of weakness and vulnerability quickly dissipating. Her thoughts flew ahead to the business at hand. "Yes, there is one more thing. Make reservations for a morning flight to Reno."

"Make it two," Mark echoed.

Kerri opened her mouth to protest, but Mark's firm look put an end to any argument.

THE FLIGHT TO RENO was a little over two hours. If Mark hadn't been sitting beside her, Kerri might have snatched a nap, but his presence was too much of a stimulant. He seemed to be in a good mood, laughing easily, and making sure that she was comfortable in the window seat. As they enjoyed the first-class pampering, she couldn't tell if he was really all that relaxed, or putting on a good front for her benefit.

As if they'd made an unspoken pact not to talk about business, they kept conversation general, touching on food, movies and, of course, sports. Kerri smiled to herself at Mark's open enthusiasm about the

Denver Broncos. "What do you say we get season tickets for next year?"

As he waited for her answer, there was something in his eyes, a kind of measuring that had nothing to do with a football contest. She realized that he wasn't just being glib about the invitation. In a way, he was really asking if there was going to be something between them beyond this moment, beyond the bizarre happenings that had drawn them together. In reality, he was asking about the future.

"Let's wait and see," she hedged. "There are too many things that are undecided."

"Maybe not as many as you think," he challenged. "Maybe you're just ignoring the possibilities."

She wasn't ready to admit that he was right. Not yet. Not when her emotions were in such a state of flux. When she was with this man, she was strangely aware of herself in a way she'd never been before. She sensed the depths of her own feelings and needs, almost like a stranger becoming acquainted with her inner self for the first time. This enlightenment was at once exhilarating and frightening. She'd never been a jealous person, but thinking of him and Lisa together created a sickening nausea that mocked her pretense of indifference. And when he was close to her and smiling at her the way he was now, she had difficulty keeping her thoughts and feelings on track. Only a large measure of self-discipline caused her to reach for her briefcase and pull out the report that the graphologist had dropped by the house the evening before.

"Are you familiar with personality profiles drawn from samples of handwriting?" she asked him.

"I've never put much stock in it," he admitted.

"Handwriting analysis is really quite fascinating, and has proven to be surprisingly reliable."

"I can see how it would be helpful in forgeries, but that's about all," he said flatly.

"I've used it in past cases to help me get a sense of the person I'm looking for," she admitted. "You can tell whether the person is bold or timid, angry, careless, has a strong ego or a weak one, and a hundred other things. Of course, more than one sample of handwriting is needed for a really thorough analysis." Kerri paused, trying to retrieve some nebulous question about the note. What was it that bothered her? What was she missing? Try as she would, she couldn't draw it out of the shadows.

"Well, what does Ardie's handwriting tell us? That she's terribly loving and maternal? Or that she's manipulative and self-centered?"

Kerri hated to admit it, but Mark was closer in his second guess. Single letters in the handwriting showed more aggressive and egocentric traits than any gentle traits or the desire to please. It was apparent from the woman's profile that Reno was definitely the place to look for someone caught up in the high living lifestyle of a gambling mecca. The graphologist had just reinforced what they already knew about the missing woman. Kerri's usual eagerness to pick up the trail of her quarry was tinged with a reluctance to bring any more unsavory details to light. As always, thinking about the children made this assignment harder than any she'd ever accepted.

Mark had been watching the tightening of her lips and the setting of her jaw. "What now, boss?"

"We find someone who knows her. If we're lucky, they'll tell us something that will show us our next move." She didn't add that there was a good chance this trip to Reno was only a dead end.

The plane began its sharp descent, and Kerri glimpsed a high-rise Hilton hotel as they landed at the airport in the middle of the sprawling town. The terminal of the Biggest Little City in the World welcomed travelers in its own special way. A myriad of slot machines stretched from the concourse gates to the baggage area, and Kerri didn't see a single vacant seat as they passed them. Clanging machines and dropping coins created a hypnotic seduction that provided an immediate fix for the gamblers arriving in droves twenty-four hours a day. Kerri hoped that Lady Luck would smile on her own gamble of a different kind.

After they claimed their baggage, they rented a car and drove to the Hilton, a short distance away. They had just entered the lobby when a good-looking redheaded man, somewhere in his thirties, sauntered toward them, wearing a bright green sport shirt open at the neck, and matching smooth-fitting slacks. His broad grin and open arms were for Kerri. "Hi, sweetheart. Long time, no see."

Mark stiffened as the man's arms went around Kerri in a bear hug that lifted her off the floor. Mark had an unreasonable urge to drop his bag and punch the man in the nose. Who in the hell was this guy? Kerri hadn't said anything about meeting anyone, but watching her laugh as the grinning redhead set her down, Mark felt like an idiot. Had he stupidly pushed himself on Kerri when she had other plans for her stay in Reno?

"Ken Nabors, meet Mark Richards." Kerri made the introductions.

"Oh, yes, the client." Ken flashed him a measuring

smile. "Well, Mr. Richards, you hired yourself the best investigator around—and the prettiest, too." He winked at Kerri. "She keeps us all in business."

"And what business is that?" Mark asked coolly.

Kerri shot a look at his glowering face, and answered quickly, "Ken is a private investigator from Phoenix. I've used him several times on other cases. He can follow up leads that would be difficult or inconvenient for my agency."

"Have badge, will travel. A roving PI, that's me." He started humming, "Just one of the roving kind..."

"You never change, Ken," Kerri said, laughing. "Thanks for coming on such short notice."

"No problem, honey. When Debbie called me yesterday and filled me in on the case, I was off and running—or flying, rather. I checked into the hotel about nine o'clock last night. I guess you'll want to get settled before we huddle?"

Huddle? Mark's itch to deliver a well-placed punch on this guy was growing with every minute.

"Why don't we meet in the lounge, say, in an hour?" she suggested.

"My favorite kind of office."

Kerri shook a warning finger at him, "I'm not picking up a giant tab as a business expense."

"Now, Kerri, honey, you never can tell when buying someone a couple of drinks will pay off," he chided and boldly tweaked her nose in a playful fashion. "Besides, you didn't call me in on the case to sit in a hotel room and read the Gideon's Bible, did you?"

"That would be the day," Kerri answered dryly as she turned toward the registration desk.

Ken gave Mark a nod of dismissal. "Nice to meet you, Mr. Richards."

"I suspect we'll be seeing quite a bit of each other," Mark replied, making the remark sound more like a warning than polite pleasantry.

Going up in the elevator to their rooms on the twenty-sixth floor, Kerri was well aware of Mark's dark mood. He was abrupt, touchy as hell. It was easy to see that Ken had definitely rubbed Mark the wrong way. She supposed she should have warned him that she had called in another investigator, but she wasn't in the habit of conferring with anyone else about business decisions. Besides, Ken was exactly the kind of PI she needed in a setting like Reno. He could move in and out of the casinos, fit in with any gambling crowd, and act the innocent playboy role to perfection.

Kerri waited until the bellhop let them into rooms across the hall from each other, before she went into Mark's and confronted him about his hostile attitude. "We might as well clear the air, right now. Unless you want to take me off the case, I intend to use Ken Nabors in this investigation. I've worked with him before, and I know what he can do."

"It's obvious that you're old friends."

"Business associates," she corrected him. "Nothing more."

"Didn't look like that to me. Anyone with eyes in his head could tell he was coming on to you."

"And anyone with eyes in his head should be able to tell that he flirts as easily as he breathes. And, maybe, being charming is Ken's secret weapon for success," she admitted. "If Ken runs into any woman that's been close to Ardie, he has a good chance of finding out what our missing mother is up to these days. I can't get as close to the sources that he can. I'm depending upon him to get me some firsthand info about Buddy Browski's ill-fated con game, and what might have gone wrong enough to get Browski killed.''

"Why couldn't you have given him the assignment over the phone? Why make the trip yourself?"

"There's plenty of other footwork for me to do. As soon as I unpack, I'll decide where to start." She paused in the doorway of his room. "If you truly think that I'm here for a tête-à-tête with Ken Nabors, you're a blind, pigheaded fool." She gave his door a punctuating slam.

LATER, WHEN HE HEARD her door open and close, he forced himself not to rush after her. He paced his room, starting to leave a dozen times, and then changing his mind. He wasn't about to admit to adolescent jealousy, but at the moment, he couldn't come up with any mature reason for acting the way he had. The fact that he'd even thought she was capable of arranging a rendezvous with someone while on business made him ashamed. She was right to hire the best man for the job, but it still bothered him that she was downstairs in the lounge with the guy.

He got on the phone and spent a half an hour taking care of business. After he hung up, he grabbed a financial journal he needed to read, left his room, and went down to the lobby. As casually as he could, he chose a chair that gave him a clear view of the entrance to the lounge. Twenty minutes later, he put down his journal when Kerri and the PI came into the lobby. They walked toward the front entrance of the hotel, and Mark thought they were leaving, but they stopped at the door. Kerri said something to Nabors and then the PI left alone.

As Kerri turned back into the lobby, she saw Mark sitting there watching her. A flash of warmth burned her cheeks as she walked over to him. "Are you spying on me?"

"No, just waiting for you," he assured her with an easy smile, as he rose to his feet. "I thought you might need a chauffeur this afternoon, and I'm at your service." He gave a mock bow that disarmed her and brought a smile to her eyes.

"All right, you're hired. I want to check out the address on Ardie's driver's license, and also that place listed in your brother's name that showed up on his telephone calls. We can knock on a few doors and see if we come up with anything helpful."

"Sounds good to me."

There was a boyish enthusiasm in Mark's tone that made Kerri smile, but she didn't say anything. He'd find out soon enough that sleuthing was mostly boring, painstaking work that wore patience down to a frazzle.

Unfortunately, their first stop proved to be a case in point. The address that Ardie had given on her two-year-old driver's license, 2712 Moana St., was a huge motel fairly close to the strip of gambling casinos on Virgina Street. They talked to the office manager who informed them that the motel's clientele was transient, the average stay only a week or two. He told them that with over a hundred units in the complex, the likelihood of anyone remembering a woman who stayed there two years ago was minute. Kerri agreed and reluctantly crossed the address off her list of possible leads.

"Forward and onward," Mark said, giving Kerri a

reassuring smile as they drove to the address he'd been able to get from the telephone company. If his brother had made repeated calls to that number after his marriage, it stood to reason that Ardie had been living there while Jason was still in California.

Kerri agreed. Maybe Jason had rented it while he was courting Ardie, and had kept it while they were working out arrangements for her to come to Los Angeles. What kind of business could have kept her in Reno for several months after their marriage?

Mark braked in front of the wrought-iron gate of the Medallion Condominiums. A security fence enclosed the exclusive complex, and a sign, Adult Occupancy Only, was clearly posted.

As they stared at the sign, neither of them said anything, but Kerri's disappointment was already setting in. She knew what the restrictions meant—Ardie couldn't have lived here with a baby and two lively youngsters.

Mark asked himself, if Ardie hadn't been living in his brother's condo, who had? For the hundredth time, he cursed himself for not having kept closer tabs on his brother's personal life.

"Well, let's see what the manager has to say," Kerri said. "Maybe we'll pick up something that will lead us in a different direction." She knew that sometimes an apparent dead end could open up some unexpected avenues.

An electronic gate allowed residents with the proper magnetic key to enter and leave the premises, but a gatehouse was positioned to monitor everyone else. Mark pulled the car close to the small window and a gaunt-looking white-haired man rose to his feet in a slow, lumbering fashion and squinted as if he couldn't quite see them through the thick lenses of his glasses.

"We'd like to talk to someone in the office about a condo that my brother occupied some months ago," Mark told him.

The elderly man cocked his head slightly to one side as if not quite hearing, and Mark repeated what he had said in a louder voice. With deliberate slowness, the gatekeeper nodded. "You'd be wanting to see Mr. Lamquist."

"Mr. Lamquist," Mark repeated. "Thank you, and where will I find him?"

He waved a skeleton hand. "He has an office in the first building. You can't miss it," he assured them, but made no movement toward opening the gate.

"Thanks for your help," Mark said, as if those were the magic words to gain entrance to the place.

"Mr. Lamquist ain't here, though. He's in San Diego."

Kerri covered her mouth to hide a smile. Mark's frustration mirrored her own on so many occasions that she couldn't help but be amused. Used to the cut-and-dried world of business, he was doing his best not to lose his temper with the elderly man's inefficiency, but she could see a cord in his neck flickering.

"We'll talk to someone else in the office," Mark told him slowly with forced patience. "Will you please open the gate?"

As if the gatekeeper were considering whether or not it was a good idea, he hesitated. Then, shrugging his thin shoulders, he finally pushed a button that let the wrought-iron gate swing open. Mark drove the car through the opening, holding his breath, hoping that the elderly man wouldn't change his mind before they got through.

Beautifully landscaped grounds surrounded ultra-modern condos that shouted six-figure incomes. Mark knew all too well that Jason had never been judicious about money, even though he had been in a position to invest wisely and accrue modest wealth. Living in a place like this cost plenty. Something didn't add up. Jason didn't have this kind of money. Even when he won at the races, he turned around and lost it as quickly as he could make the next bet.

He put a guiding hand on Kerri's elbow as they went into the building. After he had identified himself as Jason Richards's brother to a pretty lady behind a counter in the condo office, he stepped aside and let Kerri take charge from there.

She showed the woman her credentials, and asked for her help in trying to locate a missing person. "A telephone was listed at this address to Jason Richards and we want to verify that he had a residence here."

"Yes, Mr. Richards leased one of our condos for three months," the lady said with a pleasant smile.

"I see. And is his the only signature on the lease?" Kerri asked. "We understood that he was married at that time."

"I can show you the signed form if you'd like," she said graciously. With quick efficiency, she found the correct file and laid it out on the counter for Kerri and Mark. "As you can see, the condo was leased to Jason P. Richards for a period of three months. Our records show that he gave us one check for the entire amount and moved out on this date."

Three weeks before he died in the car accident Kerri

noted, and avoided looking at Mark. "And you don't have a record of anyone else living there with him?"

"No, it's listed as single occupancy," she said, and then added with a meaningful smile, "but that doesn't mean he might not have had a houseguest from time to time."

"Would it be possible for us to talk with some of the tenants who live in neighboring condos?"

"Oh, I'm sorry," she said, most apologetically. "Privacy is of utmost importance to our tenants, and unless someone willingly puts your name on their approved list, we have a strict code that prohibits non-residents freedom of the premises. You understand?"

Mark opened his mouth to protest, but Kerri put a staying hand on his arm. They'd have to come at this another way. "Thank you for your time."

Any thoughts Mark had about ignoring the rules and seeking out Jason's neighbors quickly faded as they left the office and returned to the car. He was acutely aware of two young and muscular security guards who watched them until they had driven off the premises.

Mark's hands were tight on the steering wheel, and his jaw ridged. "There's no way Jason could afford a place like that. And even if he had a run of luck and decided to pay off the lease with his winnings, why would he lease it for three months when Ardie and the kids couldn't live in it?"

"I don't know, but obviously someone was living in it while your brother was working in Los Angeles. He wouldn't have been calling an empty apartment."

"It only makes sense if Jason took the condo for Ardie and his newly acquired family."

"Ardie could have made other arrangements for the kids."

"Dumped them on somebody else, you mean," he muttered. "I feel damn sorry for those kids. I'll have a thing or two to tell the woman when I get her face-to-face. Why my brother ever took up with her, I'll never know."

"It's too early to judge her," Kerri cautioned, and then thinking aloud added, "For some reason, Ardie could have been staying at Jason's condo alone until the lease was up, three weeks before Jason's accident. If only we knew why and where she went after that, we might have a lot of answers."

"I don't see how any of it helps us find out where the woman is now."

Kerri shrugged. "Circles of the past often bring us up to the present. If we're lucky we'll find that circular path."

"I certainly hope so," Mark said without much conviction. He'd rather make a prediction on the stock market any day.

When they got back to the hotel, there was a message from Ken Nabors that seemed promising. "Good news," she told Mark. "Ken's meeting someone who knew both Ardie and her husband, Buddy. Eight o'clock at the Locust Club if I want to join them."

"You're not going alone," Mark said flatly.

Ordinarily Kerri would have bristled at his authoritative tone, but strangely enough, it felt nice to have someone determined to look after her—even when she was perfectly capable of taking care of herself.

"I didn't think you cared much for this sleuthing business," she teased as they left the elevator and walked down the hall to their rooms.

"You're not very smart if that's what you think I care about." He stopped by her door and putting his hands gently on her shoulders, turned her toward him. "In case you haven't noticed, you've put my whole life in a tailspin. I used to think that I had everything in proper order, and knew what I wanted and how to get it."

She was startled by the intensity of his expression. Her heart suddenly took an unexpected lurch into her throat. "And now you don't?"

"No. You've changed all that. Don't you realize that I can't imagine a future without you in it? I don't know how it happened, but you moved into an empty space in my life that I didn't even know existed. And you've brought me an awareness of myself that makes me want to be the kind of man that would appeal to someone like you. Do you think that's possible?"

He let his hand trace the soft curve of her cheek, and as they stood looking at each other for a long moment, she fought a battle with herself about her own feelings. She couldn't believe that this was happening to her, and yet, deep down, she'd known from the first moment Mark Richards walked into her office, that he threatened the solitary future she'd mapped out for herself.

"You can't hold me at arm's length forever," he chided softly. "And no matter how this case turns out, I'm not going to let you go. I'm being as up-front as I know how, and I'll do whatever you want to prove how I feel. Just don't shut me out of your life, Kerri."

As one of his fingers eased a wayward curl back behind her ear, an inexplicable joy began surging through her. She had a foolish desire to laugh and cry at the same time. She searched his face, and found only deep, caring commitment that swept away all hesitation, and all doubts.

She put her hand in his and drew him into her room.

As he took her in his arms, the sexual attraction that had existed from the first moment they met leaped into full blaze. With a lover's passion, he claimed her mouth, kissing her with compelling urgency, working her lips with the tip of his tongue until she opened them like a pliable rosebud.

With quickened breath, they tossed aside the impediment of clothing, and clung to each other in their nakedness as if they'd known all along that their bodies would fit together with perfection.

The soft light of the afternoon sun slanting through the windows bathed them in a rosy hue as they each delighted in the wondrous discovery of the other, touching, kissing and caressing with loving abandonment. Tumultuous waves of pure sensation crashed over them, and in the height of exploding joy, they made love.

Kerri had never experienced such total completeness, such euphoria and fulfillment. Tears of wonder filled her eyes and trailed down the soft curves of her flushed cheeks.

When Mark saw that she was crying, he was horrified. His chest tightened, and he despaired that he had pushed her too fast and too far. "Sweetheart, what is it? Why are you crying?" he asked, cursing himself for not holding back his own desire.

"I don't know," she blubbered. "It's just that I feel so happy. And I always cry when I'm happy."

"Thanks for warning me," he said with tremendous relief. He kissed her wet cheeks, and buried his face in the soft cleft of her breasts. If making love was a gauge for being happy, they were lost in blissful joy the rest of the afternoon.

AT ABOUT SIX O'CLOCK that evening, Kerri woke up with a start to find the room in darkness and Mark nestled beside her. He woke up as she slipped out of bed, and reached out with languid arms to catch her.

"No, you don't," he said, but she made it away before he could sabotage her good intentions. She turned on a lamp, and he blinked against the sudden brightness. The sight of her lovely nude body brushed with radiant light only added to his desire to pull her back into bed. "Just one more kiss."

She laughed at him. "I'm tempted, but I've got to shower, dress, and meet Ken in a couple of hours," she reminded him, turning toward the bathroom. "And if you want to be my escort, you'd better get a move on yourself."

"I'll join you in the shower," he offered magnanimously.

"Not on your life. I recognize a sabotaging offer when I get one." She blew him a kiss and shut the door.

AS IT WAS, they were a few minutes late because they had trouble finding the address. "Are you sure you want to go in there?" Mark asked as he viewed the place. The Locust Club was in the basement of an old brick building, with its entrance on an alley.

"This is the address Ken gave me. Come on, let's see if he's here. It's already past eight."

Kerri was glad for Mark's guiding arm as they negotiated some narrow steps and were greeted by a sweaty-faced bruiser who obviously doubled as a bouncer. He looked them over carefully before muttering, "Evening."

Mark's good sense told him to get Kerri back in the

car pronto. She had no business being in a place like this. He couldn't believe that this was the kind of thing she did for a living. As he searched her face, she seemed perfectly at ease, even smiling at the man as she returned his greeting. With a struggle, he reined in his protests, and forced himself to let her set the rules.

The interior of the casino made no pretense of being anything but a basement. No attempt had been made at any camouflaging decor. Unadorned lights hung from overhead rafters and some plain light fixtures dotted muddy cement walls. A rough-hewn bar stretched along one wall, booths bordered two sides of a small dance floor, and gambling tables and the ever-present slot machines stretched the length of the room. The press of humanity moving about in the congested space made the low-ceilinged room seem even smaller. A clamor of raised voices was an accompaniment to the loud clanging of slot machines and canned music coming from speakers mounted high on the walls.

"Let's rove," Kerri said in a near shout. "Ken ought to be here someplace."

As they pushed their way through an elbow-to-elbow crowd that seemed unconcerned about poor lighting and a lack of good ventilation, Mark wondered if the safety codes had been met or if somebody's palm had been greased to look the other way.

When Kerri was satisfied that Ken wasn't in the gambling end of the room, they made their way back to the bar and managed to grab a table at the edge of the dance floor. A few hearty couples were doing a two-step to some western tune that was blaring out one of the nearby speakers. A waitress, somewhere in

her fifties, whose spangled dress did nothing for her
hips and thick thighs, took their order for a couple of
beers.

"I'm glad we had dinner before we came," Mark
said, sitting beside her. As he bent his head close
enough to hers to smell the sweet scent of her hair and
the touch of perfume behind her ears, her nearness
filled his senses as no other woman could. He wished
they could shut their eyes to the rest of the world and
delight in each other. He might have said something
sweet and sloppy if Kerri hadn't glanced at her watch
and said, "It isn't like Ken to be late."

"Maybe he had trouble getting the person to come
with him?"

She frowned. "Something could have gone wrong,
but Ken usually does what he says he'll do."

They finished one beer, Mark ordered a second, and
still no sign of the private investigator. After a while,
they made several more turns around the crowded casino, then sat at the bar for another half hour. After a
two-hour wait, Mark had had enough. It was almost
ten o'clock, and obviously something had happened to
detain the redhead.

"No telling when he'll show up," Mark said, more
impatient than concerned.

"I hope he's all right," Kerri said, a worried crease
in her forehead. If Buddy Browski's killer is still at
large, anyone asking questions about his former wife
might be inviting trouble. What if Ken's inquiries had
alerted someone enough to stop him from asking questions?

She must have paled, because Mark took one look
at her face and said, "Let's get the hell out of here."

At night Reno glittered like Times Square, and the

streets were as bright as noonday. When they got back to the hotel, Kerri asked at the desk about messages, but the clerk shook his head.

"You might have some voice messages," he reassured her at her crestfallen expression.

"Yes, thank you." As she started toward the elevator, she told Mark, "Something's happened, I know it has." Kerri's intuitive alarm system was usually reliable—but not this time.

Before the elevator came down to the lobby, a familiar voice hailed them. "Kerri, luv. I've been waiting for you."

She swung around to see Ken sauntering toward them from the bar. At once, both relieved and furious, she didn't know which emotion to give vent to.

Mark didn't have the same trouble, he laid into the grinning redhead with pent-up fury. "Dammit, what's with you? You were supposed to be at the Locust."

"My plans got changed," Ken said smoothly. "My lady friend decided we should go to her place to talk." He winked at Kerri. "And you know I never argue with a lady. Anyway, I just got here. Come on, let's have a friendly nightcap and I'll fill you in." He grinned. "It's been a hard night. I had to hustle three gals before I got to the right one," he complained.

"Poor baby," Kerri said sarcastically.

Mark would have preferred to stuff Romeo's grinning face in a vinegar barrel, but Kerri took charge in her usual competent way. "I hope you've got something more than another number for your black book."

"Sure do. Papa is bringing home the bacon."

Something in Ken's triumphant eyes made Kerri catch her breath. "What is it?"

"You want it now or over a double martini?" he asked.

"Now." Her mouth went dry.

"All right." He flashed a triumphant smile. "Ardie Browski is in Blackhawk, Colorado."

Chapter Ten

Kerri stared at Ken. What was the children's mother doing there? Blackhawk was a small mountain gambling town about thirty miles west of Denver. Cupped by rocky hillsides, it was scarcely more than a wide spot in the road. "Blackhawk? Are you sure?"

"It's quite a story. Why don't we go in the bar and I'll give you a full report?" Ken suggested. "I talk better when my mouth isn't dry."

Mark was ready to grab the PI by his handsome throat and show him what a dry mouth was really like. If Kerri hadn't been there, he would have forced the guy to cut to the bottom line fast. The guy had news that they were paying him to deliver, and it infuriated Mark that they had to cater to him to get the whole story. With great effort, Mark held his tongue until they were settled at a small table in the hotel bar.

"Will one drink be enough, Mr. Nabors, or shall we buy a whole bottle?" Mark asked pointedly. "We wouldn't want to hear only half a story."

Kerri lowered her eyes at Mark in a warning gesture. *Easy does it.* She understood his impatience, but she also knew the private investigator's propensity for drama. Ken was good at his job in part because he had a flair for making the most mundane investigation something of an adventure. No doubt about it, the handsome redhead liked grabbing center stage whenever he could, but catering to Ken's vanity was a small price to pay for the kind of information he could dig up for her.

Ken ignored Mark as if he were just part of the background, and ordered his usual cranberry and vodka. "Put the drinks on my tab," he told the waitress magnanimously.

Kerri returned his grin, knowing full well the bill would be hers to pay, but when he had a drink in his hand, she was all business.

"Okay, Ken, you delivered your bombshell, now let's hear the rest." Since it was important to ascertain up front if an informant was reliable, she demanded, "Who's your informant?"

"A scrumptious little lovely who used to work at the Locust Club. A few weeks ago she moved uptown on the strip, and as I said, I had to hustle two gals before I got to her, but it was worth the effort, all around." He grinned. "If you know what I mean."

Mark's glower deepened but Kerri just ignored the double innuendo. "Go on."

"Well it seems that Betsy Marie Bertinelli, that's the lovely's full name, served drinks in the back room at the Locust. According to Betsy, a nightly poker game was set up to fleece out-of-town pigeons, and that's where she met Buddy and Ardie Browski." Ken took his time lighting a cigarette, and then added, "According to Betsy, Ardie was the one to lead the pigeon into the cage to be fleeced by her husband and two other guys, Dirk Boyd and Stu Zimmermon."

Mark set his drink down with a force that spilled the liquid over the side. "Did you say, Dirk?"

"Yeah, you know him?"

"No, but my brother may have."

"Oh, really? I asked Betsy if she knew a Jason Richards, but she couldn't place him."

Mark and Kerri exchanged glances. In a way that was good news.

"What about Buddy Browski?" Kerri asked. "Was Betsy around when he was murdered?"

"Yeah, and Betsy thinks Browski was snuffed out by a loser getting revenge. In any case, his murder put an end to the nightly poker parties." Ken raised his hand for another drink. "I guess Betsy and Dirk got kind of cozy after that. Anyway, he told her that he and Stu were going to move the old poker scam out of state. They'd decided to set up in Blackhawk, Colorado, and a neighboring gambling town called Central City."

"And Ardie agreed to this?" Mark demanded.

"According to Betsy, your brother's widow wasn't going to go along with the new scam. Apparently, she had other fish to fry, but I gathered from what Betsy said, that Dirk and Stu weren't above some heavy arm twisting to get her to go along with them."

Kerri's stomach took a sickening plunge. "Did Dirk say anything to Betsy about using Ardie's new husband or the children as leverage?"

He shook his head. "I'm convinced Betsy didn't know what was going on in Ardie's personal life after Buddy got killed and the con games stopped."

They went over everything several times as both Kerri and Mark continued to bombard him with questions, but Ken didn't have much to add, and they didn't turn up any new angles.

About two o'clock in the morning they called it quits. Mark and Kerri left Ken in the bar, and made their way upstairs. Mark pulled her close in front of her door, and lightly kissed her good-night.

"Get some sleep," he ordered gently, and made no move to light the passionate fires that had consumed them earlier in the day.

His sensitivity brought a rush of new affection. How perceptive he was to give her the space and solitude that she needed. She couldn't believe that a capricious fate had smiled on her, and brought this man into her life. He seemed to understand her better than she did herself. She could almost hear Debbie and her sister, Cathy, laughing at her.

Kerri intended to go straight to bed, but an ingrained habit of recording every minute detail of an ongoing investigation interfered. Sitting at the hotel desk, she worked at her laptop computer until she was satisfied that she'd recorded everything that Ken had related to them.

When she finally fell into bed, her thoughts still whirled with unanswered questions, but she knew she was too tired to organize her thinking in any constructive way. She fell asleep, knowing that tomorrow she'd have to put some new plans into action.

KERRI WAS STILL sleeping at nine o'clock in the morning, and Mark suspected that she hadn't gone right to bed. Not wanting to disturb her, he ordered his breakfast from room service and then got busy on the phone, making reservations for an afternoon flight back to Denver.

Now that they had zeroed in on Ardie's location, the woman's behavior began to make sense. She'd left her children where it was convenient and close to where her partners were setting up a gambling scam, using her as the lure. Most likely Jason had been one of the pigeons in her sight, but why had she ended up marrying him? Even though Mark could hardly wait to confront the woman and make her accountable for her behavior, his eagerness was tempered with a nagging reluctance. Because of his growing affection for her children, he had wanted to be proven wrong about their mother. He wanted Ardie Richards to be everything Timmy and his sisters deserved. Even now, he had a hard time believing that Jason had been taken in so completely that he'd marry such a woman. Maybe he and Kerri were still missing something important that would alter what Ken had found out about Jason's widow. A nagging suspicion remained with Mark that somehow all of this tied in with his brother's accident. He feared that there was more ugliness ahead, and he vowed to keep Kerri safe at any cost.

ON THE FLIGHT back to Denver, Mark expressed his ambivalent feelings, and Kerri admitted she was being pulled in two directions herself, wanting to find the children's mother, and dreading it at the same time. No doubt about it, Kerri admitted to herself, she'd lost her usual professional detachment. As the end to their search seemed to be approaching, a nagging disquiet ruined any feelings of jubilation. "All we can do is follow the leads, and learn to live with what turns up."

"What if the information Nabors got from his luscious Betsy is all wrong?'' Mark countered. ''We don't have anyone corroborating any of this stuff.''

''Yes, we do. There's Buddy's murder, and the police's suspicions that he was running a gambling scam.''

''But the police couldn't come up with enough evidence to charge anybody.''

''I have copies of reports that indicate they looked at Ardie very closely. She must have been in on the action.''

''We have only this Betsy's word that she's anywhere near Colorado.''

''Don't forget we have two sightings that would seem to collaborate it. Timmy was convinced he'd seen Dirk at Coors Field, and I'm beginning to be convinced that my memory is correct about seeing Ardie in the lobby of your place. That would put two of the three in the vicinity.''

''Something still doesn't add up.''

''Maybe because of the children, we don't want it to.''

He didn't answer, because he knew she was right. He'd gotten used to thinking of himself as their guardian. But they needed their own mother to take care of them.

After they'd set down at Denver's new international airport, and received Mark's car from the valet service, Kerri asked him to drop her off at home. ''I need to check on things there and then head to the office. I want to get started making inquiries in Blackhawk and Central City, see what we can turn up. It will save time if the computer does some of the footwork for us. If we get a lead on any of the three, we'll have to decide the next course of action.''

"All right, but don't you go hightailing it up to Blackhawk without me." He didn't like the way this whole thing was shaping up. He worried that Kerri might stumble into a dangerous situation as explosive as a smoldering volcano. Whatever happened, he didn't want her compromising her own safety. "As soon as you find out anything—" he landed heavily on the *anything* "—you call me."

She kissed his cheek. "I promise I'll let you know the minute I get anything positive. Now, don't look so fierce. When you clamp your jaw shut like that, you look ready to chew nails and spit them out."

"I wish we could turn this over to the police."

"And put me out of a job?" she teased. "Stop worrying, okay?"

His expression softened as he looked at her. "If you wanted to stop by my apartment first, I bet you could change my mood."

She laughed. "I'm tempted, but we Kincaids always put business first. My dear father would rise up in his grave if I ignored a hot lead like the one Ken gave us."

With reluctance, he agreed to take her home, and on the way, Mark tried unsuccessfully to make a date for dinner. The best offer he got was one to stop by her house later in the evening. A driving need to be with her made him readily accept the invitation, but he doubted they'd get a moment alone together, under the watchful eyes of her family. He knew that he had to be patient, and not overpower her with the intensity of his feelings. He'd never felt so reckless, wanting to ignore everything but the need to be with her, but caution made him hold back. He wasn't sure that he'd convinced this independent, self-reliant woman that she needed him in her life.

As they pulled up in front of the house, they saw Timmy sitting dejectedly on the front steps, lightly tossing his new baseball. When he saw Mark come around the car to open the door for Kerri, the little boy leaped to his feet. He squealed, ''Catch,'' and gave the ball a wobbly toss.

The throw was so low that Mark had to nearly go down on his knees to catch it, and before he could gain his balance, Timmy leaped into the middle of him with a force that sent them both backward.

''Hey, fella, we're playing baseball, not football,'' Mark chided, laughing as he playfully rolled with the boy on the ground. Timmy squealed and wiggled as they tumbled, his freckled face glowing with delight.

Kerri had to laugh at the two of them wrestling around on the grass. All signs of Mark's heavy mood had dissipated in abandoned horseplay with a giggling little boy. They looked like they belonged together, and she wished that she could capture the moment in a capsule for both of them. For a cowardly moment, she wanted to resign from the case, and let Ardie's disappearance play itself out without her interference. Why should she plunge the children back into the kind of life that their mother offered? *Because she's their mother. And she's done a good job with them, whether you want to admit it or not.*

Mark gave Timmy a ride on his shoulders back to the house. The tantalizing smell of freshly baked cookies led them to the kitchen. Mrs. Kincaid gave them a cheery hello as she pulled a cookie sheet out of the oven.

"Any gingerbread men, yet?" Timmy asked eagerly.

"See." Patti held up a headless one as she chomped on the missing head. "Wanna bite?"

"Timmy can have his own cookie," Kerri's mother replied, handing the boy a gingerbread man from a cooled tray. "There's enough for everyone."

"Amy and Emily, too?" Timmy asked anxiously. "Can I take some over to their house?"

Mrs. Kincaid patted him on the shoulder. "Don't worry, honey, they'll be running over here as soon as they get home." She shook her head, smiling. "You'd think the three of you were triplets the way you stick together."

"What's a triplet?" Timmy asked solemnly.

"Never mind. Just eat your cookie."

"Where's Grams?" Kerri asked. It was unusual for her grandmother's chair to be empty when anything was going on in the kitchen.

"Upstairs, taking a nap with the baby." Mrs. Kincaid eyed Mark and Kerri as she poured the children some milk. "Well, how were things in Reno?"

"I'll tell you later, Mom. Right now, I have to get back to the office. I just wanted to make sure that everything was all right here."

Her mother raised an eyebrow. "And why wouldn't it be?

"No reason," Mark said smoothly. "It's obvious that things couldn't be better. You've been an angel to do all of this. I'd like to show my appreciation somehow."

"Would you now?" she echoed thoughtfully. "Well, maybe Kerri and I can think of something."

Kerri laughed. "Mom, you are so obvious."

"Am I? Is that why you're blushing?"

"I am not blushing," Kerri protested, even as she felt heat rising into her cheeks. In another minute her mother would know everything. Under normal circumstances, she would have given her own happiness high priority, but looking at Timmy's and Patti's cookie-smeared faces, she knew that until their future was settled, her own would have to wait. "I've got to get to the office." She turned and left the cozy kitchen.

"She's a handful, my Kerri," Mrs. Kincaid warned Mark. "Just like a headstrong filly. When she gets a bit in her teeth, there's no stopping her. She needs a firm hand and a lot of gentling."

"I'll see what I can do," Mark said with a conspirator's wink.

WHEN KERRI GOT TO the office, Debbie tried her best to find out if anything romantic had happened between her boss and Mark, but she didn't have any luck. She signed in resignation. Kerri was all business, deflecting any personal questions as if she hadn't heard them— a sure sign that she was hiding something, thought Debbie, undaunted.

Kerri gave her the printed report she'd written the night before. Debbie's eyes rounded as she read it. "If this is true, our missing Ardie is up to her ears in you-know-what."

Kerri nodded. "I keep hoping that somehow it's not what it looks like." If the children hadn't been involved, she would have dropped the case without a qualm. She could have honestly told Mark that his sister-in-law could show up or not, that she didn't care one way or the other. But she did care about Timmy, Patti and the baby, and now she felt an added responsibility to try to see that Ardie took care of them before she ended up behind bars, or worse yet, suffered the same fate as her husband Buddy.

"So, what's the plan?" asked Debbie.

"If Ardie's in Blackhawk working a scam with these two guys, they have to be staying somewhere." Kerri knew that finding them easily with the office computers was not likely to happen, but it was worth a try. "If they're using false identities or staying at a private residence, we'll come up empty, but it's a place to start. Check with all the lodging places listed in both Blackhawk and the neighboring Central City. If we come up empty, the next step will be to show Ardie's driver's license photo around both places and see if anyone recognizes her."

"And if they do?"

"I'll try to make contact with her."

"She's not going to have out a welcome mat, if she's gone to all this trouble to disappear," Debbie warned. "You really ought to get some police security."

"That would really scare her off."

"But you're not going alone?"

"No, Mark's going with me." A quiver of anticipation began creeping through her and she deliberately kept her eyes lowered on the papers she held in her hand. She felt Debbie's measuring eyes on her.

"I see. And then what happens after you find her?"

"My job is finished," she said flatly. "Case closed."

Debbie smirked. "I doubt that very much."

KERRI WORKED through the dinner hour, frustrated that none of the advertised lodgings in either town netted any leads when they checked their registration lists. Finally, Kerri called everyone she knew who liked to spend time at the Colorado casinos and frequented the gambling towns. She discovered several private bed-and-breakfast homes that were not advertised, but whose rooms were rented through referrals. At eight o'clock she found the one she was looking for.

So used to negative responses, Kerri didn't quite register the woman's pleasant, "Yes, Mrs. Richards, rented my nice front bedroom for a couple of nights. She seemed quite happy with the accommodations, but I had the impression that she'd decided to stay somewhere else. I only have two rooms to rent, so if you're inquiring about them, I'm sorry to tell you that they're already booked. A nice couple from New York have the back room, which isn't quite as large as the one Mrs. Richards rented."

"Mrs. Ardie Richards? Or Ardella Richards?"

"I'm sorry, I really don't know her first name. She registered as Mrs. Jason Richards."

Kerri moistened her dry lips. "And you don't know where she went?"

"No, but she had a nice gentleman friend. He picked her up in one of those moneyed cars, you know, the kind that cost as much as a house used to."

"Did you ever see her with anyone else?"

"No, I didn't." The woman's tone changed. "What is this all about? Why are you asking so much about Mrs. Richards? Didn't you call about a room?"

Kerri wasn't about to tell her the whole story, so she just thanked her for her time, after assuring her she'd recommend her B-and-B to all her friends. After she hung up, she put a star beside the woman's telephone number and address. The successful call had firmly placed Ardie in the Colorado town, and Kerri knew she should have been exhilarated that Ken's informant had proven reliable, but she wasn't. If Ardie was in Blackhawk, then, by reasonable deduction, the information about her involvement in Dirk's new scam was also true. The "handsome gentleman" in the expensive car was probably their next mark, and, maybe, it was already too late to find Ardie before the illegal game exploited another victim. She reached for the phone to call Mark.

HE PICKED HER UP at the house at eight o'clock the next morning. After Kerri's telephone call, verifying Ardie's presence in Blackhawk, Mark had felt like a jumper on the end of a bungee cord, rising and falling with conflicting emotions. He could hardly wait to confront the blasted woman, and dump all the feelings seething inside of him, and yet, he had a sinking feeling that he would walk away from the whole thing if he could. One look at Kerri's taut face told him she was feeling the same way.

They went west on Highway 6, a narrow mountain road snaking through foothills that had once been alive with prospectors digging for gold in the rugged hillsides. Men had sacrificed a lot to seek their fortune in these hills, and not much had changed, Mark thought, as casino buses and shuttles passed him, loaded with passengers. Obviously, modern day prospectors were still seeking illusive riches in the Rockies of Colorado, only the tools had changed. Now cards, dice and slot machines had replaced axes and picks.

"What's the plan?" he asked Kerri, wishing they could keep driving to some isolated place and delight

in each other without the ugly world intruding.
''Where do we start?''

''The casinos, I think. We'll show her picture
around and maybe we'll get a lead on her present
whereabouts. If Ardie and her pals are scouting for
someone to entice into a fixed poker game, they'll cir-
culate in casinos and saloons, looking for a prospect.
Not a nickel slot machine addict, either,'' she added.
''They're after bigger game. Someone worth the trouble of a setup.''

Mark nodded, but he didn't like the plan. Kerri
might believe that she was perfectly capable of handling anything that came up, but he wasn't taking any
chances. He wasn't leaving her alone for one minute,
even though she'd probably want to split up to cover
the territory faster.

Mark had been up to the old mining towns a few
times since the good citizens of Colorado had voted
in gambling, but he was always a little angry to see
how commercial avarice had changed authentic Old
West buildings and historical streets. As they entered
Blackhawk, bawdy sounds and signs alerted them to
the hipped allure of Bullwhackers, Bronco Billy's,
Crooks Palace, and a half-dozen other casinos. A mile
farther into the mountains was Central City, the larger
of two old mining towns, but for all practical purposes,
the two gambling towns were one and the same.

Mark stuck to his vow and stayed at Kerri's side as
they maneuvered through Blackhawk's boisterous casinos, showing Ardie's license to any employee who
would look at her. All they got for their trouble were
some weird looks, or a quick, leave-me-alone response, like ''Never saw her.'' Even the young men
doing the valet parking barely glanced at the photo

before they shook their heads. Trying some of the restaurants didn't go any better. The whole day slipped by, without the slightest bit of success.

By the time they returned to the car and drove up the narrow highway to Central City, Mark's frustrations had peaked. "I don't know how you can stand being in a business like this. It's like looking for a black cat in a dark room, and not even knowing if there's such a creature around."

Kerri smiled. "Don't be discouraged. It's just a matter of time and patience before we find that dark room where the cat is hiding."

"And how much time do we have if my dear sister-in-law is up to her neck in an illegal swindle?"

"Not much," she admitted, just as much aware of the ticking clock as he was, but she knew that feeding a building anxiety wasn't going to do any good.

The sun had already set behind the western mountains, making the glittering streets of Central City looked like Santa Claus land caught between dark rising foothills.

"We'd better find a place to stay," Mark said, giving Kerri a questioning glance. "Unless you're thinking of driving back and forth."

"No, I called the Prospector Casino and Lodge this morning and reserved my room."

"Your room?" He raised a questioning eyebrow.

She looked at him with a look of total innocence. "Yes, I guess I wasn't thinking. I just reserved one room, but I think she said it was a double."

"I suppose we can make do with that," he agreed with mock solemnity.

The Prospector Lodge was a renovated stone building, a block off of Main Street. The whole lower floor had been made into a casino, with lodgings on the second level. A pretty young desk clerk, wearing the name tag, Bunny, verified Kerri's reservation.

"Yes, I remember speaking with you this morning, Ms. Kincaid," she said, with a ready, welcome-ya-all smile. "You were lucky we had a cancellation." Dangling earrings matched a spattering of golden studs on her dark blue western shirt and pants. "Usually you need to make your reservations at least a week in advance. And how long will be you staying?"

"We're not sure," Kerri answered. "We're trying to touch base with a friend of ours, Ardie Richards. Do you by any chance know if she's registered here?"

"I can check." After consulting a small computer, she shook her head. "No. Her name doesn't come up. If she'd been a guest here our records would pull her name."

Kerri reached into her shoulder bag. "Here's her picture. Maybe you've seen her in the casino?"

With only a moment's hesitation, Bunny nodded with a bright smile. "Oh, yes, she's been in quite a few times. In fact, she left a message for her friend, Mr. Tanner." She swung around and pulled out an envelope from the key boxes. "See, here it is."

Kerri bent her head so she could read the name on the envelope. It was Ardie's handwriting all right. The same bold strokes, and the name, "Thomas Tanner."

Mark smiled at Bunny with an admiring look. "You really must have a great memory. Imagine you remembering Ardie's note to Mr. Tanner. I suppose you know when he's most likely to come in."

"I really don't," Bunny said regretfully, obviously sorry about refusing any request of Mark's. "Mr. Tanner has his own home between here and Blackhawk, but he likes to stay here from time to time when he's on a roll. I'm not even sure he'll be back tonight to get the lady's note."

"Do you have Mr. Tanner's home address?" Kerri asked. "I imagine it's on his registration." She realized too late that she should have let Mark do the quizzing.

Bunny gave her dangling earrings a toss as if she answered one too many questions. "I'm afraid I couldn't give out that information." Her welcome-ya-all smile was strained.

"I understand," Kerri said. "Perhaps it would be best if I left my card for Mr. Tanner." She took one out of her purse and scribbled on the back, "See me. Very important." Then she handed the card to the girl. "Would you put this with the note, and see that Mr. Tanner gets it if he comes in?"

Bunny nodded, and put both the envelope and Kerri's card in the mail slot. Then she handed them their key. "Number 208. It's straight up the stairs, and at the end of the hall."

As they walked away from the desk, Mark bent his head toward Kerri's. "She pulled the note out of box 207, so Mr. Tanner must be across the hall from us."

Kerri gave him an approving grin. "You're catching on to this business."

"Thanks, boss." He slipped his arm through hers as they made their way through a crowd of people circulating in the downstairs casino. Bells were ringing and lights flashing as the slot machines paid off their winners. Some of the racket faded as they made their way up the stairs to a room that was strictly of the economy motel variety.

Kerri was disappointed that nothing of the original

Old West flavor of the building remained. As soon as Mark closed the door behind them, she was on her way to the phone. As she called her sister's home, she glanced at her watch. Almost six-thirty.

"Hi, Cathy, it's Kerri. Is Harry home?"

"Yeah, he just came in. Where are you, sis?"

"In Central City, at the Prospector."

"Mom said you left early this morning with Mark Richards." With a suggestive chuckle, she asked, "Whatcha up to?"

"I'm working on his case, Cathy," Kerri replied with as much patience as she could muster. "And I need to speak to Harry."

Her sister mumbled something that Kerri couldn't quite hear, but in a minute Harry came on the line, and listened as Kerri filled him in. "There seems to be a connection between Ardie Richards and a man, Thomas Tanner, who has a home between Central City and Blackhawk. Just what the connection is, I don't know, but if you could run a driver's license check on Thomas Tanner and get an address from his license, that would help a lot. We're at the Prospector in Central City where he stays sometimes, but if we don't connect here with him, we'll need to go to his home. I have the feeling that he may be the victim of a setup."

"Okay, I'll see what I can do. What's the telephone number there?" After she gave it to him, he promised to get back to her as soon as he had the information.

She put the telephone down on the stand beside the bed, and then she just sat there, staring at the ugly tweed carpet. She was so lost in thought that Mark refrained from saying anything to her. He quietly took some things out of his overnight bag and went into the bathroom.

When he came back in the room, she was standing at one of the tall narrow windows, looking out at the night sky. As she turned around, her stunned expression startled him. "What is it?"

She moistened her lips as if they were too dry to shape words. "It's been clear from the beginning and I missed it. I don't know how, but I missed it."

"Missed what?"

She said very slowly, "Ardie Richards isn't the children's mother."

Chapter Eleven

The impact of her words tightened every muscle in his body. His mind refused to accept what she was saying, and instant denial sprung to his lips. "Of course she's their mother."

"No, she's not."

"How do you know that?" What could have happened in the short time he'd been out of the room to bring about this incredible revelation?

She walked over to the desk where she had spread out papers from her briefcase. "Something bothered me from the first time that I saw Ardie's note, but I couldn't put my finger on it—until tonight." She held the note out to Mark.

He read the curt message again, but looked equally blank when he'd finished.

"See the bold strokes," she said. "The heavy *T* and *A*. The graphologist's report pointed them out. And then there's the almost perpendicular slant to all the letters."

"So?"

"When I saw that envelope tonight, the same heavy *T* was in Thomas Tanner's name. There's no doubt about it, Ardie addressed that envelope to him."

"All right, Ardie wrote the note and addressed the envelope. I don't see how that brought you to the astounding conclusion that she's not the children's mother. What am I missing?"

Her eyes flashed with excitement. "Timmy's book, *Are You My Mother?*"

Mark looked at her as if she'd taken leave of her senses. "That book tells you who Timmy's mother is?"

"Not the book," she answered impatiently. "The inscription."

"What inscription?" he asked, doing his best to try to understand how a children's book had turned all their assumptions upside down.

"On the inside cover of that book, his mother wrote, 'To Timmy Lee on his fourth birthday, Love, Mother.'" Kerri met Mark's eyes squarely. "The writing is not the same as Ardie's note, nor the address on Mr. Tanner's envelope. The *T* in *Timmy* was flowing and the letters small and uniform. The person who gave that book to her son is not Ardie."

He let out a slow whistle.

"My subconscious registered the difference in the handwriting, but I was so focused on the false assumption that Ardie was the mother, that I couldn't figure out what was bothering me about the note. I thought it was the content that was trying to tell me something, but it didn't hit me until tonight that it was the handwriting."

Mark swallowed against a sudden constriction of his throat. "But if Ardie's not the mother," he asked hoarsely. "Who is?"

"I don't know. But I'm pretty darn sure we've been asking the wrong questions," she admitted, remembering Timmy's reaction when the subject of his mother came up. The boy was obviously hurting from his mother's absence, but it wasn't Ardie who brought the flow of tears to his eyes. "When we asked Timmy about his mother, we assumed he was talking about Ardie, but he wasn't. The children are missing their real mother."

He ran an agitated hand through his hair. "Wow, this puts a whole different twist on the woman's disappearance. If Ardie's not the children's mother, where is their father? And how did my brother get roped into this whole thing?" Mark groaned. "I did my best when Jason was growing up to keep him from making stupid mistakes, so he wouldn't hurt himself and others, but he really spun out of control on this one."

"We don't know that," Kerri said as reassuringly as she could. "We know your brother married Ardie, but that's all we know."

"Isn't that enough? He's in the middle of this mess, and we both know it."

The telephone rang and saved Kerri from having to answer. "Got the address for you," Harry told her. "26 Canyon Butte Road. Blackhawk, Colorado."

"How about the statistics on the license?"

"Age, fifty-nine. Height, five foot seven. Weight, 190 pounds. His picture shows a full face, double chin, thinning hair and brown eyes." Harry added, "Looks kinda of shifty to me. I don't like the idea of you trying to run him down. Why don't I call the sheriff and have him check this guy out?"

"There's no need to bring in anyone from the outside. I'm only going after information that will help me find Ardie. Either he'll help me or he won't."

"What if he gets ugly?"

"Quit worrying. Mark is with me, if I need rein-forcements. Thanks for your help, Harry. I'll call you back first thing in the morning and tell you whether or not we found the guy."

"Okay, but I'm less than an hour away if you need me."

Kerri thanked him again and then hung up.

Mark said, "You're amazing. I've never known anyone so relentless and tenacious. I gather from that spark in your eyes you got the address."

She laughed softly. "Am I that transparent?"

"Sometimes," he admitted, not too happily. He could tell that she was going full steam ahead with the investigation until she ran out of leads.

He reached out a hand and pulled her to him. Low-ering his face to hers, he claimed the lips that parted to receive his. As he pressed her length against his, his hands molded the sweet curve of her back and waist, and he kissed her with a building hunger that blotted out everything else.

All the ugliness of the world passed them by for a brief moment. Then she reluctantly pushed away from his embrace. "We have to go," she whispered with bruised lips.

"I know," he said, kissing her one more time.

For the first time in her career, she was tempted to forget about business and linger in his arms, but a deeply imbedded sense of responsibility sent the temp-tation fleeing. She knew they shouldn't waste any time in finding Tanner. She was almost positive that he'd lead them to Ardie.

"I suppose there's no time for a leisurely dinner

before we head out to find Canyon Butte Road?"
Mark protested.

"We can pick up some food from the restaurant
downstairs and eat it on the way."

"I'll forgo the food for something else, my sweet,"
he said, kissing the tip of her nose. "What do you
say?"

"I'm tempted," she admitted. "But I have the feeling that we'd better find Mr. Tanner as soon as possible.

They left their room and knocked on the door of
207 across the hall just to be sure the man hadn't come
back during the few minutes they'd been in their room,
but there was no answer.

Downstairs, they asked the pretty desk clerk if
Thomas Tanner had picked up his messages, specu-
lating that he might have come in and lingered in the
casino or restaurant, but Bunny shook her blond head.
"No, I haven't seen him."

They were about to turn away, when she added
"But your friend who left the message for him was
here a few minutes ago."

An earthquake wouldn't have been any more of a
shock. Kerri and Mark gasped almost in unison. "She
was here?"

"Yeah, she wanted to know if Mr. Tanner had
picked up her envelope. When I told her that he
hadn't, she seemed anxious, so I told her you guys
were looking for him, too. She wanted to see the card
that you left for him but I didn't show it to her," she
said with satisfaction. "I did tell her which room you
were in, though, since you said you wanted to talk to
her, but she just took off."

Kerri swore under her breath. She hadn't considered

staking out the lobby, because there was no reason to
believe that Ardie would return so soon to see if her
message had been picked up. Blast it all! Not only had
they missed Ardie when she was under their noses,
but now she knew someone was interested in Thomas
Tanner. No telling if she'd hightail it out of the area
before they had a chance to catch up with her. Kerri
couldn't believe that they'd been under the same roof
with the woman a few minutes earlier.

Mark could tell Kerri was blaming herself. "Honey,
you're not clairvoyant, and neither am I. Who would
have guessed Ardie would come waltzing in here a
second time? We're getting closer, that's all that
counts."

Kerri held her tongue. She knew that no matter how
close she came to finding a missing person, the indi-
vidual could vanish again, could disappear as completely as the first time. Weeks of careful work would
be lost, and the whole investigation forced back to
square one. In this instance, Kerri was pulled in two
directions. Should they wait here for Tanner, or try his
home in Blackhawk?

Making her decision, Kerri said, "We can make a
quick trip to Canyon Butte Road, and if we come up
empty, we'll come back here and wait for Tanner to
show up."

"Okay. You get a map while I order some sandwiches and coffee. I don't like playing Blindman's
Bluff on an empty stomach."

He strode off toward the restaurant while Kerri
turned her attention to a rack of brochures and maps.
Once she found the map she needed, she had no trouble locating Canyon Butte Road, which snaked off
Highway 279. She knew that finding the road on the

map and finding the right house on the hillside were
two different things. Even in the daylight, mountain
homes were hard to see because they were nestled in
clumps of trees and boulders, hidden from the road.
At night, a flickering light through the trees might be-
tray a hidden dwelling, and she hoped that would be
the case with Thomas Tanner's house.

As they drove back to Blackhawk, the roast beef
sandwich she'd begun to eat didn't sit well in Kerri's
tense stomach, so she returned most of it to the sack.
Hot, strong coffee was better, and as she sipped it, her
thoughts raced ahead. She mentally calculated what
they knew about Thomas Tanner. He stayed at the
Prospector when he was in town gambling, but had a
home of his own. He was probably the gray-haired
gentleman that had taken Ardie away from the bed-
and-breakfast. And why all the urgency to find him?
Ardie was anxious to give him a message of some
kind. Was she was setting him up to get fleeced in a
crooked gambling game? Unanswered questions
swirled like dry leaves in a devil's wind.

Mark couldn't see much beyond the sweep of his
headlights, but he spotted a weathered sign on a listing
pole that alerted them they had reached Canyon Butte
Road. The car rumbled across a cattle guard, and began climbing a road so narrow that it would have been
easy to scrape the car against protruding boulders.

"I don't like this," Mark said, as the darkness
closed in around them. "It's hard enough to see anything in the trees, let alone a mailbox."

When the beam of his headlights swept past a rutted
road to the right, he wondered if he should have turned
on it. How could they know whether Tanner's house

was on this gravel road, or set back like so many others in a maze of long driveways?

As the road climbed, they passed several clusters of mailboxes, but none had the right name or address. At least they were still on Canyon Butte Road, Kerri thought, completely disoriented as the road twisted back upon itself in a series of hairpin curves. Tree branches moving darkly against shelves of rocks gave an eerie impression of waving arms. Not once did they pass a car coming or going on the narrow road.

Mark wondered if they would come to an abrupt dead end or whether the road would eventually turn back upon itself. He was about to ask Kerri to check the map when she grabbed his arm.

"Stop. Back up," she ordered, as she peered out the side window at a small wooden sign and arrow they'd almost missed: 26 Canyon Butte Road. The arrow pointed to the left where a side road made a sharp turn into an infinity of trees, scrubs and rocks.

Mark hesitated. If he'd been alone, there wouldn't have been any question about going ahead, but putting Kerri in any kind of danger made him cautious. "Are you sure you want to tackle this tonight? Now that we know where Tanner lives, we could come back in the daylight and talk with him."

"We could," she granted, "but waiting until tomorrow might mean the difference between finding Ardie and losing her again. We may already be too late. She may have taken off like a bird in flight, and if she has, we'll need to move fast. If she's trying to contact Tanner, he could be our lead to her next move."

Mark knew it was useless to argue, so he ignored an uneasy feeling in his stomach and headed the car through a tunnel of trees. Rocks spit out from under the wheels as they climbed sharply up the side of a hill. When they reached top, the road made an abrupt descent down the other side, and they saw the house.

Kerri felt some of her tension ease as brightly lighted windows spilled a yellow glow out into the night. Made of logs, the ranch-style house was fashioned with a wide veranda circling the front and sides, and a wide driveway led up to the front entrance. Thomas Tanner must be at home, she thought, and if the three cars parked in front were any indication, he must have company. *What kind of company?* The thought made her shoot a quick look at Mark. Maybe he'd been right about waiting until the next morning. And maybe, she should have taken Harry's advice, and brought someone in authority with them. As quickly as the doubts came, she shoved them away.

Mark sensed her uneasiness, and spoke as lightly as he could. "Looks like we might be crashing a party. I wouldn't be surprised if they're turning away unexpected guests."

"I guess we'll find out. All I want is a few minutes conversation with Mr. Tanner." Her frown deepened. "But if Ardie was expecting him at the Prospector, he may not even be home."

Mark looked at the brightly lighted house. "But somebody sure is. Come on, let's find out who."

He opened the car door for her, and slipped his arm through hers as they walked up a flight of steps to the front door. He pushed the doorbell button and a melodic chime echoed from inside.

After a long moment, the door opened and Ardie stood there in the doorway, looking straight at them.

Mark and Kerri stared in disbelief.

"Who is it, Ardie?" A man shouted from the depths of the house.

She turned halfway and called back. "Just someone needing directions."

The lie took Kerri so much by surprise that she couldn't find her voice, but Mark recovered much faster. He guided Kerri past Ardie into a small foyer. Then he closed the door and positioned himself in front of his brother's late wife. "Well, well, life is full of surprises, isn't it?"

"Please, we can't talk now." She gave a furtive glance down a hall that ran the width of the house.

"Oh, I think we can," Mark countered with a stubborn jut to his chin. "I've got three kids that belong to someone. You'd better start talking, Ardie, and the truth would be nice this time."

"Easy, Mark," Kerri cautioned. She could tell the woman was running on adrenaline overload. Her eyes were darting in every direction like a cornered animal. "We need to talk, Ardie," Kerri said quietly in a non-threatening tone.

Ardie hesitated, and then motioned toward a closed door a few steps down the hall. "In there, but be quiet," she ordered in a hoarse whisper. "Don't let them know you're here. I'll tell you everything and then you've got to leave, quick."

As they crossed the hall, they could hear men's voices coming from a room at the back of the house. Ardie stealthily opened the door, turned on a small light, motioned them in, and then quietly closed the door after them.

The room was a small study with bookshelves, leather chairs and a sofa banking a fireplace. Ardie quickly drew the blinds, and nervously sat on the edge of one chair while Mark and Kerri faced her from the couch.

She was a smaller woman than Kerri had visualized, and crow's feet which didn't show in the license photo marred the beauty of her blue eyes. A haunted expression deepened the lines around her mouth, and she seemed to be searching for a place to begin as she wiped sweaty hands on tight-fitting jeans, and pulled her lower lip between her teeth.

Mark waited as long as he could, then asked the question that topped his concerns, "Whose kids do I have?"

Kerri was afraid Ardie was going to refuse to answer. Ardie stared at Mark as if he were someone who had asked a question in a foreign tongue, but after a moment she moistened her lips and said clearly, "My sister's."

"Your sister's?" Mark said loudly enough for Ardie to put a warning finger up to her lips.

"And you have custody of them?" Kerri asked, wishing she had a tape recorder to validate everything that was being said.

Ardie nodded.

"What happened?" Kerri coaxed. "Three little children are a huge responsibility for anyone."

Ardie looked relieved as she turned to Kerri, obviously grateful that someone finally understood. "My sister, Irene, died a couple of months before I met Jason. Her husband was killed in a small plane crash when she was two months pregnant with the baby, and I think she died of a broken heart, although the doctors said it was an aneurysm. Anyway, there was no one else to take the kids, and when I met Jason, he really took to them, so I decided to marry him. My own husband was dead, and I thought I could change my life for the better." Her lips quivered. "But I only brought Jason down with me."

"What do you mean—brought him down?" Mark asked, wondering if he was really up to hearing the truth about his brother.

"Dirk and Stu used him to rent a condo for their gambling scams. He thought the place was for me, and I was afraid to let him know the truth. They threatened to hurt him if I didn't play along." Her eyes filled with tears. "And then he got himself killed in that car wreck, and I never knew for sure if it was really an accident."

"Why didn't you go to the police and tell them everything?" Kerri asked softly.

"I couldn't. God knows, I wanted out of the whole stinking mess, but it would be just my word against theirs, and nobody would believe Buddy Browski's wife—not when she'd been a part of his gambling scams. I'm positive Dirk killed Buddy because he wanted to take over, but he threw the suspicion all on me. I think that's why they wanted to keep me around, I was a good one to take the heat if things went wrong."

"So Dirk and Stu decided to move their con game to Colorado, and they made you come with them?"

She nodded. "They knew I could lure addicted high rollers into their gambling trap, and they used the children as the leverage to force me to do what they wanted." She looked at Mark with pleading eyes. "Dirk's been keeping an eye on them, but I knew they'd be safe with you, and I had no other place to leave them."

"Did you come back to Denver to check on them?" Kerri asked.

"Yes, but Dirk got to Mark's place before I did and checked it out. He said it was empty. I didn't believe him and was going to check on it myself."

Someone had *been in the loft that day.* "I saw you in the lobby, didn't I? And Dirk hit me on the head when I came out of the building."

"Yes, he was afraid you might recognize him. He saw you with Timmy at the ballpark. He wanted to make sure he could still get to the kids if I refused to cooperate."

All of it was beginning to make sense, Kerri thought as Ardie verified a lot of things they had already suspected. She'd tried to protect the kids by leaving them with Mark, and her warning not to try to find her had really been for their benefit.

The three of them had been so engrossed in their whispered conversation that they hadn't noticed the door had slowly opened. They jerked around when they heard an ugly laugh. A dark-haired man with a ponytail and sideburns stood there, listening.

"What a cozy little gathering," he said. "I'm ashamed of you, Ardie, keeping company all to yourself. And telling such lies. You really ought to watch your tongue."

Mark stood up. "And you ought to watch yours, Dirk."

The man's dark eyes flickered over Mark, "And who are you to be giving me orders?"

"I think you knew my brother, Jason Richards." Mark's glare dared him to deny it.

"Oh, yes, of course. Very sad, your brother's death. Leaving Ardie a widow before her time. Those California highways are death traps, aren't they?'' Dirk's smile was blatantly smug.

Kerri remembered Jeff Elders saying someone had called for Jason just after he'd left work on the day he died.

"I promise you, the police will be looking into his accident more closely. You won't mind answering a few questions about where you were that night, will you?" Mark's voice and expression were grim.

"Your car," Ardie gasped. "That's why it needed a new paint job. You said that you scratched it sideswiping a post. Oh, my God," she whimpered. "Jason…Jason…"

"Shut up! You're off your rocker if you think I had anything to do with that. And you—" He shook his fist at Mark. "You get yourself and your girlfriend out of this house while you're still on two legs."

"We're going," Kerri said quickly, stepping between the two men. This was no time for male heroics. The advantage was all on the other side—Dirk knew they had no real evidence against him, and if he was letting them go, they'd better walk while they could. Enough words had been exchanged to light a bonfire. But they couldn't leave Ardie to disappear with Dirk. "We're taking Ardie with us, if she wants to come."

"The hell you are. She stays here."

"But that would amount to a kidnapping charge, wouldn't it? If you keep her here against her will?"

"And who's going to bring the charge? You? By the time the law gets here, she'd swear on a stack of Bibles that she wanted to stay. Wouldn't you, baby?"

Ardie covered her face with her hands and her shoulders shook. Whatever strength she'd mustered to keep going under such dire circumstances was all gone.

Glaring at Dirk, Kerri said, "You can't blackmail her with the kids any more. We have them in protective custody." Kerri said, stretching the truth a bit.

Mark had helped Ardie to her feet. "Come on, let's get out of here."

"Don't be a fool, Ardie," snapped Dirk. "Two more poker hands and this whole place will be ours. This is the payoff. Tanner is down to his last pot tonight, and fading fast."

Ardie's head came up and surprised everyone by lashing out at him, "I told you not to go through with this. I tried to find Thon..s and warn him that you were taking him down tonight, but you already had him sucked into a game."

"A game you helped set up, sweetheart, don't forget that, but if you want to pull out, fine. Go." He gave a dramatic sweep of his hand toward the door. "All the more for the rest of us, but remember, sweetheart, this was just a friendly little poker game, with the luck running against Tanner." His glare was threatening. "You're not stupid enough to put a noose around your own neck by spreading a bunch of lies about your old friends, now, are you?"

With Kerri on one side and Mark on the other, Ardie cowered against them as they walked out of the study.

At that moment all hell broke loose.

The sharp report of a gunshot came from a room at the back of the house, and in the next instant a man staggered out into the hall, blood spurting through the hands he held to his chest. He spun on his heels and then crashed to the floor.

"Stu!" Dirk shouted, reaching for his own gun

tucked in the back of his belt, but Thomas Tanner came through the door and had Dirk in his sights before he could raise it to fire.

"Drop it, you cheating bastard." Tanner shouted.

"Hey, take it easy," Dirk soothed, as he lowered his arm to his side, the gun still in his hand. "What's going on, man?"

"You dirty, cheating bastards! The game was rigged. You were going to take me for everything. Everything."

"Thomas, listen," Ardie begged.

"No, I'm done listening. Oh, the three of you were smooth, real smooth, but nobody makes a fool of me and gets away with it." He aimed his gun at Ardie.

Mark flung himself at Tanner, grabbing him around his fat legs in a flying tackle, and bringing him to the floor.

Dirk swung his gun toward Ardie and fired. Kerri screamed as Ardie grabbed her chest and slumped to the floor.

Grabbing Tanner's revolver, Mark ordered, "Drop your gun, Dirk, or I'll shoot."

With lightning speed, Dirk grabbed Kerri, pressed his gun against her neck, and held her as a shield in front of him. "Come on, baby, you're my passport out of here."

"Let her go!" Mark shouted as Dirk yanked her backward toward the front door.

"Stay back!" Dirk growled.

"Do as he says," Kerri told Mark. She was afraid that he might rush them and get himself shot.

Dirk jerked opened the front door and pulled Kerri out of the house and down the steps.

"Call an ambulance and 911, now!" Mark shouted

down at Tanner, still sprawled on the floor. As the man stared up at Mark pugnaciously, instant fury made Mark want to kick him. He settled for pointing the gun threateningly. "Do it! Now!"

Mark made toward the front door, just as gunshots sounded in rapid succession outside. Forgetting all about caution, he burst out onto the porch.

"What the—?"

He couldn't see either Dirk or Kerri.

Where were they?

He bounded down the steps just as a dark car parked at the corner of the house burst into life. With engine roaring and tires spitting gravel, the car raced by. The glimpse he had into the front seat stunned Mark as if someone had hit him in the stomach with a doubled fist.

Kerri was driving.

Mark was stunned and horrified. He sprinted toward his car, and then stopped short when he saw rubber fragments on the ground. That's what the gunfire had been. Dirk had shot out the tires on the remaining cars so no one could follow him and Kerri.

The taillights on Dirk's car faded out of sight as the automobile disappeared over the crest of the hill.

LEANING OVER the steering wheel, Kerri was relieved, on some detached level, to get the gunman away from the house and away from Mark, even though her own safety was in jeopardy.

The gun poking into her side had prevented any argument on her part when Dirk had ordered her to drive. "Burn rubber if you want to live," he had growled. "Don't forget I can blow you to bits, and dump you out of this car any time I want."

Kerri swallowed back the sickening bile rising in her throat. She knew that Dirk had already killed Buddy and Jason, and maybe Ardie. What would one more victim mean to him? Once her usefulness as a hostage was over, he could easily dispose of her in these rocky hills, and it could be weeks, even months, or years before anyone found her body. Colorado's crime reports were full of such murders. A pricking shiver trailed up her spine.

"You won't get away, Dirk," she said with more bravado than she felt. "You're just making things worse by running."

"Shut up and drive."

"The police will be waiting for us when we reach the highway at Blackhawk," she warned, trying to ignore the gun in her side.

He shot her a triumphant sneer. "We're not going to Blackhawk. When we get to the bottom of this hill, turn right."

"But the highway is the other direction."

"Hell, I know where it is," he snapped. "I've been all over these hills. There's another paved road that comes up to Blackhawk from Boulder, and we'll hit it in a couple of miles. Always pays to have an exit plan if something goes wrong."

"What went wrong?" Even in these dire circumstances she couldn't contain her curiosity.

He swore. "I don't know what in blazes tipped Tanner off. We were taking a break from the game. Dammit, we had the guy where we wanted him. Stu must have done something stupid."

"And now he's dead," she reminded him. "And you're going to be on the run the rest of your life."

He jabbed the gun barrel so viciously into her side

that she winced with pain. "Save the sob stuff! And shut up!"

He kept looking out the back window, but she knew from the reflection in the rearview mirror that there were no car lights following them. Once they reached the paved highway, he could be out of these hills in twenty minutes, and then he wouldn't need a hostage to get him out of the state. If she was going to save her life, she couldn't wait until they reached the paved road.

"Turn here," he barked as they came to a junction of two dirt roads.

With her mind racing ahead, she gave the steering wheel an abrupt turn and scraped the side of the car with some scrub oak bushes as she took the corner too close.

Dirk swore. "Where in the hell did you learn to drive?"

"Not in the mountains," she lied, hoping he wouldn't know she'd been raised at the foot of the Rockies, and had chalked up plenty of hours of mountain driving, summer and winter. She gunned the car, and swerved it dangerously close to the edge of the road.

"I can't see," she wailed.

"Watch it!" he yelled, looking out the window at a drop-off of several hundred feet. He grabbed the steering wheel and turned it back toward the center of the road, and as he did, she braced herself, and slammed on the brakes.

He lunged forward. Off balance, his fingers slipped off the gun as he tried to catch himself with both hands. In that instant, she grabbed the revolver.

Before he could straighten up, she brought the butt

of the gun up in one swift movement and crashed it down upon his head.

As he slumped unconscious in the seat beside her, she remembered the blow he'd given her on her head. "Now we're even," she said, with childish satisfaction.

Chapter Twelve

Kerri had no idea if the highway Dirk had talked about was straight ahead or if she'd have to make the right twists and turns to reach it. Getting hopelessly lost while Dirk regained consciousness did not seem worth the gamble, so she turned the car around and headed back toward Tanner's house.

She kept hoping that she would meet someone else on the narrow dirt road, but she didn't. Dirk's breathing was heavy, but steady, and she had no idea how long he'd be unconscious. Not long, if her own experience of getting hit in the head was any indication. Even though he might be weakened and fuzzy when he regained consciousness, he was still big enough to make two of her.

As far as she could remember, she'd only made one turn, and that was at the bottom of the hill where the sign pointing to the Tanner house had been. She prayed she wouldn't miss it coming from this direction.

Keeping her eye on Dirk and the nighttime view out the side window, she drove as fast as she could. The gunman remained slumped forward with his head resting on the dashboard, his arms dangling listlessly at his sides. His body bounced slightly as she hit washboard stretches in the road.

Please, God, don't let him wake up before I get there.

As Kerri hunched over the wheel, she tried desperately to see the side of the road. Her back and neck muscles were rigid with tension. Where in heaven's name was the turnoff? An eternity of time went by, and still she didn't see the sign pointing to the side road that led to the Tanner house. With Dirk urging speed, she must have driven a lot farther than she thought—or she'd passed the turnoff already, she thought with rising despair. Yes, she was almost certain now that she'd driven too far.

When she saw Dirk's arm move, instant panic nearly paralyzed her. He must be coming back to consciousness. In a few minutes he might be alert enough to wrestle her for his gun. What should she do? She couldn't bring herself to hit him again while he slumped forward. Maybe she should open the door and push him out, and hope that he wouldn't be able to get very far away before they caught up to him?

At that moment, a squeal of brakes and the slashing beam of headlights just ahead stopped all further thought. She skidded to a stop as an ambulance roared by her. Immediately, another pair of headlights hit her. A police car following the ambulance pulled up alongside of the Subaru, and a uniformed cop got out. He shone a flashlight in Kerri's face, and ordered. "Get out of the car."

She'd never heard such blessed words in all her life.

A WEEK LATER Kerri stood at her office window late in the afternoon, looking at the Denver skyline. Her

mood was pensive as she remembered the day Mark
Richards had walked into her life and heart. Even
though she'd known at the beginning that it wasn't
going to be an ordinary case, she'd never expected it
to change every facet of her life.

A file on her desk was stamped Case Closed. The
missing person had been found, and it would seem that
Finders, Inc. had successfully brought everything to a
satisfying end, but nothing was further from the truth.
Too many important aspects remained unfinished, and
Kerri felt a heaviness in spirit that denied any sense
of victory.

Three children were still without a mother, and the
woman who held their future was in the hospital re-
covering from a nearly fatal gunshot wound. Dirk was
in jail, charged with gambling fraud and attempted
murder. And Thomas Tanner was facing manslaughter
charges.

On a personal level, her romantic relationship with
Mark was at a standstill. The recent events had been
an emotional drain on them both. Mark had gone to
California, determined to bring pressure on the au-
thorities to find enough evidence to connect Dirk with
Jason's fatal accident.

The police were holding off charging Ardie, and
Kerri knew that her next challenge would be visiting
her at the hospital. Even though Mark seemed to have
softened his attitude toward the children, he hadn't
indicated any intention of being personally involved
in their upbringing. Something had to be done about
their future. Kerri couldn't expect her family to care
for them indefinitely.

"You look awfully thoughtful," Debbie said coming into the office. "Lonesome?"

"Yeah." What was the use of denying it? Everyone knew what was going on between her and Mark. At least, they thought they did. She wasn't all that certain herself what was happening. Now that the search was over, and they were back to their normal routines, she wondered if the bond between them would hold. The passion between them was genuine enough, she readily admitted, but a lasting relationship demanded more. She wasn't sure how much compromising they would have to do to create a satisfying life together. Could two people with such different backgrounds marry and be happy? Maybe she was old-fashioned about love, but she wasn't willing to settle for anything less than a lifetime commitment.

"When is Mr. Richards coming back?"

"I'm not sure. Maybe in a day or two." Kerri pulled her thoughts away from the empty ache his absence had created. "I'm going to have a talk with Ardie this afternoon. I'm not sure when they'll release her, but we need to have some things settled about the children."

"You mean, ship them off to somebody else? From what you've told me, Ardie left them with Mr. Richards because there wasn't anybody else in the family to take them."

"I'm not sure what the situation is. I know that Mark will be willing to support the kids financially, but he's not the type to take on a ready-made family."

"What man would? I mean, let's be honest. A guy wants his own kids, not somebody else's thrust on him." Debbie eyed Kerri suspiciously. "Are you thinking of creating some kind of a package deal, you and the kids, all or nothing?"

"No, of course not. That wouldn't be fair to Mark."

She smiled wanly. "He's really tried to fit into my crazy family, but I can tell that kind of zoo is not for him. I'm not certain that there's a happy future for us when we're starting out so far apart."

"Good grief, if you love the man, what else is there to think about?"

Kerri laughed and shook her head. "You're a true romantic, Debbie. I think you honestly believe that love conquers all."

"Doesn't it?" she asked with such sincere honesty that Kerri turned away without answering.

BECAUSE OF Kerri's recent stay at Saint Joseph's Hospital, she knew where the gift shop was located, and where the bank of elevators were to take her up to Ardie's private room on the tenth floor.

With a bouquet of roses in her arms, Kerri knocked lightly on the door and poked her head into the room. "May I come in?"

Ardie was visibly startled to see Kerri in the doorway. Instant color seeped up into her pale cheeks, as she nodded.

"I hear you're one lucky woman," Kerri said brightly, as she came over to the bed.

"Yes, very lucky."

Kerri handed her the flowers, and Ardie buried her nose in the fragrant bouquet. Then she smiled wanly at Kerri. "Roses are my favorite."

"Mine, too. Let me put them in a vase so you can have them by your bedside. I remember how much I enjoyed some when I was in the hospital after—" Kerri broke off, silently cursing herself for being so stupid.

Ardie's mouth quivered. "I'm so sorry—"

Kerri brushed the apology aside. "It wasn't your fault. Now, tell me, how are you doing? I hear the bullet missed all the vital organs, and you got through surgery in terrific fashion."

"I've had good care."

She did look surprisingly well, her eyes were bright and her mouth relaxed. "You really look more at peace with yourself," Kerri said honestly, remembering the frightened, tearful Ardie who had let them into Tanner's house.

She nodded. "I am. No matter what happens, I'm glad it's all over. I think I've got the courage now to change my life. I married Buddy when I was a starry-eyed dancer, trying to make my way in Las Vegas, and didn't have the sense to see what he was until it was too late to pull away. For eight years, he treated me like a puppet and I let him."

"And how did you meet Jason?"

"Oh, he gambled at the Locust Club, and Buddy told me to find out if he had money enough to make it worthwhile pulling him into a fixed poker game. It didn't take long to discover that he wasn't the kind of mark that Buddy was looking for so he told me to drop him, but by then Jason and I had started to like each other, and after Buddy was killed, he was a god-send. When the care of Irene's kids fell to me, he really took to them." Tears flowed into her eyes. "I admit our marriage wasn't the stuff romantic novels are made of, but we had something to give to each other."

Kerri squeezed her hand. "I know Mark would appreciate knowing what you've told me. He loved his brother very much."

"I can't thank Mark enough for paying all my bills.

And he's promised to make sure Irene's kids get everything they need. Did he tell you, he's setting up some kind of trust fund for them? That means that whoever takes them won't have to worry about money. I know they'll find a good home somewhere. Mark said that Colorado Social Services do a good job finding guardians for displaced children.''

"I'm sure they do," Kerri responded with a smile that had an edge to it. "And what about you? Have the authorities brought any charges?"

"Not yet, but they tell me that if I agree to testify against Dirk, and plead guilty to a lesser charge, I could get off with a reduced sentence. My testimony could even open up the investigation into Buddy's murder and Jason's accident. I want to make things right with everyone." Ardie eyes sought Kerri's approval. "I'm so glad you found me."

"So am I," Kerri replied. *What if I hadn't taken the case?* The answer filled her with mixed emotions. She'd discovered some things about herself that had nothing to do with her business.

She left the hospital, and cursing the slow rush hour traffic, she used her cellular phone to call the office and check on her voice mail. She was disappointed that Mark hadn't called.

The last two nights, he'd called late, and seemed to have his mind on other things. She felt the distance between them widening every day that he was gone. The close bond that had been between them during the investigation was dissipating as their lives got back to normal.

When she got home, her mother asked her what kind of day she'd had, and Kerri just grumbled an answer.

"Oh, so it's like that, is it?" Her mother nodded knowingly. "Well, you know what they say, 'Absence makes the heart grow fonder.'"

Kerri wasn't up to challenging any of her mother's homilies, but she thought that one was a crock. She pulled a wine cooler out of the fridge, and took a deep swig.

"Grams and the kids are over at Cathy's. I guess it's just you and me for supper, honey. Why don't you go upstairs and freshen up a bit. You're looking a wee bit wilted."

Her mother's use of *wilted* was a euphemism for "you look like hell." Kerri finished her drink, went upstairs and threw herself across the bed. About a half hour later, she was on the verge of taking a nap when she heard her mother calling from the bottom of the stairs. "Somebody to see you, Kerri."

She sat up slowly. She couldn't think of anyone but Mark who would seek her out at home, and he was still in Los Angeles.

"Coming," she called back as she went over to her dressing table. Giving her dark curls a quick brush, she frowned at the reflection of her listless face. Feeling let down after a difficult case wasn't all that unusual, but Kerri knew that her blues had a wider base than just business. It was almost as if she'd had a dream within her reach, only to have it grabbed away.

Squaring her shoulders, she started down the stairs, but she didn't even make it halfway before her visitor bounded up to meet her.

"Mark," she gasped. "I...I thought you were in Los Angeles," she stammered.

"Ever heard of planes, darling?"

"But why didn't you call, let me know?"

"There wasn't time." He halted any more questions with a possessive kiss that nearly lifted her off her feet. Then he grabbed her hand and guided her down the rest of the stairs. "Get your jacket. We're going for a walk."

Her mother was watching from the kitchen doorway, and laughing, shook a finger at them. "Now, don't be late for dinner, you two. We're having Irish stew and biscuits."

"Sounds wonderful," Mark said over his shoulder, as he guided Kerri out the front door.

She slipped her arm through his, and her ailing spirits made a miraculous recovery. The brisk evening air touched her cheeks, and as they walked down the street together, the colorless mood of her day disappeared. Life suddenly seemed as bright as the autumn leaves crunching under their feet.

"And what have you been up to since I've been away?" he asked, smiling down at her and drawing her close to his side.

"I visited Ardie today," Kerri said, hesitating, not wanting to spoil the mood by bringing up her concern for the children, but anxious to get the matter cleared up. "Ardie told me that you'd made financial arrangements for the children."

"That's right. So, everything's in place to move them."

"Move them where? Have you already made arrangements with Social Services?"

He nodded.

She was stunned by the explosive fury that swept over her. How could he do this? Be so callous? So unfeeling? Stopping in the middle of the sidewalk, she jerked her arm away from his. "And just where have you arranged to move them to, if you don't mind my asking?''

''I don't mind at all.'' Raising his hand, he pointed to a Victorian house that stood at the corner of their street. ''Right over there.''

She stared at the beautiful empty house with a Sold sign stuck in the front lawn. Her eyes jerked from the house back to him, and then back to the house again.

''Well, what do you think?'' He grabbed her hand. ''Let's go take a look. It looks like a nice house for raising kids. And I like the neighborhood, don't you?''

They crossed the street and he laughed at her stunned expression as he put a key in the lock. She held back as he opened the door. ''What are you up to?'' she asked in a breathless whisper.

He put his hands on her shoulders. ''It's simple. I love you. I want to marry you, Kerri Kincaid. And if you'll take a chance on turning a bachelor into a family man, I promise you, we'll live happily ever after.'' His caressing eyes bathed her face. ''Will you have me?''

Later, she couldn't remember whether she actually answered him, but there wasn't any need for words as he lifted her up in his arms and carried her inside. Then, as if she were already a bride, he kissed her soundly before he set her down.

''Wait 'til you see the place. Timmy's going to love the backyard, and there's a playhouse for Patti. Ardie signed all the papers. The children will be ours once we're married. I told the real estate agent we had to have a house in this neighborhood—near *our* family.''

As they walked through the beautiful, spacious house that only needed the bustle of children to make it complete, he searched her misty eyes. "You like it, don't you?"

With a smile filled with love, and her lips raised to his, she said softly, "Yes, I like it. It's home."

Lost & Found

All new...and filled with the mystery and romance you love!

SOMEBODY'S BABY
by Amanda Stevens in November 1998

A FATHER FOR HER BABY
by B. J. Daniels in December 1998

A FATHER'S LOVE
by Carla Cassidy in January 1999

It all begins one night when three women go into labor in the same Galveston, Texas, hospital. Shortly after the babies are born, fire erupts, and though each child and mother make it to safety, there's more than just the mystery of birth to solve now....

Don't miss this *all new* LOST & FOUND trilogy!

Available at your favorite retail outlet.

HARLEQUIN®
Makes any time special™

Catch more great

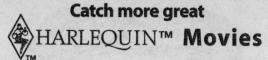

HARLEQUIN™ Movies

featured on **the movie channel** tmc

Premiering October 10th
Loving Evangeline
Based on the novel by *New York Times* bestselling author Linda Howard

Don't miss next month's movie!
Premiering November 14th
Broken Lullaby
Starring Mel Harris and Rob Stewart.
Based on the novel by bestselling author Laurel Pace

If you are not currently a subscriber to The Movie Channel, simply call your local cable or satellite provider for more details. Call today, and don't miss out on the romance!

the movie channel tmc   HARLEQUIN®

100% pure movies.
100% pure fun.

*M*akes any time special ™

COMING NEXT MONTH

#489 SOMEBODY'S BABY by Amanda Stevens
Lost & Found
Nina Fairchild's accusations were almost too incredible to believe—
but as Grant Chambers stared into her haunted eyes, something in her
gaze touched his soul. He had to uncover the truth, for Nina claimed
someone had stolen her baby—that Grant's new nephew was hers....

#490 NEVER LET HER GO by Gayle Wilson
A bullet took undercover agent Nick Deandro's sight and his
memories. But it couldn't erase the feeling that he knew Abby Sterling,
his temporary bodyguard, from somewhere....Could he remember in
time to protect *her?*

#491 SPENCER'S SECRET by Laura Gordon
The Spencer Brothers
Logan Spencer was back in town to find his best friend's killer. But
he hadn't expected his passion for his friend's widow to resurface—or
that her secrets had kept him from being a father to his own child....

#492 UNDER THE MIDNIGHT SUN by Marilyn Cunningham
A lonely stretch of frozen tundra, a stranger's body buried in the
snow—and Brian Kennedy's life became enmeshed with the life of
beautiful Malinche Adams. She needed his help to solve her brother's
murder.... But if he helped, would he risk losing his bachelor's heart?

AVAILABLE THIS MONTH:

**#485 REMEMBER ME,
COWBOY**
Caroline Burnes
#486 SEND ME A HERO
Rita Herron

#487 MYSTERY DAD
Leona Karr
**#488 THE ARMS OF THE
LAW**
Jenna Ryan